"Touch me. Please

She pressed his hands to her and Chase ignited. If he didn't stop now, there would be no stopping. And he had to.

"I can't do this, Haley. Not when you belong to someone else."

He saw the wounded expression in her eyes. "It's not me your brother owns. It's you, Chase."

It didn't make sense. No one owned him.

"Haley—"

"Just go back to your room."

He did as she asked. But he didn't sleep. He had to admit snatching Haley without any authority and forcing her to go with him to find his missing brother had been reckless.

Now it was too late. As long as there was any risk to her, he had to remain at her side. Which was a big problem when she was a walking temptation. And now it looked as if she was also attracted to him.

So, what the hell were they going to do about it?

***

If you're on Twitter, tell us what you think of Harlequin Romantic Suspense! #harlequinromsuspense

Dear Reader,

Have you ever heard of Svalbard? I hadn't either until a few years ago when I learned it's an archipelago halfway between Norway and the North Pole. There, on an uninhabited island, is located what may well be mankind's most important structure—a state-of-the-art storage facility built inside a frozen mountain. To store what? Seeds. Millions of varieties of seeds collected from around the world. If a monumental disaster, natural or man-made, should ever occur to our crops, here are preserved in this Global Seed Vault the seeds to begin anew.

The more I read about Svalbard, the more intrigued I became. Those who have read my romantic suspense books know that I like to build my stories around unique subjects. *The Bounty Hunter's Forbidden Desire* is one of those stories. It concerns a man and a woman who race to save an international seed vault threatened with destruction by a megalomaniac—a seed vault that in my novel is situated in Alaska, not Norway. As fast-paced as the plot is, this is not its major theme. That deals with a guilt-ridden hero searching for his missing brother and the romance that was never supposed to happen. Here's a hint before you take this journey with Haley and Chase. You won't need a dogsled. It can be quite warm in Alaska in the summer. And with Haley and Chase heating up the environment...well, you get the idea.

Jean Thomas

THE BOUNTY HUNTER'S FORBIDDEN DESIRE

Jean Thomas

⬧ **HARLEQUIN**® ROMANTIC SUSPENSE

Recycling programs
for this product may
not exist in your area.

ISBN-13: 978-0-373-27912-8

The Bounty Hunter's Forbidden Desire

Copyright © 2015 by Jean Thomas

Printed in U.S.A.

www.Harlequin.com

Jean Thomas, aka Jean Barrett, lives in Wisconsin in an English-style cottage on a Lake Michigan shore bluff. The view from her office window would be a magnificent one if it weren't blocked by a big fat computer that keeps demanding her attention.

This author of twenty-six romances was a teacher before she left the classroom to write full-time. A longtime member of Romance Writers of America, Jean is a proud winner of three national awards and has appeared on several bestseller lists. When she isn't at the keyboard, she likes to take long walks that churn up new story ideas or work in the garden, which never seems to churn up anything but dirt. Of course, there are always books to be read. Romantic suspense stories are her favorite. No surprise there. Visit Jean at jeanthomas-author.com.

Books by Jean Thomas

HARLEQUIN ROMANTIC SUSPENSE

AWOL with the Operative
The Lieutenant by Her Side
Lethal Affair
The Bounty Hunter's Forbidden Desire

Visit the Author Profile page at
Harlequin.com for more titles.

To my good friends
Bobbie Finn and Kathy Mueller
for their loyal support

Chapter 1

Chase McKinley sat behind the wheel of his black SUV, watching the couple in the gray Chevy. The sedan was parked diagonally across the street from him, its position allowing him to observe the occupants without giving them a reason to be suspicious of his presence. In any case, they were too engrossed in what appeared to be an intense dialogue to be aware of him.

There was no way for Chase to hear what they were saying. Nor did he worry about that. What the woman looked like was his only real concern at the moment. At this angle, and with the width of the street between them, that was hard to tell.

The PI whom Chase regularly used had emailed a photo of the brunette, but it had been a blurry, disappointing result. Far more interesting was the investigator's description in his report. He'd referred to her simply as "a hot number." An exaggeration? Maybe. Chase looked forward to finding out.

The Chevy's front passenger door opened. A pair of long, shapely legs swung into view. They were followed by the rest of the woman who owned them. Chase sucked in a lungful of air. Holy crap! The PI had been right on target. Haley Adams was one dark-haired, gorgeous filly.

She was joined by the guy behind the wheel of the Chevy, who had rounded the rear of the car to meet her. Chase couldn't say much for her taste in men. Not bad looking, he supposed, but too ordinary to make any impression. And with an extraordinary-looking woman like her, he would have expected something more.

Whoever he was, he had his hand on her arm, prepared to escort her across the street to her door. The place was one of those row house affairs, nothing to distinguish it from its adjoining neighbors. Like the homes above it on the ridge, it looked down on the valley where Portland's downtown high-rises were packed along the Willamette River rimmed with cargo ships at anchor.

Chase cared about neither the boats nor the office towers. His only focus was Haley Adams and the guy close at her side, who, now that he had a better view of him, wore an unhappy expression on his narrow face. Chase got a look at their parting at her front door. Enough of it, anyway, to tell it involved an embrace. A spiky evergreen blocked the rest of it. Damn shrubs grew like weeds here in the Pacific Northwest.

Chase was willing to bet, though, the embrace ended in a kiss of the passionate variety. Who'd part from a woman like her without one? After his farewell, the guy retreated to his sedan and drove off down the street.

Chase didn't wait until he was out of sight to emerge from his SUV, race to Haley Adams' door and ring her bell. He was counting on her thinking her anxious boyfriend had returned. He'd used this kind of tactic before with success, and it didn't fail him this time.

Her wide blue eyes registered a concerned surprise when she opened the door to find a strange man on her doorstep. Chase had his foot in the opening before she could close the door on him.

Haley realized at once that she'd made two careless mistakes. She had failed to secure the chain on the door behind Bill Farley's departure, and she neglected to check the peephole before opening the door. Not that the neighborhood—or Portland in general—had a reputation for crime. But still…

Make that three mistakes. Bill had left in such a state that she'd assumed he was back for a last session of pleading. Wrong.

"If you're selling," she brusquely informed the rangy figure, "I'm not interested. And if you're collecting for a charity, I prefer to do that by mail. Now if you'll take your foot out of my door…"

"I'm not selling or collecting."

No, she decided, he didn't look the type. Too tough for anything like that. More like a longshoreman. He still hadn't removed his foot. He was making her uneasy. Did she have something to worry about here?

"Look, whoever and whatever you are, you have no right to push in here like this. I'm going to ask you again to take your foot out of my door so I can close it after you. Because if you don't go away, I'm going to call the police."

"You do that. I may need them here to conduct my business with you."

"I think you've made some kind of mistake."

"They all say that. You are Haley Adams, aren't you?"

She was surprised he knew her name. "Yes, but I may very well not be the only one in a city this size."

"Any other Haley Adams living at this address?"

"Of course not."

"Then you're the Haley Adams I want."

"How do you know me and my name? And just what is this so-called business you're supposed to have with me?"

"About time we got around to that."

He moved the rest of the way into her foyer. Before she could tell him to leave the door open behind him, he'd nudged it shut with his elbow and was opening a folder tucked under his arm.

She didn't like this. Didn't like it at all. It wasn't anything he might have in that folder that had her nervous. It was the presence of the man himself inside her house— when she hadn't let him in. Why hadn't she called the cops immediately? That tall, solid figure could be anything, anybody. Bad things happened to women in situations like this.

He must have understood she was concerned. "Relax," he said, the timbre of his voice deep and husky, not at all conducive to relaxing. "If you don't give me any trouble—and believe me, plenty of them try it—then you have nothing to worry about."

Nothing to worry about? Give him any trouble? Who was he? What was this all about?

"Come on, Haley," he said, "you shouldn't need any explanations. You know what this is all about." Did this guy read minds? "No? You want to play hardball, do you? Well, we can do that."

He had an official-looking document inside the folder. He held it out to her. "This is your copy. Mine stays inside the folder."

She hesitantly took it from him, looked down at it in her hand and scanned it in disbelief. It was a legal order for the apprehension of Haley Adams, residing at this address, who had failed to appear in court on the scheduled date of her arraignment and was therefore in violation of her bail bond. She looked up at him in bewilderment. He nodded solemnly.

"I need to bring you in, Haley. Afraid that's my job. Says so right here. See?"

He'd produced a wallet from the back pocket of his jeans, folded it back for her inspection and was now tapping at the identification it contained with his forefinger. "Chase McKinley," he read, "licensed bond enforcer. That's me."

She looked at the ID, then at his square-jawed face. For a moment she had no reaction. Then she understood. "You're a bounty hunter."

"Well, that's one term for it. There are others. Skip tracer. Fugitive apprehension agent. Take your pick."

"You're a bounty hunter," she repeated, "and your name is Chase. I get it now. Chase, hunter." She began to giggle. This was exactly the kind of prank her friend Kelly was forever pulling. Her giggle escalated into outright laughter.

She waited for him to grin, to snap a "gotcha" at her.

That didn't happen. He wasn't grinning. He was staring at her in mild astonishment. "I've got to hand it to you, lady," he drawled. "I've seen all kinds of reactions when I show up, but you're the first to try something like this. Have to warn you, though, it isn't going to work. So why don't you just stop stalling and come with me peacefully."

He was serious. This was no joke. "There's been some

kind of mistake," she insisted. "I haven't committed any crime. And I certainly haven't applied to any—any—"

"Bail bond agency," he supplied for her.

"Yes, if that's what it's called to post bonds for people in order for them to keep out of jail while they wait to go to trial."

"That's what it's called."

"You have to believe me. This is all crazy."

"No, Haley, I don't have to believe anything you tell me. My only assignment is to bring you in. You got arguments, you save them for police headquarters."

This man had no patience and no sympathy. If he'd ever had them, they had been drained out of him long ago. But there was someone who *would* listen to her, who would straighten out this whole absurd mess. She started to reach for her purse, but he anticipated her move. "Nuh-uh-uh," he cautioned, snatching it away before she could claim it.

"But my cell phone is in there. I need to call my lawyer."

"No phone calls until you're booked down at the main station, and then you get to call your lawyer. That is, if you behave yourself. Meanwhile, I'll take charge of your purse."

What was going on?

Everyone knew Portland was famous as the City of Roses. But with all its bridges across the Willamette and Columbia Rivers, it could just as easily be the City of Bridges. Or, for that matter, Chase thought, the City of Fountains, since water attractions were everywhere in the parks and squares. It was a beautiful place.

Which should have been a reason for him not to be distracted by the woman beside him in the SUV. Trouble was, Haley Adams was a hell of a lot better looking than the gorgeous streets he was driving through. He couldn't help casting glances in her direction, admiring that alluring body in the summer T-shirt and clinging jeans; the clear, ivory skin; and the deep blue eyes that, whenever they turned his way, unfortunately looked at him as though he were something that had slithered out of a hole.

Yeah, Chase could see why Josh had fallen so hard for this tempting package, but he wasn't going to let himself be fooled by all the wrapping. She was plainly cheating on Josh in his absence with this other guy. That tight squeeze he'd witnessed at her door when they'd parted was evidence of that. His PI, too, had caught them in a couple of similar cozy sessions.

Bill Farley. That was the man's name, and according to the investigator's report, Farley was connected with some very questionable people. There was no proof Haley Adams was associated with the same crowd, but Chase wouldn't be surprised to learn she was.

Josh will have my ass if he ever finds out I hired a PI to spy on his girlfriend, he thought. Tough, because right now she was his one and only link to Josh, and he wasn't going to hesitate to use her.

Once the traffic thinned, sweet little Haley was bound to notice she wasn't going where she thought she was. So far she hadn't been particularly observant about their route. Too busy silently smoldering over her situation and the man who was responsible for it—him. But any minute now, her fuse was going to ignite.

A couple of blocks farther on, he sensed her sudden awareness. *Here it comes*, Chase thought, bracing for the blast.

"What are you doing! This isn't the way to the main police station!"

"I know where I'm going," he told her serenely.

"I'm telling you, this isn't right! You're going in the complete opposite direction!"

"Don't think so."

"But you're wrong! Don't you suppose I know my own city? Turn around," she insisted, "and go back!"

Chase kept on driving.

"Why aren't you listening to me? If you keep on going this way, we'll be headed out of Portland!"

"That's the general idea."

Her gasp wasn't a loud one, barely audible in fact, but it was sufficient enough to register her alarm. "Just where are you taking me?"

"Like I said, police headquarters."

"That can't be possible! You lied to me!"

"Oh, Haley, Haley, accusations like that hurt me. I wouldn't lie to you. It's not only possible, it's true. If you'd taken the time to read the order for your apprehension carefully, you would have seen that is exactly where I'm taking you. Seattle Police Headquarters."

"Seat— Are you out of your mind? Seattle is hours away!"

"Uh-huh. Well, there's nothing unusual about that. You wouldn't believe the considerable distances I've had to travel to haul FTAs back to the right places. Means 'failed to appear,' in case you're wondering. Once I had to go all the way to Chicago. Man, was that guy a pain."

"You still aren't listening to me, are you? Why aren't you listening? Why aren't you understanding that if I didn't break the law in Portland, I certainly didn't break it in Seattle?"

"Take it easy, Haley. You go on like this and you're

apt to pop a blood vessel. And that couldn't be good. How about some music? You want some music? Great way to relax."

Useless, Haley finally decided. He wasn't listening to her pleas and arguments. She was simply wearing herself out trying.

He was *actually* taking her to Seattle. Portland was already behind them. They were in Washington now, rolling north on Interstate 5. There were mountains and lush forests of hemlocks, firs and pines on either side of the highway. Far ahead, off to the right, it was possible to make out what was left of Mount Saint Helens after its famous volcanic explosion.

Magnificent, all of it. If you cared to gaze at it. Haley didn't. She was too busy thinking what a nightmare she'd landed herself in when she had so innocently opened her front door to the man at her side. He was currently whistling under his breath to some old Frank Sinatra song on the radio. Casual as a barefoot boy headed down to the river to land himself a mess of fish.

Not a very sensible analogy, she told herself. Chase McKinley was a bounty hunter, wasn't he? Something she only knew about from movies and television. What did that require? Probably all the qualities of a rough-neck. Things like a well-built, long-limbed body, big hands made to deliver a punch, a deep, commanding voice. Yeah, he had all those and more. Rugged features, dark hair that could use both a trim and a comb. Even darker eyes that had the sexy—

Stop right there.

Whatever he was or wasn't, she refused to permit herself to think of him in those terms.

But there was one thing…what? What was it that

had been bothering her every time she glanced at him? A vague familiarity, wasn't that it? Only that was nonsense. She couldn't possibly have encountered him before. She would have remembered someone as distinctly different as he was.

None of this mattered, of course. Because familiar or otherwise, Haley had made up her mind. Whatever it took, she was getting away from Chase McKinley at the first opportunity.

Chapter 2

The more Haley thought about it, the more she was convinced there was something wrong about this whole thing. She knew she wasn't guilty of any wrongdoing. Then why was she being made to go to Seattle, of all places?

An error of some kind. Had to be. So why not just go on to Seattle and straighten it all out? Why this resolve to give Chase McKinley the slip? It wasn't because she was no longer afraid of him. And that was another puzzle. She should be terrified in a car with a strange man on the way to another state. Why wasn't she more than just worried about being with him? She couldn't figure that out, either.

Haley had only one certainty about this man. It would be a mistake to underestimate him. He wasn't going to stand by and let her just walk away from him. He would take measures to prevent that. Did he have a gun? she wondered. He probably did and would use it if it became necessary.

Well, maybe he wouldn't need a gun. Not with a woman. For a man of his size and strength, there were other easier ways to stop a woman from running.

Better not think about those, Haley, she instructed herself. They would just bring up unpleasant images. Things like physical overpowering. He didn't seem violent or dangerous. Just determined to control his…what did he call them? FTAs. A polite term for fugitives.

Anyway, it didn't pay to speculate about what might happen. All she could do was be ready to act whenever the chance to escape came her way.

That such an opportunity could actually occur was not very likely. Haley knew that, but she refused to surrender the possibility. Meanwhile, she kept as much space between her captor and her as the seats permitted, speaking to him only when he addressed her. She tried not to fret as the SUV ate up the miles, putting Portland farther behind her with every one of those dismal miles.

It was difficult, though, not to worry. She had a life, job commitments, friends who would wonder about her. What would they think, do when they couldn't reach her? She would have to contact them somehow when she got the chance. Probably through her lawyer. Hadn't Bounty Hunter here said she was entitled to a phone call when she was booked? After which she'd be slapped behind bars. Maddening, all of it. And for something she didn't do—whatever it was.

Minutes later, Haley was shaken out of her reverie by his grumbled curse of displeasure. "Damn it all to hell, wouldn't you just know it?"

This was the first time in over an hour he'd spoken to her. Only he hadn't, really. His curse was directed elsewhere.

"What? What's happened?"

He didn't answer her. He didn't need to. All she had to do was follow his gaze up the highway to realize something was happening ahead of them. The traffic seemed to be backing up on both lanes. They themselves had no choice but to slow to a crawl.

"An accident?" she asked.

"I doubt it. Wanna bet it's a construction tie-up? I swear, there isn't a road in this country that isn't being worked on somewhere along its length."

He sounded like it was all a conspiracy directed personally against him. Were men always this grouchy when they were inconvenienced by road repairs?

"I didn't see any signs announcing construction," she said.

"You will."

He was right. It took some considerable stop-and-go before they spotted it, but eventually they were advised by an orange caution sign that, within a half mile, they would need to move into the left lane.

The heavy traffic eased forward at a frustrating pace, seemingly inch by mere inch, each vehicle waiting its turn to squeeze over into the designated lane. But long before that shift arrived, the lines halted altogether. They sat there without moving.

The unexpected. What she'd been waiting for. If it worked out.

"This has got to be eating up the gas," she commented.

He grunted. She waited. The stalled traffic waited.

"Hope you've got enough in your tank that we don't get caught out here on empty. It could be a long while yet before we move out of this trap."

"You let me worry about that."

But he looked down at his gauge. And, hallelujah, the

gas must have been just low enough for him to decide it might be smart to conserve it. That was what the expression on his face seemed to register, anyway.

Come on, McKinley, act. Don't just think about it. Do it.

She restrained herself from a sigh of thanksgiving when, after lowering the window on his side, he turned off the engine.

The keys sat there in the ignition, beckoning to her.

Perfect. Or would be, if—

Ah, another break. He had his head out the window, muttering as he tried to see around the line in front of him in an endeavor to learn what was holding them up.

This was the moment she'd been waiting for. And feared she would never get. But somebody upstairs must have been listening to her prayers. Haley didn't hesitate.

Unsnapping her seat belt, she leaned forward, snatched the keys out of the ignition and, with a pitch worthy of the Seattle Mariners, sent them flying out the open window, managing to just miss his head. With satisfaction, she heard them striking the pavement.

"Whoops."

Chase's ears were red with righteous anger when he withdrew his head. "Why, you little—"

He must have choked on whatever would have followed, because she never heard it. He couldn't have been thinking clearly, or for that matter thinking at all, when he opened his door and exited the SUV. On the other hand, there was no other way for him to recover the keys. Haley had counted on that.

Chase was quick, but she was quicker. Before he could get the keys and stop her, she was out the door on her side, dashing across the shoulder, plunging into a ditch and scrambling under a rail fence. She was busy losing herself in the pine woods on the other side before it struck her that he had her purse. She had no money. No cell phone. What was she going to do on her own in a place where she knew no one?

Her escape hadn't been so clever after all.

Chase ignored the blasts of the car horns behind him. Now that his brain was functioning again, he figured those blasts meant the traffic was rolling once more but the vehicles stuck behind his SUV weren't.

Too bad. Let them squeeze around the SUV when they got the chance. He had a task more important than going back and moving it out of the way. He had Haley Adams to hunt down. When he caught up with her, and he would, he was going to blister her with language she wouldn't forget. And that was the very least he was going to do.

She had disappeared into the woods on the other side of the fence. He had seen that much and was able to enter the forest at the same spot. Beyond that, he didn't know. From here she could have chosen any direction, weaving her way through the ranks of the tall pines.

He looked for some flash of movement ahead of him. There was none. That slim figure was nowhere in sight.

Where are you, Haley?

The dense canopy of the trees cast a cool, damp shade below. Chase stood still, hoping to catch some sound that would betray her. All he heard was the distant call of a dove. Sounded like a dove, anyway. But what did he know? He had a limited knowledge of birds.

Silence followed. Nothing to hear now. And nothing to smell but the sharp fragrance of the pines. So it was his sight he needed to depend on.

Training in the army rangers had taught him tracking.

He used that now, walking in a circle, gazing down at the forest floor for signs. It wasn't long before he picked up the partial footprint of a tennis shoe in the moist earth. The toe pointed the way for him.

After that he was able to spot other signs, several places where the pine needles had been recently disturbed, sticks just as recently snapped underfoot, more prints where there was clear earth.

He figured she wanted to leave the forest behind her as soon as possible. It looked like once she'd chosen her direction, she had managed to stick to it. It didn't take Chase long to discover bright sunlight ahead of him.

Clearing the last of the trees, he reached another rail fence. On the other side was an open pasture. He was disappointed not to see her in the pasture or the field beyond it. Damn. Had he lost her altogether?

He stood there, trying to decide what to try next. Off to one end of the pasture was a horse shelter, enclosed against the weather on three sides, with the fourth side left wide-open for the animals to enter.

No sign of any horses in the pasture now, just the silent shelter. Chase wondered. Did it bear investigating? With no other alternative, it seemed like a good idea.

Hand on one of the fence posts, he vaulted over the top rail, cleared the barrier and strode toward the shelter. The dung in the pasture, though not recent, was evidence horses *were* grazed here at one time and apparently had been moved elsewhere.

He reached the shelter and looked inside. It was deserted. Nothing in there but a stack of hay keeping dry under the roof. Wasted moments, he told himself. He needed to get back to his search.

Chase was just turning away, ready to look elsewhere,

when out of the corner of his eye he saw the hay quiver slightly. Or had he imagined it? Must have. All the same…

He went back inside and squatted on his heels beside the mound, waiting quietly. There was no further movement. He was about to get to his feet when he heard it. A faint rustling inside the pile.

Probably a small creature. Maybe a mouse. At least he hoped it was nothing large.

Willing to take the risk, he plunged his hands into the stack, where his fingers probed around in the vicinity of the rustling. Almost immediately he encountered warm flesh. Yep, something *wild* had burrowed into the hay all right. Except it was of the human variety. No doubt of that when his hands closed around a pair of very nice, smooth-skinned ankles.

Grasping them tightly, because the body they were attached to began to resist, he dragged Haley Adams out of the hay where she'd been hiding.

"Now just look what we've turned up here," he gloated.

He was pleased with what he'd hooked, but once she spit the bits of hay out of her mouth, she was anything but a docile catch. Managing to twist her legs free of his grip, she flipped over on her back, and when he tried to grab her again, she fought him like the animal he'd been worried about.

She kicked, she clawed, she punched, she jabbed, she writhed and rolled and heaved. She even managed to yell language at him that he hadn't heard since the army, though never from the women in the ranks, tough as some of them were. No question of it. Haley Adams was one pissed-off female.

The only way Chase could subdue her in the end was to pin her down by lowering his body full length on hers. She went totally still then. Maybe because she was as instantly aware of their intimate contact as he was. And God help him, that soft, womanly flesh beneath his weight not only felt good, it smelled good.

There was a long silence. Their gazes met and locked in a battle of wills. Or was it that? Was it maybe not so much a conflict as it was a shared desire? Chase's gaze drifted down to her parted lips. He might not have even considered kissing those lips if she hadn't used that moment to start squirming.

It was a bad movement. He felt himself beginning to grow hard.

"Let me up," she whispered. "You're suffocating me."

His only defense against her breathy plea was a dry "You could have suffocated inside that hay."

"The hay wasn't heavy. You are."

He was suddenly angry with his arousal. Angry with himself for his urge to kiss that seductive mouth just inches under his. And angry because he had to remind himself he'd forgotten to give her hell for her escape.

Levering himself off her, he got to his feet. Once he was standing, he reached down, caught her by the wrist and pulled her up.

"You can let me go now."

His laugh was a husky one. "What? And watch you take off again?"

"Oh, now, you're not going to hang on to me all the way back to the car."

"That's exactly what I'm going to do, sweetheart. Only it's not going to be by the wrist."

Before she could object, Chase shifted his grip higher on her arm, whirled her around, bent his knees low enough to collect and balance her weight and slung her up and over his shoulder.

When he came erect again, she was swinging head-first down his back with her lower half dangling down his chest. It was a maneuver he'd learned in the rangers and used effectively a couple of times to transport wounded soldiers to the nearest dressing station.

Holding the load in place was achieved by splaying the fingers of one hand firmly over the rump. It was just a position when it came to a wounded buddy, but it took on a whole new meaning with this cargo. Haley Adams had one hell of a spectacular bottom for a man to hold on to.

"I'm not going to ride like this! Put me down!"

"Not a chance."

He struck off across the pasture, knowing she couldn't be comfortable bouncing along with each of his steps. Too bad. She didn't deserve comfort.

"How you doing back there, Haley? Comfy enough?"

He missed her muffled reply, but from the sound of it, it couldn't have been very friendly. Managing to scramble across the fence while still bearing her over his shoulder, he achieved a more or less direct path through the woods. She was just as tightly in his possession when they crossed the second fence and arrived back at the highway where his SUV safely waited for them. Thankfully, the cops hadn't gotten there yet to tow it away.

Nor did he release her until his free hand produced the keys from his pocket, unlocked the doors, opened the front passenger one and flung her down into the seat with a warning.

"You try any more dumb stunts like that, and I'll handcuff you."

His promise had merit, Haley reluctantly decided when they were rolling up the highway again. It had been stupid of her to make a run for it without money, then hide in a pile of hay like a child.

She would do better the next time. Like, for instance, avoiding his body on top of hers. There had been something much too effectively sensual about both that and his hot hand pressed against her backside afterward. She much preferred him in an unpleasant mood. Safer, right?

But she wasn't certain of that. There was an element of danger about him.

It was better not to look at him. She turned her head away, staring out the window. Off both sides of the four-lane were high, forested slopes. Even though many of them had been denuded in long, vertical swaths by lumbering, there was a beauty about them enhanced by the majestic Cascade Range behind them.

"You feeling okay?"

He hadn't spoken a word in miles. His deep voice coming out of nowhere like this startled her. She stole a glance at him. The man had no heart, and yet she swore she could see a guilty expression on that square-jawed face.

She assumed he was referring to the way she'd been treated when he caught up with her at the horse shelter. "How would you feel if you'd been tossed around like a sack of potatoes?"

"You saying the merchandise ended up bruised?"

"Let's just say it's a bit tender."

She hoped she was wearing a wounded look on her face. There was nothing frail about Haley, but he deserved to think he'd been too rough on her.

"I did warn you."

She kept up her pretense, this time with a martyr's sniff. Had she gone too far? Was that suspicion she read in his sidelong gaze?

They were silent again. Haley returned her attention to the view. They didn't go far before Chase spoke up once more.

"I'm pulling off at the next exit."

"Is there something wrong?"

"Yeah, my stomach. It's empty. I can't remember when I've last eaten. How about you? You hungry?"

Haley admitted she could do with a meal. Counting the long backup with the construction tie-up and her break for freedom, they had been on the road for hours. They had left Portland this morning, and it was now midafternoon.

She wondered at first if this stop would provide another opportunity for her to escape. Not a chance, she quickly realized, because it was a fast food restaurant he selected. They never left the car. Chase ordered take-out from a drive-up window. They ate their food in the parking lot.

He was working on fries and a hamburger when, looking at her thoughtfully, he asked, "Is it true you're self-employed?"

"How did you hear that?"

"I have my sources."

"Uh-huh. So, tell me, is it part of a bounty hunter's job to know what the FTAs he grabs do for a living?"

He shrugged. "It can be."

He was being evasive, Haley thought, inserting the straw into her drink and drawing on the soda.

"What is it you do specifically?" he wanted to know.

She had no reason to conceal anything. "I'm an independent contractor." The expression on his face told her he thought she was messing with him. "No, not that kind of contractor. What I construct I do at home on my computer."

"Such as?"

"Whatever I'm hired to do. Like, for example, report development for public school systems or creating detailed websites for professional, private outfits looking for my kind of training and certification."

"How do these people find you?"

"Online, of course. Most frequently on sites where you post things like your training, your credentials and your recommendations."

He actually looked impressed and that pleased her, although she couldn't exactly say why. Maybe just because it would make him question whether someone with her record would have needed to post a bond for breaking the law and then failed to appear in court. On the other hand, she supposed anyone could be guilty of something like that.

Letting herself be pleased by this man for any other reason was not a good idea.

"Satisfied?" she asked him.

"Yeah, thanks."

Haley wanted him to know she wasn't hiding anything about herself, but that wasn't true of him. There was a secretiveness here, as if this sexy roughneck was protecting something. And that's when it struck her again. Crazy as it seemed, he was somehow, someway familiar.

Haley seldom traveled in this direction. When she did, she always hoped to see that Mount Rainier for once was free of cloud. It never was on any of her visits.

She was prepared to be disappointed again, and instead was treated by nature to a splendid sight. Twilight was already closing in, but still some distance away, far off to the right, the head of the perfect cone that was Rainier was bathed in a golden glow. Haley was enchanted.

She turned her head to see Chase's reaction. He had none. She could only suppose this meant he lived in Seattle and Mount Rainier was a familiar sight. Or maybe he simply wasn't moved by nature. Either way, there was no reason why it should make any difference to her.

What did matter was the decision he made fifteen minutes later. "I'm taking us off at the next exit."

"Are you hungry again?"

"No, sleepy. We'll spend the night at a motel."

"We are *what*?"

"You heard me. It'll be morning before you know it."

Haley knew it was true that early summer at this latitude meant long days and short nights. But even so…

"I don't want to spend the night at a motel," she announced stubbornly.

"Oh, you don't? I suppose instead you'd have me fall asleep at the wheel."

"Don't be silly. I've been dozing, and I'm perfectly capable of taking a turn at the wheel."

"While I what? Go bye-bye?"

"Why not?"

"Sure, why not? Listen, sweetheart, we both know what destinations you get off to when you're turned loose."

"All right, you don't trust me. But Seattle can't be far now. Can't you just go on?"

"It's farther than you think. We've still got the traffic of Olympia, then Tacoma, and after that the whole long urban crawl into Seattle. And all after dark. No, thanks. We're going to a motel."

The last faint glow of twilight was leaving the sky when they exited the interstate. There were three motels to choose from. Chase selected the nearest one, pulled up in front of its office and shut off the engine.

Haley drew back when he reached for the glove compartment, holding her breath as his hand brushed across the side of her breast. As brief and innocent as the contact was, it was like a flame licking across her.

When she was breathing normally again, he had extracted a pair of handcuffs from the glove compartment. Haley stared at them. This was going too far.

"Oh, you're not going to—"

"Handcuff you to the wheel here while I go into the office? That's exactly what I'm going to do."

"But that isn't necessary. Just take me with you."

"And have you make another break for it the minute I turn my back? I don't think so. Of course, I could always handcuff our wrists together and drag you in there. Might scare the attendant, though. Nope, you're safer out here."

Before she could raise another objection, he had snatched up her hand and clicked one of the bracelets over her wrist and the other one to the wheel. It was a humiliating situation, made worse when he removed the keys from the ignition and dangled them in front of her nose with a little grin. He was reminding her of earlier when she'd thrown away the keys, taunting her.

Haley fumed while he was gone. She had counted on this mix-up getting settled sometime today. Then she might be released so she could go home. Now that wouldn't happen before tomorrow. The more she thought about it, the more insane the whole thing seemed. None of it made any sense.

When he finally emerged from the motel office, he was carrying a plastic sack loaded with something.

Opening the door on her side, he dumped the sack into her lap.

"Here, you take charge of it," he ordered as he leaned across her to unlock the handcuffs.

Whatever the sack contained, the lumpy contents weren't heavy enough to crack him over the head with. Because that's what she would have liked to do to this insensitive gorilla.

"I suppose it won't be enough to just lock me inside my room. You'll insist on handcuffing me to something in there, too."

"That won't be necessary. We'll be sharing a single room."

"Please tell me you didn't."

"Naw, just kidding. I was able to get you a room of your own with no windows and only one steel door I get to lock from the outside. Kind of like a cell." His voice changed instantly then from pleasantly jocular to something that sounded like the crack of a whip. "One room, Haley. That's what we've got. And guess what? It has only one bed, too. Should be fun, huh?"

Chapter 3

Like most motels, there was little to distinguish it. Clean and impersonal. And, as promised, just one bed.

Chase had brought his athletic bag in from the car. A wary Haley watched him place it on the desk chair, open it and remove a tube of toothpaste and an unopened toothbrush.

"Here," he said, holding them out to her.

She hesitated to accept them.

"Go on, take them. I have a spare toothbrush for me."

"Thank you," she murmured coolly, taking the two items.

She watched him cross to the bathroom and spread the door wide, his hand reaching around the jamb for the light switch. He looked inside without going in. *He's checking to make sure I can't get out.*

He must have been satisfied, because he stepped to one side, sweeping a hand in the direction of the open doorway. "You take it first."

Chase could have given her a little more room to enter—but he didn't. The man knew that any contact with him, even a slight one, made her nervous.

"And don't lock the door behind you," he called after her. "Unless you want me busting in there on you."

Jerk!

Even if she'd wanted to escape, Haley realized she couldn't have managed it. The solitary frosted window was too high and too small. She used the toilet, cleaned up at the sink and brushed her teeth.

When she emerged from the bathroom, he was seated on the edge of the bed. "Join me," he said, patting the spread on his side. "Come on. You're safe."

She wasn't so sure of that, but she didn't want him to think she was afraid of him. Nervous, yes, but not afraid. She sauntered over to the bed. He'd left room for her between himself and the railed footboard. She perched on the spot, making sure to leave several inches between them.

"I have a little job for you," he said before she could ask him why he wanted her sitting here. "Something to keep you occupied while I take my own turn in the john."

That's when she noticed he had the plastic sack she'd brought in from the car. Turning it upside down between them, he dumped its mystery contents out on the spread.

"I'm afraid it's the only supper we get. You get to divide it out for us."

This was the explanation for his long absence in the motel office. There must have been snack and soda machines in there. It looked as if he'd bought at least two of everything.

"And while you divide and I visit the john…"

The hateful handcuffs, of course. She should have realized he wouldn't leave her alone in here without cuffing her to something. In this case, it was the footboard rail, leaving her with one hand to divide the haul and the other hand secured and useless.

She was half-afraid that when Chase reappeared a little later, he would be stripped down to his underwear, ready for bed. Or something more extreme. Because there was the possibility he was in the habit of sleeping in the raw, in which case... Well, in other circumstances, that might have been an interesting, even enjoyable spectacle. But not in her current situation, even if she still didn't feel afraid of sharing a room with a stranger.

As it was, she needn't have been concerned. He was fully dressed when he walked out of the bathroom. And eager.

"Time to eat!"

Haley rattled the handcuffs. "Do I rate both hands for that?"

"You do."

He unlocked the cuffs from her wrist and the rail, pocketing them along with the key. Together, they carried their separate piles of food to a table beside the front window, seating themselves in chairs across from each other.

"Not exactly a nutritious meal," Chase apologized, "but it's the best the chef could manage."

The machines he'd taken advantage of in the motel office had provided packaged crackers filled with cheese and peanut butter, nuts, chocolate bars and cans of cold soda.

"I was thinking," Haley said, biting into one of the cheese crackers, "that since there's only the one bed, and since you need the rest more than I do, why don't I curl up in the easy chair there?"

His slow reply couldn't have been more wry if he'd rehearsed it beforehand. "Now that's a plan."

"You didn't let me finish. Naturally, you aren't going to just turn me loose."

"Naturally. How do you recommend we handle that?"

"You can handcuff me to the pole of the floor lamp."

"Right. Problem with that is, I can see you walking out of here in the middle of the night dragging the floor lamp with you. Maybe even managing to flag down a lift from a truck going south on the freeway. Bet you could even invent a believable story for the driver just why you happen to be attached to a lamp."

She adopted an injured tone. "I was only thinking of your comfort."

"And I'm touched by that. But this is how it's going to be, Haley. You're going to be attached to me, my right wrist to your left. Both of us flat on the bed side by side, not under the covers but safely on top of them. Hope you can sleep on your back. What do you think?"

"You don't want to know."

"Hey, if you're worried about seduction, you can relax. Any other time I'd be happy to oblige, but tonight all I'm interested in are some hours of solid sleep. The only thing we'll be removing are our shoes."

She might have believed him…if his gaze wasn't fastened on her mouth as if he'd like to own it before he took possession of a few other areas of her body. And to her surprise, she realized she might not mind.

As it turned out, Haley couldn't accuse him of not behaving himself. He fell instantly and deeply asleep and remained that way. She, on the other hand, didn't behave herself. Not emotionally, anyway.

She wasn't happy with herself for the way she was

letting him affect her. His necessary nearness to her on the bed had her far too aware of the disturbing heat of his hard body. Conscious, too, of the distinctive, masculine scent of him.

Not happy, no.

Haley didn't expect to sleep at all. She kept picturing what she had discovered when he'd leaned toward her during the latest cuffing. He had a small scar on the outside corner of his right eye. Funny she hadn't noticed it before then.

She could see it now just by turning her head in his direction. It was a roguish thing, the kind of souvenir a scoundrel would get in a duel.

What is wrong with you? You've been reading too many pirate novels.

This was ridiculous. She turned her head away from the tempting sight of him, shut her eyes and willed herself to relax. It took a while, but eventually she drifted off.

Haley had no idea how long she slept, but when she came awake, the first thing she did was check on her captor. He was still hard asleep, breathing softly. Without any evidence of snoring, she was pleased to note. The lamp on his bedside table continued to burn.

What time was it, anyway? She glanced at the watch on her unrestrained right wrist. It was probably an hour or so until sunup. She'd slept longer than she had imagined.

If it hadn't been for that breathing, the rhythmic, slow rise and fall of his broad chest, she might have thought he had died on her in the night. Because there was no sign he had moved so much as an inch either way since he had stretched out beside her. How did he do that? Eerie. As far as she knew, Chase McKinley was legitimate. And unless she gave him any real grief, she didn't think he was a danger to her. All the same, her resolve to get away from him was stronger than ever. And if by some miracle that chance should present itself again, this time she'd need to be smarter about it.

What did she need most of all? *Money.* She'd have to get her hands on some cash if she were to get back to Portland and the people she could count on to help her out of this mess.

Money, she realized, that was waiting for her on his bedside table.

Chase had locked her purse, containing her wallet and cell phone, inside the SUV, placing it far out of her reach. But his own wallet, which he'd removed from his back jeans pocket, presumably because it would have been uncomfortable to sleep on, he'd placed on the edge of his bedside table.

What's more, the handcuff key was inside the change section of that wallet. She had watched him tuck it there.

Had she any prayer of getting the wallet without disturbing him? It wasn't very likely, but nothing ventured…

Concentration. She would have to exercise extreme concentration, starting now. Her first step was to lie there quietly while she formed a plan. By necessity, it had to be a rough, simple plan.

She began by willing her left arm to go limp, absolutely motionless, as if it were no longer a part of her body. Only this way could she prevent the wrist of that arm from tugging in the slightest fashion on the cuffs, a fatal action that would be almost certain to rouse Chase.

This achieved, and bracing herself with her right elbow, Haley slowly elevated her body from the waist up. She was satisfied when she was sitting without having stirred any part of her lower body.

Now comes the hard stuff.

In slow, patient degrees, she twisted herself in Chase's direction until she was facing the wallet. Could she manage this next challenge, leaning over his body while stretching her right arm out far enough to snag the wallet?

All, she reminded herself, without the use of her left arm to prop herself in place. Even though that arm had been available, there was such strain on it from holding it steady, it had gone to sleep. Like it was no longer her own limb.

What Haley needed right now was the skill of a contortionist. The best she could do was to will herself across the gulf with a combination of balance and strain. Out went her right arm, reaching, reaching.

Contact. Her forefinger on the surface of the wallet. Applying pressure, she was able to drag the wallet toward her just far enough to capture it with both forefinger and thumb. Holding her breath, she lifted it off the night table and drew it slowly, carefully toward her.

Apparently not carefully enough. She watched in horror as it slipped and landed on his waistline. She expected him to surge up off the bed, yanking on the chain between them. To her relief, there was nothing from him but a low grunt. He didn't move, didn't open his eyes. He was still asleep.

She waited a few seconds before plucking it off him and dropping it into her lap. Victory! She could breathe again. Her fingers were trembling now, which was why, when she parted the wallet, it fell open not to money or the handcuff key but a photograph in a clear plastic sleeve.

Haley wasn't interested. She was ready to move on when something about the picture captured her attention. The photo showed two boys, one a teenager and the other much younger. Although the two of them were looking out at the camera with almost identical grins, it was not a posed shot. It must have been taken in midaction, with the teen just having boosted the younger boy up on a horse, where he was helping him to stay firm in the saddle.

Funny how the picture seemed to tell a story. Even odder was that it should mean something to her at all. Like, for instance, what? Haley took long seconds she couldn't afford to examine it more closely. First of all, she could tell these two kids were related. But although they resembled each other strongly enough at that stage, the resemblance hadn't followed them into full adulthood.

Wait a minute. How did she know that?

The explanation struck her all at once. There was just enough of a slight likeness remaining, maybe in their similar grins, to tell her why Chase McKinley should have seemed familiar to her from the beginning.

The man beside her and Josh Matthews, the man she'd dated before he left Portland, were brothers. She didn't know how she could be certain when their surnames were different, but she was sure of it.

An unrestrained hand reached out and snatched the wallet away from her.

He was awake, was he? Good!

"Get these handcuffs off me, you son of a—"

She was so angry she choked on the rest.

Son of a bitch was right, Chase thought. He'd messed up by placing his wallet where he had thought she couldn't possibly get at it. He had forgotten, too, that the snapshot was in there.

The mistake with the wallet, although bad enough, was nothing by itself. This whole effort was a disaster. He hadn't been thinking clearly when he'd taken her. Crazy of him. On the other hand, it had seemed the only way to get the truth out of her. She was all he had, and now he'd blown his cover.

She rattled the handcuffs binding them.

"Take these cuffs off of me before I shout the motel down!"

Since there didn't seem to be any wisdom in hesitation, Chase got the key out of his wallet and removed the bracelets. She couldn't thrust herself away from him fast enough. Springing feetfirst off the bed, she whirled around to confront him, her blue eyes sparking with fire.

"I want answers, and I want them fast!"

"Hey, take it easy."

"Do I get my answers, or do I go to the office and ask them to call the cops?"

"Look, you'll get your answers, but don't you think they might wait long enough for us to take turns in the bathroom? I don't know about you, but, uh, I could use the facilities."

Eyes narrowed at him suspiciously, she seemed to think about it a minute before deciding. "All right, but make it quick."

Quick was exactly what Chase needed. Flushing the toilet afterwards, he washed his hands at the sink, splashed cold water on his face and was drying himself when he glimpsed his reflection in the mirror. Jeez, he looked like hell, bleary-eyed, unshaven, clothes rumpled from a night of sleep.

She was waiting for him when he emerged. "You took your time," she grumbled.

She had a comb in her hand. As a matter of fact, it was his comb. She held it up. "I helped myself to this in your bag. Hope you don't mind."

"Oh, sure, why not? Come to think of it, there's some shaving cream in there you might like."

She sailed by him into the bathroom, rounding on him just before she shut the door behind her. "You *will* be here when I come out, won't you?"

Now that was funny, considering that until a short while ago, this was exactly the kind of question he would have been asking *her*. But then she no longer had a reason to escape.

Chase was ready to handle her when she came out of the bathroom. Or maybe not. He knew he looked crappy. She looked great. His comb had done wonders for that mass of dark hair. And although she might figure she could benefit from makeup, he felt her beauty was natural enough not to need it.

That face of hers was the kind a man yearned to—

Don't go there, McKinley. This is no time for getting all worked up.

He'd left their room long enough to bring her purse from the car, passing it to her now in hopes she would regard it as a peace offering. Apparently not. She swiped it out of his hand without a word of thanks.

Damn, she was still mad as blazes.

"Your cell is there in your purse," Chase assured her.

"Do I make my calls right now, or wait until after you talk?"

"I'm going to explain everything to you, I promise, but could we—"

"Are you going to start stalling again?"

"Hell, no, I'm— Well, yeah, I am, kind of. But, look, can't we do this over breakfast? Haley, I'm starving. There's a diner next door already open and serving. What do you say?"

It took Chase some time to convince her, but he finally had them in a corner of the diner seated across from each other in a booth where they could talk in privacy. She was ready to listen, calmer by then. To a degree.

Haley waited until the waitress poured coffee and retreated with their orders to accuse him. "You're not what you say you are, and there is no legal order for my apprehension, is there?"

"Half-right."

"And which half is that?"

"I am a licensed recovery agent. The ID I showed you is genuine."

"Which makes the apprehension order a forgery."

"Afraid so," he admitted solemnly.

"Why? What is this all about?"

"It's a little...complicated."

"Uncomplicate it for me. There are a couple of things I need to know. We've established what you are. What we haven't settled is *who* you are."

Chase nodded, understanding her confusion. "The photo in my wallet. You're wondering why Josh is a Matthews and I'm a McKinley. We're half brothers."

"Mmm, I kind of thought that might be the case. You look alike."

"What else? You said there were a couple of things."

As if fortifying herself, she brought her coffee mug to those beguiling lips of hers. He watched her swallow the brew, following it down that perfect throat.

"Yes, the second thing," she said, lowering the mug. "About what you're going to tell me... I want to know right now if I have a reason to think I'm being involved in something I'll have to worry about just by hearing it. Of course," she added quickly before Chase could reply, "you could lie about it. You did before. Only then I didn't have a choice about going with you."

"And now?"

"Now if I decide you're not telling me the truth, I'm going to get up from this booth and walk out of here."

"Then I hope this time you'll believe me, because I need your help. No risk to you." It was true—he had no reason to think she was in any personal danger.

There was no denying she was suspicious of him and his motives. Who could blame her? He could tell that by the way she gazed at him silently and how her fingertips beat a slow tattoo on the edge of the table before she made up her mind.

"All right, let's hear what you have to say. Just what is this help you need from me?"

"Josh is missing."

Her blue eyes widened. "Says who?"

"I do." He bent toward her. "Look, you know Josh is a freelance investigative journalist. I know you know because no one could spend any time with him and not learn that. He would have talked your head off about it."

Haley nodded. "He did."

"I bet he also told you that for years he's been looking for the big story that will make his reputation."

"He mentioned it."

She's being cagey, Chase thought. *Unwilling to give me more until she hears just what I have to say.*

"Some weeks back," he said, "Josh emailed me that he'd found that story. He was excited as hell about it, but he didn't share any details. He would, eventually—but he always kept it to himself until the words poured out on the page. All he told me was that he'd be gone for a while. Not where or for how long. Not even the subject of the story. Just that he was following a trail, but he'd keep in touch."

"Only he didn't." She was perceptive.

"I haven't heard from him in all the weeks he's been gone. Not a single word. When I started to worry seriously, I tried to reach him on his cell. No response."

"Did you stop to consider he could be out of the country? Maybe in some remote area where there's no reliable service."

Chase shook his head. "Believe me, I thought of all the possibilities. No, something is definitely wrong. I can feel it."

"And that qualifies as missing?"

Before he could answer her, the waitress arrived with a tray. There was the delay of the soft-spoken young woman setting out their orders—fresh grapefruit and steaming oatmeal for Haley, bacon and pancakes drenched in melting butter and maple syrup for Chase.

Before she went away, the girl poured more coffee into their mugs, leaving him aware that Haley was staring at his plate. "I don't know how you all do it," she said, making a face.

"Who?"

"Men. Well, most of the men I know, anyway. You eat all those calories and don't gain an ounce. We women add pounds just looking at it. I'm surprised you didn't ask the waitress to add a glazed doughnut to your order."

"I might get around to that yet," he said, tucking into his breakfast.

She waited until he'd put away a couple of slices of bacon and half of one of his pancakes before reminding him, "You still owe me an answer."

He cleared his mouth. "Hell, yeah, I think he's missing."

"And you think I can help you? Why? Why would you suppose I might have information you yourself don't have?"

"Why not? Why wouldn't Josh have shared his plans with you? Isn't that what lovers do?"

Chapter 4

"What in the world," she demanded, dropping her spoon into the oatmeal in startled surprise, "made you think your brother and I are lovers?"

"Well, aren't you?"

It was what Josh had implied in his last emails before he'd disappeared, that he was crazy about the woman he'd met in Portland on one of his assignments. Sweethearts. That was the quaint word he'd used to describe Haley Adams and him. That they were sweethearts.

It was this eager confidence to Chase, the brother Josh loved and trusted, that had gotten Chase into trouble. You weren't supposed to be attracted in any measure, even minimally, to the woman your devoted brother deeply cared for, maybe even hoped to marry. Chase had felt like a heel, still did, for thinking lusty thoughts about her.

"I can't imagine what impression Josh gave you about

us," Haley said, "but it seems to be an exaggerated one. We went out often, that's true, had a lot of fun together, even became very good friends, but it didn't go beyond that."

Not as far as she was concerned, but he was convinced his brother felt otherwise. Poor Josh. He apparently didn't know about that other guy in Portland, the one who might have been hanging around her before Josh and who, after Josh left the scene, had moved in on Haley. He'd seen it himself.

Haley sighed. "If you wanted my help, why didn't you just ask me? Why all this elaborate nonsense about bringing me in because I'd violated a bond on some fictional court appearance?"

She would smell a lie if he didn't tell the truth. "Simple. I didn't trust you."

"You didn't tr—" She broke off there, looking very confused. "How could you mistrust me when you'd never met me?"

"I had a reason."

"What reason?"

"I'd learned you had connections with some very questionable people."

"Me? What? That deserves explaining. Like, exactly what did you learn and from whom?"

"You want the long version or the short?"

"Make it brief, but don't leave anything out."

Now there was a challenge, Chase thought. He had no choice but to answer it. "There's this private investigator I use sometimes whenever the bail bond company I work for back in Seattle overloads me with FTAs and I need his help in locating the tough ones."

"Wait a minute." Haley wore an expression that said

she was not pleased. "Are you telling me you actually had a PI following me?"

"After Josh vanished, yeah."

"You think I had something to do with that?" No, she was definitely not pleased.

"I didn't know what to think. I just wanted information."

"You had some nerve! And what did your PI tell you?"

"For one thing, that you were cheating on Josh with this Bill Farley. My PI had photo evidence of the two of you being cozy around Portland, and I saw it for myself when I arrived and took over."

"Uh-huh. And what else?"

"That your boyfriend, Farley, is actively associated with some Vegas-type racketeers."

"Well, thank you for that very incisive report." Her voice had turned to ice. "Now if you don't mind hearing some advice…"

"I'm always open to suggestions," he drawled.

"That's good, because that's exactly what I have. When you get back to Seattle, McKinley…when you get back there, the first thing you should do is fire your private investigator, because he definitely stinks. Then after that, I think you need to find a good ophthalmologist and have your eyes examined."

"Hey, I'll have you know I have twenty-twenty vision."

"I don't see how either you or your PI possibly can. Because the both of you have badly judged the relationship between Bill Farley and me."

"Yeah? What is the truth?"

"That poor Billy happens to be desperately in love with my friend Jennifer Donaldson. Only she's given him back his ring and refuses to see him until he's broken all contact with the crowd he's been hanging around with. That much is fact."

"So, why have *you* been meeting him? And don't tell me you haven't."

"Wouldn't dream of it. Yes, I've been meeting him. For one reason only. Bill knows how close I am to Jennifer. He's been pleading with me to intercede for him. But Jennifer is right. He needs to break away from these people. They're a rough bunch, though, and Bill is afraid of how they'll react. Anything else?"

"There was that intimate parting on your doorstep."

"What? The hug of sympathy? Oh, no, don't tell me you assumed it involved a kiss behind the shrub."

Chase raised both hands in surrender. "I give up."

"Not yet you don't, mister. I gave you the truth. How about yours? Were you ever going to tell me before I discovered that photo in your wallet?"

"I was waiting until Seattle."

"Why Seattle? Why force me to come all this way? Why didn't you just explain everything in Portland and save us the trip?"

"I didn't trust you."

"You didn't trust me in Portland, but you would have trusted me in Seattle? How does that make sense?"

"It doesn't," Chase admitted. "All I wanted…all I had in my mind was to get you on familiar turf where I was in control, away from any possible interference from what I was convinced were your mob friends who would rush to your rescue with big guns. Look, the fact is I just wasn't thinking straight."

"And now? Are you thinking straight?"

"Let's hope so."

Chase looked down at what remained on his plate.

It had to be cold by now. Neither one had touched their breakfast after the conversation had become so intense.

"I'm not hungry any longer," he said. "What about you? You want them to bring you a fresh oatmeal?"

She shook her head. "I'm ready to leave."

"Good. I was hoping for a chance to stretch my legs before we headed back to Portland."

"You're in the mood for exercise?"

"It wouldn't hurt after all those hours yesterday and today that we've been sedentary. Also…"

"What?" she urged him.

"I was hoping for a chance to explain to you just why I haven't been thinking straight."

"And you feel a walk would be suitable for that?" The look on her face told him she was considering it. "I wouldn't mind," she decided.

Chase left a tip on the table, paid the bill at the counter and accompanied Haley out of the diner.

Considering the wild circumstances that had landed her in both the company and control of Chase McKinley, Haley could have been making a mistake willingly going off with him like this in a lonely place. She sensed, however, that she had nothing to fear. She remembered that she hadn't feared him this entire time. Despite his bounty hunter swagger, there had been a gentleness lurking within him.

On the other hand, her trust could have more to do with the morning than the man. The sun had risen over the mountains in the east while they were in the diner, promising another feel-good day for Washington. It was still cool, though, with dew on the grass.

Just past the diner, on the access road off the interstate that had brought them first to the motel, was a posted trail to a nature preserve. It was the perfect place for a stroll, lined with the glossy-leaved rhododendrons that were native to the Pacific coast. Even now, past their bloom, they were magnificent shrubs.

"Before you begin," she said, "there's something I'd like to know. Josh told me he had this half brother who was an army ranger and stationed overseas. And here you are, a bounty hunter and not overseas."

"Yeah, well, that's past tense." Hands shoved into his pants pockets, he paused to watch a bald eagle circling slowly high overhead. "The thing is, our dad—Josh's biological father to put it accurately—died from a ruptured aneurysm just a couple of weeks before my current enlistment was up."

"I'm sorry about your father." She paused. "They sent you home for the funeral, I suppose."

"That and to help Josh settle affairs. By the time that was done, I'd decided not to reenlist."

"I see." Haley nodded, and then almost as a part of the same action shook her head. "No, I don't see. Didn't you care for the army?"

"Sure, I liked it just fine. It was my career."

"Then why…"

He walked on, changing the subject. Or seeming to. "I bet Josh never mentioned to you that after I quit the army, I joined the ranks of the bounty hunters."

"Come to think of it," she said catching up to him, "he never spoke at all about you after that one time."

"No, he wouldn't. Josh liked to boast of his big brother's service record, but I think he thought there was something just a little disreputable about being a bounty hunter. But it suits me. I was trained in search and recovery, and I needed something temporary until I could decide what I wanted to do for the rest of my life."

"Fascinating, McKinley, except I don't see what any of this has to do with you not thinking straight."

"Hold on, we're getting there."

Chase stopped again on the trail, this time to discover a willow goldfinch flitting from holly bush to holly bush.

"Waiting," Haley sang.

He turned his head to favor her with a grin. "I'm gonna bore you with some more history."

"How much?"

"Probably more than you're going to like, but it's necessary."

"Going back how far?"

"To when I was very young. I have no memory of my biological father. He walked out on us when I was a baby. The only father I knew was the man my mother married when I was about four. Brian Matthews was everything my biological father wasn't. I got every kind of attention a kid could want from both him and my mother. That all threatened to change when I was eight years old. Are you cold? It's a little chilly out here still."

"I'm fine. Go on. What happened when you were eight?"

"Mom and Dad told me there was going to be a baby, that I was going to have a brother. I figured I wouldn't have all the attention anymore. Or maybe any attention at all. I hated this kid before he was even born."

"I detect that didn't last."

"I had very smart parents. They knew I was jealous, and they knew what to do about it. Not long after the baby came home from the hospital, they sat me down and placed him carefully in my lap. They said his name was Josh and that I was to be someone very important in his life. I would matter to him. Matter? I wanted to shove the little intruder right back at them."

"And did you?"

"I would have, except before I could do that, this tiny thing looked up at me with…well, I don't know that I could call it anything like trust. I don't suppose the vision of a baby that young is developed enough to be capable of any sort of recognition of that kind."

"Probably not."

"Didn't matter. He looked up at me, I looked back at him, and I was lost."

"Magic?"

"Yeah, an instant connection. You understand it, huh?"

"I don't know why I should. I'm an only child. No siblings." But she did understand. She remembered the photograph he carried in his wallet of a teenage boy helping his young brother to ride a horse. "So, from then on?"

Chase nodded. "I looked out for him. Came to his rescue when he needed it."

And you're still doing that, she thought. *No wonder you came home and stayed home.*

Josh had mentioned that his mother had died of breast cancer some years ago. Now their father was gone, and the brothers were the only family left.

The whole thing was clear to her now. Chase was convinced his brother was missing and in trouble, and that had him wild with worry. He was willing to do anything to find him—including what could easily be defined as kidnapping an unarmed woman.

After checking out of the motel, they filled the SUV with gas and started back to Portland. Now that Haley had her cell phone back, she called a couple of her closest friends who might have been worried about her absence. She was ready to explain it as business, but they hadn't known she was gone.

Chase was silent during these calls and silent for some minutes after. She couldn't be unaware of his sidelong glances and the speculative look in his eyes.

"I seem to be the subject of your thoughts. You're wondering something about me. Do I get to know what it is?"

"It's just that I shared practically everything with you about my past except the crush on Miss Sheldon I had in the second grade. Heck, I still remember how I admired her breasts in a certain blouse she wore."

Haley affected what she considered to be a genuine case of shock. "In the *second* grade!"

"What can I say? I guess I was a budding lech even back then. But Miss Sheldon did have an impressive bust. Anyway, to get back to the moment… It occurred to me I know nothing about *your* background."

"What's to know? It's nothing as dramatic as yours. I already mentioned I'm an only child. Both my parents are retired high school teachers living now in Arizona where it's dry. My father used to complain about the damp, raw climate in Portland. Living in Seattle, you know what that's like."

"Yep, going whole winters without seeing the sun."

"Exactly. Dad is as happy now as a hound on the scent of a possum. You see, all very ordinary and boring."

"Maybe, but I think there are depths to Haley Adams she's not sharing."

"She aims to fascinate, all right."

In truth, Haley concluded, Chase McKinley was the one who currently fascinated. She still wondered about that scar near his eye. It would have been easy enough just to ask him about it, except she didn't want him to think she was interested in him like that. Bad enough she couldn't stop inhaling that heady, masculine scent of his and she liked the way he quirked one eyebrow whenever he was questioning the veracity of something.

They were silent again. Haley might not consider it safe to get personal with him on any man-woman basis, but she couldn't stop thinking about his relationship with his brother. She had told herself earlier it wasn't her business or something he would appreciate discussing in any depth.

Now she couldn't resist risking it.

"Chase?"

"Huh?"

"About Josh."

"What about him?"

"I was just wondering how he feels about you still playing the big, protective brother. I mean, he's— what?—well into his twenties and on his own now. I was just, you know, wondering."

"Don't wonder."

There was a bite to his words that bordered on the severe. She'd been right. He didn't like anything that approached criticism about his concerns for Josh.

Haley immediately dropped the subject.

Chase parked in front of Haley's terrace house, shut off the engine and went around the SUV to see her to her door. The trip back to Portland had been as uneventful as the one before it had been action-packed. As far as he knew, she had been honest with him, giving him everything he'd asked for about Josh and his brother's departure from Portland. Chase had no reason to linger, but he suddenly found himself reluctant to part from her.

He knew that examining that reluctance would be

a mistake. It was better just to apologize for having wrongly apprehended her, thank her for helping him and leave her here and now before making a fool of himself.

She was digging her house keys out of her purse when he remembered something. "Would you mind taking this?" he asked her, removing one of his business cards from his wallet and handing it to her. "My address and phone number are there. I'm thinking that if you should hear from Josh, you'd do me the favor of contacting me. There's no guarantee that he'll write or call me, but you…"

"Yes, of course," she said, accepting his card. "And having my own address and number as you did before you turned up here yesterday, maybe you'd return the favor if Josh should get in touch with you first. I would like to know he's all right and how he made out with the big story he was so eager to hunt down."

"I'll do that," he promised her.

She had the key inserted in her door and was unlocking it when a woman with a helmet of tight curls and a long nose flew out of the house adjacent to hers. She had a packet in her hand and was waving it as she hailed Haley. "Saw you pull up and decided I'd better run out and deliver this. Old Faithful went and pushed it through the wrong slot in the wrong door."

"This is my neighbor, Phyllis," Haley introduced Chase, accepting the packet. "Don't tell me we're having that trouble again, Phyl?"

"Yep, we're going to have to talk seriously to that man."

Haley turned to Chase, explaining, "Our postal carrier is forever mixing up our mail."

The neighbor lifted her hand in farewell. "Gotta fly. I promised Eddy I'd be on hand for his soccer game."

"Thanks, Phyl," Haley called after her.

Chase was prepared to make his own farewell when his gaze was caught by the address on the front of the packet in her hand. The sight of it locked him in place where he stood.

"Can I see that?" he asked.

"It is *my* address," she assured him.

"It isn't that. It's the handwriting."

She passed the brown packet over to him so he could look at it up close. There was no mistaking the familiar scrawl. "This is from Josh."

"I never had any occasion to see his handwriting, so I couldn't have recognized it. You're sure of that?"

"Positive." He gave the packet back to her.

"You'd better come in, then, while I open it."

He made an effort to contain his excitement as she pushed the door open, scooped up the rest of her mail from the floor of the foyer where it had landed from the mail slot and indicated he should follow her into the house.

It was a modest-sized place. Comfortably furnished, Chase noted, with appointments that spoke of its owner's tastes. Country-style fabrics, traditional art work on the walls, potted green plants and a minimum of ornaments.

Chase permitted himself no more than a quick visual sweep. He was too eager to see the contents of the packet to be interested elsewhere. Haley placed her mail on the living room coffee table and perched with the packet in hand on the edge of the sofa while Chase hovered over her. He watched as she slid open one end of the thin package with a sharp fingernail.

Upending the packet, she shook it to dump out its contents. Three clear, very small plastic envelopes slid out onto the surface of the coffee table. They could have been sealed pill pouches for traveling. But they didn't contain pills.

Chase and Haley stared down at them, neither one of them speaking. It was Chase who found his raspy voice first.

"Seeds! My brother sends you three little pouches of seeds? What in hell! Does this have any meaning for you?"

Haley could only wordlessly shake her head.

"There must be an explanation. Look inside the packet. See if there's something else."

Her fingers burrowed into the packet, withdrawing a folded note. She spread it open, scanned it silently and then thrust it at him. "I can't read this scrawl of his. See if you can make it out."

"It's worse than usual. He must have been in a big hurry when he wrote it." Chase read it aloud for her. "'Take care of these for me, will you, sweetheart? Believe it or not, they're very rare and valuable. I don't want to take any chances with them. I thought maybe you wouldn't mind locking them away at the bank in your safety deposit box. *Please.*' And that's underlined."

Haley gazed up at him, mystified. "And that's all? Not even a signature?"

"Afraid that's it."

"Well, I have to say this is the damnedest gift I've ever received. This half brother of yours…he couldn't be half-baked as well, could he?"

"I don't think Josh meant these seeds as any kind of a joke. I think he was totally serious when he sent them."

"I'd like to go on sitting here trying to figure out what they mean, but right now my brain could use a stimulant." She got to her feet. "Would you drink some coffee if I made it? It'll only take a couple of minutes."

"Coffee would be welcome."

"Make yourself comfortable. I'll call you when it's ready."

He watched her walk away toward the rear of the house, the slow sway of her perfectly rounded backside sending a shaft of arousal to his groin. Presumably she was headed to the kitchen, and he was headed to hell if he didn't learn to control these desires for his brother's girl.

He was starting to settle himself on one of the easy chairs when a revelation struck him. A return address! Had Josh included any kind of a return address? Neither one of them had thought to look for that. If he could find a return address, learn where Josh was…

Chase snatched up the empty brown paper packet from the sofa where Haley had discarded it. He searched both sides of it. Haley's address was there on the front, yes. But no return address either there or on the reverse of the packet. He even felt inside in case Haley had missed something. Nothing.

It occurred to him that, considering how rare and valuable Josh claimed these seeds were, he'd been very careless in getting them to Haley. They had arrived by ordinary mail. No special delivery, nothing registered or requiring a signature.

There was something Chase suddenly realized he was overlooking. A postmark. He turned the packet back over to the front. Yeah, there it was, a little blurred but still readable.

Anchorage, Alaska.

Josh was in Anchorage, Alaska! Or had been when he'd mailed this. What in the world was he doing way up in Alaska? And connected with seeds of all things?

A reasonable theory right about now would have been

nice. He didn't have one. Or even a few seconds to come up with one. He was startled by the sound of breaking glass from the direction of the kitchen, followed by a sharp cry.

Chase discarded the packet and raced toward the noise.

Chapter 5

He found Haley in the country-style kitchen, staring in dismay at the shattered pieces of a glass carafe on the floor. The carafe must have belonged to the coffeemaker on the counter. The water she had apparently filled it with was spreading across the brick tiles.

Chase went to her immediately, expressing his concern. "Did you cut yourself?"

"Not a scratch. What you heard, my dropping the carafe and crying out, had nothing to do with an accident. It was the result of my discovering *that* when I turned from the sink."

She indicated the *that* she'd referred to by nodding toward the back door. Chase looked. The door was slightly ajar.

"Was it locked when we left here yesterday?"

"Absolutely. And no one has a spare key."

"And you watched me—"

"Take my front door key from my purse and securely

lock the front door before you hustled me off to what was supposed to be Portland's main police headquarters."

"Any other outside doors?" he asked her.

"Just the two."

"Then whoever broke in here, and obviously some-one did, either forced the door or picked the lock and afterward found he wasn't able to close it again tightly." Chase crouched down, examining both the door and the lock without touching them. "I can't see any evidence of either forcing or picking," he said, standing straight again. "But then I'm no detective. Haley, I think you need to report this to the police."

"Would you do it for me? Please."

"Of course, yes." Unhooking his cell phone from his belt, he dialed 911.

"They're sending an officer," he reported to Haley when he rang off.

She nodded without comment. There had been a change in her while he'd looked at the door. She had been fairly composed before that. Now she was visibly shaking.

Chase didn't hesitate. He went to her and folded her in his arms. She didn't object, not then or seconds after when he began to rock her slowly. They were both ready to explain the action as a form of innocent comfort.

"I'm sorry," she excused herself. "I'm not usually a wimp like this."

"You're entitled."

"I guess it's the shock of realizing that someone has violated your privacy, maybe been all through your house handling your things."

"Try not to think about it."

"I mean, you hear that's the behavior of people when their living quarters have been broken into, don't you?"

"Sure, it's understandable."

What am I doing? Chase asked himself. Pretending this is all normal, holding her like this, expressing sympathy. Initially, that had been true, but it had quickly altered into an intimacy. An emotional awareness of how soft she was in his arms, how fragrant. And of how much he wanted this woman to whom he had no rightful claim.

Haley must have realized at the same time as he did that their tight closeness was a mistake. They broke away from each other simultaneously.

She prattled nervously, "I need to clean up this mess on the floor before that officer gets here and thinks it's some part of the break-in he can count as evidence."

"Want my help?" Chase offered.

"Sure, you can sweep up the glass while I make a start on mopping up the water."

He watched her open a closet with a haste he thought might be the result of their embrace, her need maybe to forget it. She removed a broom and a dustpan and handed them to him before securing a sponge mop for herself.

By the time the uniform arrived, the kitchen floor bore no trace of Haley's accident. The thick-waisted officer, who had a friendly, understanding manner, drew on a pair of latex gloves and inspected the back door. Afterward he had Haley accompany him through the house to check for any missing valuables.

Chase saw no need to accompany them. He had a feeling she wasn't going to find anything missing. Nothing psychic on his part. He didn't believe in that kind of thing. This was something based on reason, something that had occurred to him just after the cop arrived.

It didn't bear mentioning. Not yet. But he wanted to think about it, which he did while standing with his backside against the counter, his arms folded across his chest.

He met Haley's look when they returned. She shook her head. "Nothing seems to have been taken or disturbed. Not even my computer."

"Looks like whoever was in here didn't get whatever he hoped to find," the officer said. "I imagine he wore latex gloves like mine. I could find no sign of prints on either the door lock or the handle. Afraid that lock is too damaged to repair. You'll have to get a locksmith in here to replace it."

"I will," Haley promised him.

"Meanwhile, Ms. Adams, you've got a bolt there. You need to keep it in place until the new lock is installed. I'll file a report, but with nothing to go on it won't produce results, I'm afraid."

"I never did get that coffee made for us," she said after the officer left.

"Doesn't matter," Chase told her.

She looked at him, puzzled. "What I can't figure is why a thief would break in here and then take nothing at all. Doesn't make sense."

"I think he, or she as the case might be, was looking for something specific."

"Like what? I don't have any valuables. Even my jewelry is all costume."

"You're wrong. You do have something valuable."

"You're very sure of yourself."

"That's because, while you and the cop were checking the house over, I had the time to figure it out. The seeds, Haley. If Josh is right, and they are valuable, then that's what the burglar wanted."

"But they weren't here when he broke in."

"They would have been if your mail carrier hadn't screwed up with the delivery. And don't ask me how the thief knew about the seeds or that they were sent here. That's still a mystery."

"You might have mentioned all this to the cop while he was still here."

"What was the point? Even if it's a good one, it's still a theory, something he might have considered too far-fetched to take seriously. Besides…"

"Yes?"

"He might have wanted to confiscate the seeds, insist they be examined by a forensic team."

She tilted her head, gazing at him with a little smile. "You don't believe that."

"No, I don't believe that."

"Then what do you believe?"

"That those pouches should go straight to where my brother asked you to put them. In your safe deposit box."

"I agree, although I find it awfully hard to believe any seeds could be so rare and valuable that someone would want to steal them. I mean, *seeds*. It's not like they're diamonds."

"I know. You think we could go now?"

"You're awfully anxious."

"I trust Josh when he writes he doesn't want to take any chances with the seeds. Your bank still open?"

"Should be for at least another half hour."

"Then let's go."

They were out of the house and headed for the SUV, the pouches tucked inside Haley's purse, when Chase remembered to tell her, "By the way, I found out Josh is in Anchorage, Alaska. Tell you about it on the way."

Chase found a spot to park at the curb next to a small park, directly across the street from the bank.

"Would you mind going in alone?" he asked Haley.

"I don't like the idea of letting you go off that way, but there's something I need to take care of, and I think it had better not wait."

She looked as if she would like to ask him what was so urgent but kept silent about her curiosity.

"I'll explain it to you when you get back. Meanwhile, I'm going to sit right here by the wheel and watch until you get safely inside."

"Chase, despite how I behaved when I saw that kitchen door ajar, I don't need protection. I'll be fine. It's just across the street, and once I'm inside, there's the bank security guard on duty. You do what you have to do while I get these seeds inside my box."

As he'd promised, Chase stayed at the wheel, keeping his gaze on Haley as she crossed the street. Frustratingly, he lost momentary sight of her as a passing truck passed between them.

When his view was clear again, she was on the sidewalk outside the bank. She was not alone. To his alarm, Haley was struggling to keep possession of her purse. The would-be snatcher had the appearance of a hoodlum. Where the hell had he suddenly come from out of nowhere?

As during his days in war zones, Chase was not for a second inactive. With his first glimpse of Haley in trouble, he was out of the SUV and charging to her rescue. He never got the chance to engage with this enemy. The bastard saw him coming, abandoned his target and fled up the sidewalk.

There was no point in going after Haley's assailant. A car was waiting for him, its passenger door already open. Chase saw nothing more than his back disappearing into the vehicle, which immediately tore up the street and around the corner, out of sight.

In any case, his first concern was for Haley.

Before he could ask her if she was all right, she faced him with a stubborn "I wasn't going to let that little punk get my bag."

"I saw."

Her valor sufficiently demonstrated, she seemed to wilt then. Chase put his hand out, ready to support her. She waved it away.

"I'm not going to go all to pieces this time like back at the house, but I admit I wouldn't mind sitting down. What I can't figure is whether I keep running into trouble or whether it keeps running into me."

"Let's go into the bank," Chase advised her. "There'll be a seat for you there."

"And a lot of fussing to go with it. I'm all out of 'oh, yes, I'd love some attention, please.' There's a bench over there in the park. Let's go there where we can be private. We need to talk."

"Haley, I think what we need to do is let the bank know what happened out here so they can inform the police. Plus, we've got to get those seeds into the safe deposit box before the bank closes."

"The police will want to question us. I was too busy fighting off my attacker to get any useful description of him. What about you and the getaway vehicle?"

"Too fast for me to get a license number."

"There you are."

"We should still—"

"Park bench," she insisted.

Two minutes later, after being escorted across the street by Chase, Haley found herself gratefully seated on one of the park benches facing the bank.

"Better?" he asked from his own seat beside her.

"Much."

They were silent for a long moment while she recovered herself. She turned to him then, wanting to talk. "You know perfectly well this wasn't some random mugging. Not with the waiting car that must have followed us from the house. The odds are high they're the same people who broke into my place. They somehow know about the seeds." She patted the side of her purse. "They want them, and they were willing to risk a daylight snatching to get them."

That scar so close to his eye seemed more vivid than ever. Anger, she thought. Anger with himself.

"I should have anticipated something like that. I should have crossed the street with you and gone into the bank. It was unforgivable of me."

"How about I listen to your self-recriminations later? Right now I'd like to hear about the something important that couldn't wait. You did promise to explain it to me when I got back to the car. So, what is this important something?"

"It was a phone call I needed to make to Seattle. I'm away so much of the time hunting down bail bond jumpers that my mail used to pile up. That's when I hired my neighbor, Andrea Nelson, to collect it for me daily from my mail office store and hold it for me at her place. I got to thinking on the way over here that if Josh sent you what he considered a vital packet…"

"Then," Haley said, understanding, "there was a good chance he sent you a similar packet, and if this Andrea Nelson were to collect it for you—" She covered her mouth with her hand in concern. "Oh, Chase, you were going to phone to warn her of a possible threat. Do it now. Call her and tell her what's been happening here. Say she should stay away from your box at this mail office store until she hears from you again."

She watched him stand, unclip his cell from his belt and punch in the number that would connect him to his neighbor in Seattle. Haley listened tensely as he spoke to whomever answered on the other end.

"Hi, Richard, this is Chase McKinley. I'm calling from Portland. Is Andrea available to come to the phone?"

Haley thought from the grim expression on his face and his long silence that he must be listening to a complicated explanation, one that had her fearing the worst.

Chase finally spoke. "Yes, of course, I understand. No, I wouldn't dream of bothering her. Like you say, she needs to rest. Tell her for me how deeply sorry I am that something like this happened. It's all right. I'll call the store and have them hold all of my mail until I get back. Could I ask this one quick thing before I let you get back to your wife? Was all of it taken?"

There was another answer from the other end of the line, Chase punctuating it with a "Yeah, I see," and a muttered "Uh-huh," then an understanding "Well, of course, she's in no way to blame."

This was followed by more dialogue from Andrea's husband. Chase ended the call with a sympathetic, "I'll call again tomorrow just to see how she's getting on. Thanks, Richard."

Haley watched him clip his cell back on his belt. The grim expression had turned to a sorrowful one.

"I'm guessing you were too late for a warning," she said.

He nodded slowly. "She was attacked coming away from the store this morning. Struck on the head from behind and suffered a lump, but she'll be all right. They called the police, but she never caught a glimpse of her attacker. So, like here, there's not much chance of catching these guys. Her husband doesn't want her doing any more mail pickups for me. I'd feel the same if I were him."

"*Was* all of your mail taken?"

"Afraid so. Richard said Andrea remembered one of the envelopes was a thick one with no return address."

"Which must mean that Josh *did* send you a duplicate."

"Looks like it."

"Chase, whoever took it couldn't be the thieves operating down here, not way up in Seattle on the same day."

"No, but they were probably working together, maybe a hired gang. Who else would want to steal seeds? This whole thing is insane, getting nuttier by the hour. How can something as ordinary as seeds involve this kind of desperate effort to get them?"

"Apparently, these aren't ordinary seeds."

"Which is why we've got to get them locked up in your safe deposit box."

"Not today, we won't. While you were on the phone, I saw the guard over there locking the doors. Seems like banking hours are over for the day."

"Leaving us wondering what to do with these seeds until tomorrow."

Haley tapped the nail of her forefinger against her front teeth. "I think I have the solution for that. I should have considered it back at the house, but I was too fixated on Josh's request to get the seeds into the bank for it to occur to me until just now."

"Explain."

She did just that while he listened with growing interest. "His name is Anton Rostov. He's a professor here at the university. A very sweet man."

"Sounds Russian."

"He was born there, but he's an American citizen now. I worked on computer projects for him from time to time. That's how I met Josh. The professor had asked me to stop in at his lab to discuss a new project. Josh was there, and the professor introduced us."

"I wondered how that connection happened."

"*You* wondered? I did, too, when he didn't waste any time asking me out on the first of our dates. I asked myself where all that brashness of his came from." She eyed Chase critically. "I think I know now where he got it."

"I don't deny it. I was an effective role model."

"The professor would appreciate that. He thought your brother and I made a very cute couple. His words, not mine."

"Okay, but why was Josh visiting the professor?"

"He was consulting him about this story he's chasing. He was vague about it, and at the time I didn't pay much attention. Now it makes sense."

"Why?"

"Because Professor Rostov is a prominent botanist."

"Seeds," Chase said.

"Exactly. He may be able to account for the seeds I've got here in my purse, explain what this mystery is all about. But there's something just as important as that."

"Like?"

"Professor Rostov has a safe in his office where he locks away all his important documents."

"A substitute for a bank safe deposit box, huh?"

"That's what I'm thinking."

"What are we waiting for?" Chase handed her his cell phone. "Call him. See if he's available and whether he'll agree to meet with us."

Haley learned the professor was available and would be pleased to meet with them. She fed Chase directions along the way to the university. Both of them tried to watch for any vehicle that might be tailing them, but since rush hour was underway and the streets were dense with traffic, that was an impossible undertaking.

Almost as impossible, Haley thought, as Chase's inability to stop worrying about Josh.

"How in hell did he get mixed up in something as incredible as this?"

She had no answer for him.

They found Professor Rostov in the greenhouse that adjoined his laboratory. The greenhouse was so jammed with plants it was like a jungle. At the moment, the professor was carefully manicuring one of his beloved plants.

Haley never looked at his enormous figure without thinking of a great Russian bear. He hugged like a bear, too, crushing her in his arms. Even his deep, hearty voice was a growl.

"How are you, sweet pea? It's been too long," he complained.

A bear, yes, but a very gentle one.

"It's good to see you, Professor." She turned to Chase behind her. "This is Josh's half brother, Chase McKinley, whom I told you about on the phone."

The professor extended his big paw, shaking Chase's hand with such force and vigor that an amused Haley saw Chase's dark eyes widen with surprise.

"Welcome to my garden," he greeted Chase, his Russian accent scarcely noticeable after all his years of living in America.

"Thanks for agreeing to meet with us."

"No trouble. Come on out to the lab. I have tea ready. Do you like tea? It's one Russian custom I've never traded for coffee. In my boyhood, we used to fix it in a samovar. Now I just boil the water in a microwave."

They assured him tea was fine, following him into the lab and seating themselves on mismatched chairs around a scarred table. There were a few other odd assorted pieces here and there that seemed out of place in a laboratory and were, so rumor had it, put out for trash pickup at curbs, where the professor had collected them. It was common knowledge he was an eccentric.

He poured the tea into mugs, handing the beverages to them before passing a plate of cookies. The tea was wonderful but so hot that Haley had to drink it in tiny sips to prevent burning her tongue.

"Now, what can I tell you about Josh's visit to me?" the professor asked.

"You can begin by telling us how he came to find you and why," Chase said.

The professor gulped his tea as if it weren't scalding and nodded. "As Josh explained it to me, he's an investigative journalist who makes it a practice to search online regularly for unusual story ideas. That's where he discovered a particular subject that fascinated him. As for coming to me…well, I'm a botanist known to be an authority in the field." He paused there, looking at each of them in turn, his bushy eyebrows raised in curiosity.

"I have to wonder why you're questioning me about this. I'd have thought Josh would already have explained all of this to you both."

"No," Chase said, "Josh liked to keep his stories strictly to himself until he wrote them. That never bothered me. What concerns me deeply this time is that he just seemed to vanish on the trail of this mysterious story without telling either of us his destination. We haven't heard from him in weeks."

"Until today," Haley added.

The professor looked suddenly solemn. "I see. And now you'd like to know what that subject is. He spoke with me in confidence, so I shouldn't confide what he trusted me with, but this sounds serious. Have you heard of the International Seed Vault? Yes, you must have. It's no secret."

He explained it to them. "Some years ago, scientists in various countries expressed concern about the possibility of worldwide disasters occurring, natural as well as man-made. Disasters so widespread and so terrible they could wipe out the food supplies needed by those who survived."

He paused to drink more tea before continuing. "It seems the stuff of science fiction, but I assure you that, historically, it's happened more than once in the past when crops have failed. The nineteenth century potato famine in Ireland is an example. Not worldwide, but thousands died from starvation all the same."

"And if all the food crops failed," Haley said, "then they couldn't produce—"

"Viable seeds to grow new ones," Professor Rostov finished for her.

"And that," Chase guessed, "is why an International Seed Vault was born."

"Exactly. Those funding it built it on a remote, uninhabited Aleutian island. It was sunk into a hillside cliff there and equipped with the latest technology to keep its contents safe for the possible needs of future mankind. Millions of seeds were gathered from around the world—there are thousands of varieties of grain alone—and stored in the vault."

"Sort of leaves you with your mouth hanging open in wonder, doesn't it?" Haley asked softly.

The men found no need to comment on her observation, leaving the three of them sitting there silently for a long moment while consuming their tea and cookies.

The professor finally continued. "I was pleased to share with Josh all I knew. It was there anyway for those who cared to research it. And others have written stories about it—mostly for scientific journals, but stories all the same. Which is why I was puzzled by his excited interest. I warned him it would hardly make a fascinating story for the general public."

"That's what I'm thinking," Chase murmured.

"And your brother realized that. I remember him telling me, 'I know, Professor, but I make it a habit to keep my ear, so to speak, listening to what's out there on the internet. Fact is, I picked up some chatter online about this seed vault, and if there's any truth in the buzz, it could alarm a lot of people.'"

"Did he explain that?" Chase asked.

"I'm sorry to say he didn't. All he would tell me was, 'If I can validate it, Professor, it will make one hell of a spectacular story.' I don't think I'll ever forget the little smile he wore when he said that. There was something…well, frankly, almost chilling about it."

Chapter 6

It chilled Haley just to hear Professor Rostov say that. This was not the Josh she knew. Rostov was relaying another side of him she'd never experienced during any of the times they'd gone out together, a side Josh had kept from her.

"And he didn't disclose any more than that?" Chase asked.

"He didn't, no." The professor must have finished his tea, because there was a note of finality in the click of his mug when he set it down. "So, we come to the moment when you tell me why it's so necessary to meet with me today."

Chase looked at her. She understood the question in his gaze and nodded her approval for him to speak for both of them. "This is not good," Professor Rostov said gravely when Chase finished his account of robbery, assault and mail theft. "This is bad."

"You don't get any argument from us there," Chase said.

"I can't believe your brother would send either of you any package with content that could put you at risk."

"No, that would be totally unlike Josh even with a stranger, never mind two people he cared for. And yet…"

"Yes," the professor said, "there was that reference to something he picked up online that, if true, could be alarming."

Chase turned to Haley. "I think it's time you showed the professor what we brought for him to look at."

She opened her purse, removed the three clear plastic pouches and put them into Anton Rostov's hands. "We hoped you could identify the seeds for us."

The professor turned the pouches over in his hands, gazing for some time at what each one contained. There were aspects of both awe and excitement in the way he handled them. "I can't name these seeds except to speculate that they appear to be of the legume family. Where Josh could have obtained them, I can't imagine. Did he write anything of their origin?"

"Just a very brief note saying they were rare and valuable and asking me to put them away in my deposit box for safekeeping." She defended Josh before Chase could. "But Josh couldn't have believed that either his brother or I could come to harm because the seeds were in our possession. Who would even know we had them?"

The professor had no answer for her, just another question. "Was there a return address on the wrapping?"

"Only a postmark," Chase said. "Anchorage."

"Yes, he would go there. It's where the headquarters for the International Seed Vault is located."

"Why isn't the vault itself there also, instead of some remote Aleutian island?" Haley asked.

"Anchorage is relatively close by and one of the largest cities in the region. The island is hardly appropriate for offices but it does, I understand, have near-perfect arctic conditions ideal for preserving seeds over an extended period. As I will protect your seeds if you entrust me with them. I have a good safe here. But before I put them in it, I'd like to examine the seeds out of their plastic envelopes under microscope and run some tests on them. If you'll come back tomorrow morning—say around nine, before I have my first class—I may have some definitive answers for you."

Haley readily gave her permission, relieved, in fact, to have the seeds out of her hands and in Professor Rostov's capable care.

The sun was heading toward the horizon when they emerged from the science building. The day had been a long one, so crowded with events that Chase knew he'd be foolish to try to drive all the way back to Seattle tonight.

Besides, he knew he could never make himself leave Haley on her own. Not after the threat to her outside the bank. She needed his protection now, for her own sake as well as for Josh's. He wouldn't admit to himself that he had a need to guard her for any reason of his own.

Chase stopped her on their way to the car. "I've made the decision not to go home just yet. After what's been happening here, Josh would never forgive me if I left you alone."

She looked at him as if his justification displeased her, which made what she had to say seem contradictory. "Your intention does make sense. And don't forget, the professor is expecting *both* of us to turn up here tomorrow."

"That's true. There is something else you should know, though."

"Oh?"

"I ought to check into a hotel, but that would defeat the purpose. Your house was already broken into. If the people after these seeds believe you still have them, what's to prevent them from trying to break in again?"

"I see what you're proposing. You want to stay in my house with me."

"Don't you think I should?"

He expected an objection from her, and again he was surprised.

"Why not? I have a guest room next to mine with a comfortable bed."

"Tell you what," Chase said. "In exchange, why don't I take you out to dinner?"

"Not necessary, but I won't refuse the offer."

She suggested a seafood restaurant downtown. They went there and had baked salmon freshly caught off the Oregon coast. They accompanied it with a mild local wine and a pleasant conversation that avoided any contentious subject.

"Good for the digestion," she maintained.

It was dark when they arrived back at Haley's place. Carrying his suitcase, Chase followed her into the house. He went through the rooms with her, turning on lights and checking the windows to be sure they were locked. The back door was secure with its bolt snugly in place.

"Would you like that coffee I promised earlier and never got the chance to make?" she offered. "I have another carafe."

"No, nothing. All I want is a shower and a bed to fall into."

"I'm ready to turn in myself."

Except for a few lamps they left burning, they extinguished the lights on the first floor. Haley led the way upstairs, pointing out the master bedroom that was hers and the smaller guest bedroom next to it that Chase would occupy.

"You can see the bathroom and laundry room are across the hall. I'm sorry about the scarcity of furniture in the bedrooms. Mom and Dad insisted I have the house, but the furnishings had to go with them to Arizona. I've been replacing everything as I can afford it. The downstairs is pretty much taken care of, but I still have the bedrooms to fill. I have my eye on some traditional pieces for that."

She chattered on, showing him the bathroom shelves where he could find towels, a new bar of soap and a tube of shampoo, then leaving him to shower while she made up his bed with fresh sheets.

Chase scrubbed himself under a hot spray, feeling restored when he stepped out of the stall and dried off. He had neglected to bring a clean pair of shorts into the bathroom with him. All he had to cover himself while he went back to the guest room and his suitcase was one of the large bath towels. He wrapped it around his hips, tucking its ends into place.

When he left the bathroom barefoot, his hair was still damp and uncombed, and the towel was low now on his hips and threatening to slide off altogether unless he held onto it with one hand. He found Haley at the head of the bed, vigorously shaking a pillow down into a pillowcase.

Her back was to him, but she must have been aware of his entrance. She was still in a cheerful mood when she spoke to him. "If you wake up in the night and decide you'd like another blanket, you can find one—" She had turned to face him. And stopped midsentence.

He was conscious of her gaze locking on him, a flush heating that smooth ivory skin as her deep blue eyes traveled his near-nude length, lingering on the dark, curling hairs of his chest before moving on down over the towel to his legs, whose strength had benefitted from his years with the rangers.

"Sorry," he apologized, looking down at himself. "I didn't unpack before I closed myself in the bathroom. I need to trade this terry cloth sarong for something more dependable."

When he looked up again, she was clutching the pillow against her breasts as though it were an object meant for self-defense.

"I'll say good-night, then and leave you to do that," she murmured. Casting the pillow onto the bed, she brushed by him and escaped into her own room.

He didn't know her very well, of course, but that self-conscious discomfort seemed totally unlike the Haley he had so far experienced.

Chase had expected to fall asleep the second his head hit the pillow. That didn't happen. Instead, much to his annoyance with both himself and the woman next door, he lay awake in the dark.

He knew it wasn't fair blaming her. She couldn't help what nature had gifted her with: that raven hair, the clear blue eyes fringed with long lashes, the intriguing cleft in her chin below a sensual mouth. It was his fault he couldn't sleep, because all he could seem to do was spin pictures of all those seductive assets just a wall away from him.

What had Haley started to say to him? Something about there being an extra blanket if he needed one in the middle of the night. That was pretty damn funny considering he had long ago kicked off the thin summer blanket that had covered him. He was naked now except for a pair of shorts, and his skin was still warm and moist. He didn't think it had anything to do with the air temperature either inside or outside the house. It was his own body that was controlling the heat he was feeling. Or at least, that part of his head that insisted on conjuring up images of Haley Adams stripped down to her soft, fragrant flesh.

He had to stop this. He had no right to these images. He had to remember what he and his brother had agreed to, even if that agreement had been sworn to long ago when they were very young, Chase still considered the rule in effect: Whatever the temptation, they would not steal each other's girlfriends.

Sweetheart. That was how Josh had referred to her in the brief message that accompanied the seeds. Josh considered Haley to be his girlfriend.

"And you're going to respect that," Chase ordered himself.

It was the only way he was finally able to fall asleep.

He had no idea how long he slept. It could have been many hours later when he was abruptly awakened by a noise next door. Propping himself up on his elbows, immediately alert as his overseas training had taught him to be whenever there was the possibility of danger, he listened intently.

He'd left his bedroom door open in case Haley needed him in the night. She must have left hers open also, because although there was a moment of silence now, the sound suddenly came strongly again. This time he identified it. Moaning. A woman's moaning.

He didn't stop to wonder if someone had gotten into the house again. Haley wouldn't be moaning like that if she weren't under some kind of threat.

Flying off the bed, he raced barefoot out into the hall, burst into her bedroom, fumbled for a switch on the wall and found it. The overhead fixture blazed into a light that had him blinking for the few seconds it took to clear his vision.

There was no one in the bedroom but the woman who was supposed to be here. She had rid herself of her own blanket and was lying on her side, legs drawn up, hair spilling over her face. The moan sounded again. It was definitely not one of pain or fear.

He chuckled. Haley was dreaming, and it was no nightmare. From the tone of it, he was willing to bet it was an erotic dream. Whatever its content, he had a sudden guilty longing to be a part of it. A *major* part.

Chase listened to what this time he realized were pleading whimpers. He knew he had no right to be standing here hearing them. He needed instead to relieve her of a dream that might be more upsetting than enjoyable.

Padding swiftly across the room on his bare feet, he perched on the edge of the bed and leaned over her. "Haley," he called to her softly, "you need to wake up now."

No audible response. Her only reaction was a slow wriggling of her perfect bottom, a performance that had him yearning. Man, that must be some hot dream! Just the sight of her had a certain lower portion of him stirring, coming to life. He could see her bikini panties, no more than a silky scrap beneath a thin nightshirt. She wore nothing else.

Chase managed to master self-control and made himself try again, this time speaking more forcefully. "Come on, Haley, you're having a dream, and it's got you disturbed."

Hell, it was sure disturbing him.

Success. That's what he believed, anyway, when she muttered something he didn't understand, turned over on her back, opened her eyes and gazed up at him in confusion.

"A dream, Haley. That's all it was."

He couldn't have convinced her of that, because in the next second it all went haywire. She suddenly surged up to a sitting position and fell forward, leaning against him. He had no choice but to hold her in his arms, supporting her. She buried her face against his chest, as if hiding it in embarrassment.

"Hey, it's all right," he assured her. "Whatever the dream was, you won't remember it five minutes from now."

"Your chest is bare," she said. "Feels nice." Her hands flattened against the hard muscle, which seemed to him to be steaming under her fingers that began to sift through the dusting of hair there.

Chase didn't know whether the dream was somehow still with her or whether she was on another trip now. He didn't mean to join her, but the temptation was too much.

Catching her under the chin, he lifted her face up, dipped his head and searched her gaze. He found no objection there. Reading it as permission, he lowered his mouth to hers in a slow, tender kiss. A kiss that involved his lips nibbling on hers before stroking her mouth from corner to corner with the tip of his tongue.

God, she smelled good, like the roses Portland was famous for. He could get drunk on her scent alone. What did she taste like? he wondered. He would like to know what she tasted like.

As if she sensed his longing, her mouth parted under his. A clear invitation. Only, he hesitated. He hadn't touched her yet, not with anything that might qualify as a form of penetration.

But the opportunity was here, and it was too good to miss. All his self-reproaches earlier, all his promises to himself vanished as if they meant nothing. His tongue thrust into her mouth like a warrior's sword. Except this weapon wasn't intended for an enemy but something infinitely better.

She was all wet and sweet and tasting of heat. Could heat have a flavor? He couldn't see how that was possible, and yet Haley's did. A very intimate, wet heat, and he loved it. Loved playing with her tongue.

He didn't remember it happening, or how it happened exactly, but at some point she broke their embrace without breaking the kiss. The next thing he knew she was searching blindly for his hands. When she found them, she brought them up to her breasts.

That's when she ended the kiss in order to whisper urgently, "Touch me. Please."

She pressed his open, willing hands against the soft mounds beneath her nightshirt. And Chase ignited. The fire went straight to his groin, and almost instantly he felt himself grow heavy, thick and very hard. He knew if he didn't stop here and now, within seconds he would be pulling the nightshirt over her head, stripping her of her panties, shedding his shorts and pushing her flat on the bed.

There would be no stopping then. And he had to stop.

As gently as possible, Chase withdrew his hands from her breasts and removed himself a few necessary inches from her.

"God help me for wanting you as much as I do," he rasped. "But I can't. Not when you belong to someone else."

She looked at him squarely for a long moment. There was no denying the wounded expression in her eyes. "Oh, no," she said softly in the end. "It's not me that Josh owns. It's you, Chase."

He didn't know what to say. It didn't make sense. No one owned him. He wouldn't have allowed that.

"Listen to me, Haley—"

"Get out of my way. I want the bathroom."

Not as a bathroom, he realized, but as a safe retreat.

She didn't wait for him to move off the bed. She scooted around him, and before he knew it, she was off the bed and out the door. Chase followed her across the hall, but he was too late. She was already inside the bathroom, the door closed and locked when he tried it.

He knew she was angry. And why shouldn't she be? He hadn't just hurt her with his rejection. He had humiliated her, and she hadn't deserved that.

"Haley," he pleaded, "talk to me, please."

"We have nothing to talk about," she said from the other side of the door. "Go back to your own room, and I'll try not to bother you with any more dreams."

Left with no other choice, Chase returned to the guest room. He made sure he left his door open before he climbed back into bed. He could only hope that Haley would continue to leave hers ajar. There was always the slim possibility she would need him again.

He turned out his light and tried to go back to sleep, but his mind refused to shut down long enough for that to happen. He kept thinking about the three of them— Haley, Josh and himself. She had accused him of letting his brother own him.

That was absurd. Josh was too much of a free spirit to permit himself to own anyone. But Chase had to admit that Haley had a point. Ever since his stepfather had died and he had come home to be there for Josh, he'd let himself make reckless judgments ruled by his emotions. The kind of judgments he would never have made while serving as a ranger, like snatching Haley without any authority and forcing her to go with him because he had convinced himself she was the key to finding his missing brother.

He knew better now, but it was too late to part himself from her at this stage. As long as there was any risk to her, real or otherwise, he had to remain at her side. And that was a problem, a *big* one, when he had to contend with the perpetual temptation of her. Now it looked like she was also attracted to him. So what the hell were they going to do about it?

Haley was setting the bar for breakfast when Chase appeared in the kitchen the next morning. He looked a bit bleary-eyed, as if he'd slept badly.

"Morning," she greeted him cheerfully.

His mouth didn't open in surprise, but she thought the bobbing of his Adam's apple might be registering a reaction to something he regarded as pleasant but totally unexpected.

"There's coffee made." She invited him to help himself to the pot and the tray that held the sugar bowl and the creamer. He thanked her, but the way he kept himself from coming too close to her as he fixed a mug of the coffee for himself had her wondering if he was afraid she might enact some kind of punishment for last night.

"What did you expect?" she teased him. "The silent treatment or a blow from a frying pan? Relax, McKinley. I don't believe in holding grudges. Anyway, I'm the one who invited your attention."

"And I jumped at it and then handled it badly. I'm sorry about that."

"Look, as far as I'm concerned, last night is history. Let's agree to forget it."

He seemed vastly relieved.

"So, what can I fix you for breakfast? I have eggs and bacon."

"Actually, all I'd like is cereal and toast."

She listed the cereals she had in the cupboard. He chose cornflakes. Haley decided that was all she wanted herself, although she would start with a glass of orange juice as she did most mornings.

She was perched on the stool opposite his, drinking her juice, when between sips she asked, "What comes next for you, Chase? Have you got any idea about that?"

He didn't answer her for a minute. He finished pouring milk on his cereal and set the carton beside his bowl, then gave her an indefinite, "I'll make up my mind after we see Professor Rostov. Could be he'll have something useful that will determine where I go from here."

He's stalling, Haley thought.

She had the feeling he'd already made his decision. After all, what information could the professor provide them about the seeds that would lead Chase to Josh? It was a possibility, of course, but not likely.

Why Chase should choose to withhold his decision from her, she couldn't imagine. She would just have to be patient until he was ready to tell her, although she'd already guessed what it was. There was really only one thing it could be.

They arrived at the university well before nine o'clock, the time the professor had specified. Parking on any college campus was always a problem. There never seemed to be enough spots, which was why Haley had suggested they come early.

But to her chagrin, as well as Chase's, the lot in front of the science building was already congested this morning.

"This can't be normal, can it?" he asked.

"I wouldn't think so."

Something isn't right, she thought. She could already feel it, but Chase didn't try to pursue it. He was too busy circling through the lot, searching for an empty slot for the SUV. It wasn't until he found it and they'd parked and started for the main entrance of the science building that they realized something was terribly wrong.

A high wall of shrubbery had prevented them from seeing what was going on outside the front doors. They rounded that green wall and discovered the excited crowd of buzzing spectators along with the collection of official vehicles blocking the entrance—police cars, a medical transport, a TV news van from one of the local stations. Already guessing the worst and feeling her stomach drop, Haley's hand seemed to clamp automatically on Chase's arm.

A uniformed police guard prevented anyone from entering the building, and that included them. Neither of them spoke until Chase, looking grim, stopped a young man who, from all appearances, had to be a student.

"Can you tell us what's going on in there?"

"Oh, man, it's bad. The word is Professor Rostov was murdered in his lab sometime late last night. It wasn't until this morning that a janitor discovered his body and called it in."

Haley's reaction was a sick *Oh, dear God, no! Not that wonderful old man!*

"They're saying his safe was open and robbed," the young man continued. "Sounds like the work of some druggie, but I hear all the prof had in there were papers. I suppose the term paper I turned in is already toast."

No, not just papers, Haley knew. But seeds that were now gone. She was convinced of that.

Chapter 7

Her hand must have tightened on Chase's arm. "We need to find some place for you to sit down," he said.

"Not this time." She knew it wasn't possible for people to be immune to shocks, although they could be strong for them, and she was determined to be just that.

She wondered a moment later if she was being premature about that. As they continued to stand there with the crowd, watching, two men in lab coats emerged from the building wheeling a gurney. On it was a black body bag. Haley realized it contained the remains of Professor Rostov on his way to the medical examiner.

Hating herself for gawking along with the rest, she turned her head away, her eyes brimming with tears, not wanting to see the body loaded into the police transport and driven away.

Either Chase figured she needed his physical support or her death grip was giving him bruises. Managing to free his arm, he slid it around her waist and drew her close against his side. She was grateful for his solid body. And his warmth.

"What's this all about, Chase?" she pleaded. "It's one thing to steal to get your hands on some packets of seeds, but to murder someone for them… Can they be worth that much?"

"I wish I knew."

She'd realized he wouldn't have the answers any more than she did, but she'd had to ask. If for nothing else because it was a way to release an extreme frustration over a desperate need to understand what she considered absolute madness.

"You know," she said, "we can blame ourselves for his death. We involved the professor in this thing."

"We can't take on that guilt, Haley. We had no way of knowing that whoever is responsible would go to these lengths. Or somehow learn the professor was in possession of the seeds."

"But we might have prevented it if we'd reported to the police the effort to snatch the seeds from me yesterday outside the bank. I think the mugger and his accomplice must have managed to follow us here without our being aware of it and then last night confronted the professor in his lab. How else could they have known where the seeds were going?"

"Yeah, not reporting it was a mistake," he admitted. Although he didn't argue with the rest of her conviction, it seemed his admission was as far as he was prepared to go at the moment. All he would say was, "I'm so sorry about the professor. He was a fine man, and those bastards—" He broke off here, unable to go on. "There's nothing more to see here. We need to go, Haley."

"Wait. Look at the man there coming out of the building."

"What about him?" Chase asked, watching the tall, balding figure stop to speak to the uniformed cop posted at the entrance.

"He's wearing a suit."

"So?"

"So he's standing like guys do when they're passing the time, with his weight on one leg and his hand pushing his suit coat back on the other side."

"Your point?"

"Well, isn't that a badge clipped to his belt?"

"What are you saying, Haley?"

"That he must be a plainclothes detective assigned to the case." Why was he being so exasperatingly slow to understand her? Or was he just reluctant to get them involved? "Chase, don't you think we need to speak to him? Tell him everything we know? It's information that's sure to help him find Professor Rostov's killer."

"Or make us persons of interest." He was silent for a minute, thoughtful before making up his mind. He'd spotted the detective before she'd brought it up. "You're right. We do owe it to the professor to help the police get this bastard."

With the excitement diminished, the spectators were melting away, making it less of a problem for Chase and Haley to work their way to the front steps of the building. Chase, in front of her, halted when she dragged at his elbow to get his attention.

"You do the talking first. He looks like the kind of cop who'd listen more seriously to what a man has to say."

"Shame on you, Haley. Accusing the poor guy of being a chauvinist before you've even met him."

"Just do it, huh?" she mumbled.

It was no problem drawing the detective's notice

when they arrived at the entrance. "Can I help you folks? If you're looking to enter the building, I'm afraid we haven't finished with it yet."

Chase shook his head. "If you're a detective in charge here, then it's you we need to speak to. We have information that will interest you."

The man was immediately alert. "And you are?"

Chase gave him their names. In turn, the detective introduced himself. "I'm Homicide Detective Steinmetz. We need to go somewhere quiet where you can talk and I can listen. The forensic team hasn't finished with the crime scene yet, but we should be able to use one of the classrooms."

He led the way into the building. Haley was at once aware of the emptiness. At this time of day, the halls should have been busy with students and teachers coming and going, rooms occupied and classes in session. Instead, there was this forlorn silence.

Steinmetz conducted them into one of those deserted rooms, settling them at a table near the windows.

"With your permission," he said, withdrawing a minirecorder from an inside breast pocket of his suit coat, "I'm going to tape this interview. It's standard procedure."

They gave their approval, stated their names, addresses, emails and phone numbers as directed and by turn told their stories as concisely as possible.

Even with the brevity of their accounts, there was so much to include, along with Steinmetz's periodic questions, he had to stop and insert a fresh tape. When they were finished, the detective had everything that mattered, starting with Josh's visits to Professor Rostov, the arrival of the seed packets Josh had sent from Alaska to

Chase and Haley and both the theft and attempted theft of the allegedly valuable seeds.

Haley's emphasis of the break-in at her house, and how a report had been turned in by the police officer they'd called to the scene, had been as deliberate as was her abridgment of the incident outside her bank. Her hope was Steinmetz would forgive their neglect to report that one. He didn't look happy about it but settled for their descriptions of the mugger and his accomplice, inadequate as they were.

Chase had hurried on from there to describe their visit to Professor Rostov yesterday, the reason for it and how they had left Haley's seeds with him. They'd returned today to learn the professor's findings.

"Looks like you're out of luck there," the detective said. He'd already admitted to them the seeds were gone. The expression on his face in this moment was as somber as Haley imagined hers was. She was truly sorry about Rostov's death. "Make yourselves available to us," he cautioned them. "I'll get in touch if I have any further questions for you. Same applies if we have answers to share with you."

Thanking them for their help, he released them.

"I'm ready now to sit down," Haley said when they exited the building.

"What do you call what we were just doing in there?"

"An unhappy necessity."

"All right, where would you like to go? Someplace where we can have coffee or a soda? It's too early for lunch."

"Nowhere with people. Out there," she indicated, her arm stretching toward the smooth green lawns that had been freshly mowed.

"I don't see a bench in sight."

"I don't want a bench. I just want the grass."

"You're easy," he said with the hint of a smile, the first one he'd worn this morning.

"That's me. Simple pleasures."

They strolled away from the building side by side. When Haley judged they'd come far enough, she sank down on her knees, sitting back on her heels.

They were alone here. It was a pleasant spot with the sun warm overhead and the aroma of the sweet grass.

"It's nice, isn't it?" she observed.

Chase, who had hunkered down beside her, agreed.

"I had a literature class in my junior year in college," Haley reminisced. "On especially fine days like this, our instructor would bring us outside, and we'd sit in a circle on the grass, taking turns reading poetry aloud and then discussing it."

"Happy memory, huh?"

"Yes."

They fell silent, lost in their own thoughts of sorrow about the professor's death. She waited a moment to see if he would finally answer the question she had asked at breakfast: *What comes next for you, Chase?*

She watched him pick a blade of grass longer than the others, pinch one end of it between the thumb and forefinger of his left hand and with his right hand draw it slowly out until he reached the other end of the blade.

Haley prompted him, "You told me that when we were done here, you'd decide what you were going to do."

He turned his head to gaze at her solemnly. "And share that decision with you. No, I haven't forgotten. But that was when I was counting on learning something useful from Professor Rostov. Something that would help me to find Josh, and now..."

"You've come to a dead end?" She shook her head.

"No, I don't think so. I think whatever the professor—may he rest in peace—was able to tell you or not tell you, you'd already pretty much settled on what you meant to do. You're going to Alaska. With help or without help, you're going to track your brother down. I'm right, aren't I?"

"You are."

"The only thing that puzzles me is why you kept this decision from me until now."

"Because it involves you."

"How? How do I figure into it?"

"I can't leave you behind, Haley. After all that's happened, you're vulnerable. Josh would never forgive me if something happened to you and I wasn't around to protect you. But how can I take you with me when you've got a life and a job here in Portland?"

"Isn't this part of the decision mine to make, not yours? Staying behind, if that's what I choose, doesn't necessarily make me at risk now that whoever wanted the seeds seems to have them. I'm not helpless, and I have friends. But if I go with you, it doesn't mean leaving my job behind. The work can travel with me on my laptop."

"Now you've got *me* in a state of suspense," he complained. "What is your choice?"

"We're in this thing together, Chase. That's been clear from the start. I care about Josh. I want to find him, too, and that means going with you."

"You sure?"

"Sure. There's just one thing."

"Let's hear it."

"Are we going to be in trouble with Detective Steinmetz by leaving Portland?"

"Probably. But if we come back with answers, it's just possible we'll be forgiven."

"Good enough. What are we waiting for?"

"Nothing but whatever arrangements the two of us have to make." Dropping the blade of grass, he stood, reached down for her hand and helped her to her feet. "Let's go."

Haley was working on a project for one of Portland's technical schools. She'd been busy with it for a number of hours, in fact ever since their plane had lifted off and headed north for Anchorage.

She should have been tired after yesterday's flurry of activity—arranging for her mail to be held at the post office until her return, letting her friends know she would be gone, packing a couple of bags, taking a moment here and there to mourn the kind professor. She hadn't felt the need to rest on the flight, however.

Now, though, she realized she could use a break. Backing up her work, she shut down her laptop, closed it and slid it under her seat. Earlier, feeling warm, she'd shed her jean jacket and stored it in the carrier overhead. She wasn't sure whether it was the airplane's air system or her body's moody temperature making her too cool this time, but she wanted the jacket again.

Make up your mind, Adams, she scolded herself, getting to her feet, retrieving the jacket and managing to stretch away her stiffness at the same time she fitted herself into it.

The jacket was the matching upper half of a jeans outfit, its medium blue a contrast to the red top she wore underneath. The casual pairing of pants and jacket suited her and was perfect for travel.

It was summer in Alaska, but she wasn't sure what the

weather was like so far north. Hot? Cold? Some of both depending on what the days brought? Haley had been uncertain what to bring with her in the way of clothes. In the end, she'd decided if she had to, she could buy anything else she needed in Anchorage.

Settling back in her aisle seat, she checked on Chase seated beside her by the window. Unlike her, he'd gone to sleep the moment their plane had reached cruising altitude and hadn't stirred since.

He was sprawled in his seat, chin resting on his chest, dark hair tousled and looking far too sexy for her comfort. His light blue oxford shirt was open at the neck, and the cuffs had been turned back, exposing several inches of his strongly corded forearms and the curling black hairs that complemented his masculinity.

Feeling much too conscious of his male allure, she looked quickly away. A flight attendant was coming down the aisle. Haley stopped her.

"Can you tell me how much longer it is to Anchorage?"

"We should be starting our descent in about twenty minutes. There's still time if you'd like me to get you something."

She thanked her and declined. The young woman went on her way. Haley put her head back against the headrest and, against her better judgment, continued to think about Chase.

She hated to have him guess the erotic dream from which he had aroused her the night before last might have been about him. Let him suppose she could have thrown herself at him because, having so suddenly awakened, she had been confused about his identity. Like thinking it was Josh she'd been dreaming about. It wasn't, of course, but the whole thing was humiliating.

Confusion. Something that was bad enough in a dream and its direct aftermath, but she was experiencing just that right now in reality. Haley had wanted to accompany Chase to Alaska because she did care about Josh and needed to share in helping to find him. Needed to know he was all right.

But there was something more. She had to stop comparing these two men. Stop worrying about which one she preferred, Josh or Chase. Or neither one. Why, for example, should she be attracted to Chase when she'd had her share of experiencing some dark qualities about him? When Josh, on the other hand, had always been a cheerful free spirit?

Haley feared none of it, along with her feelings, would be resolved until they found Josh.

Chase was awake by the time their plane was in its later stages of descent.

"Look out the window, Haley," he invited her. "You can see not just the Gulf of Alaska but also the first sight of land ahead."

She leaned over to share his view and caught the faint but intoxicating scent of him, a whiff of shaving scent blended with pure masculinity. Why did he have to smell so good?

Around them she could hear the other passengers gathering their things for departure. A moment later, the bell dinged to draw their attention to the lighted board instructing them to fasten their seat belts for the plane's imminent landing.

Chase had phoned ahead from Portland to reserve both hotel accommodations and a car. Once they'd landed, disembarked from their plane at Anchorage's airport terminal and collected their luggage from the baggage carousel, they headed for the car rental desk.

There was a stout woman ahead of them at the counter accompanied by a teenage girl, who looked like she was probably her daughter.

The mother was telling the young male attendant behind the desk that she wanted an ordinary sedan, nothing with a lot of fancy features. "I need it for only a couple of hours to drive up to Denali and back. Friends back home told us we shouldn't miss a close look at the park, especially Mount McKinley. Or I guess they're calling it just Denali these days like the park itself."

"Ma'am," the attendant corrected her, "I'm afraid you'd need much more than a couple of hours to get to Denali and back."

"That doesn't make sense. Just look at it. As it is, you can practically reach out and touch it." The woman waved toward the broad window behind the attendant. Through its expanse of glass loomed an immense mountain range that towered above the downtown high rises.

The young man maintained a patient expression on his face. As if, Haley thought, he'd been dealing with this same objection far too many times from far too many tourists but always managed to be polite about it.

"Ma'am, Denali is to the north of Anchorage. You're looking east. Those are the Chugach Mountains you're seeing, and they are close to us here."

"So then," the woman demanded, as if finding it difficult to believe him, "how far are you saying the park actually is?"

"Over two hundred miles."

"That would make it more than just a day trip."

"I'm afraid so. I'm sorry."

"It's certainly a disappointment."

She marched off without thanking the young man, as if he were responsible for personally spoiling her plans. Her clearly embarrassed daughter trailed after her, eyes rolling. Haley felt sorry for the teenager.

She and Chase took the woman's place at the counter.

"What can I do for you, folks?"

"You'll be relieved to know," Chase told him with a grin, "that we don't want a car to drive to Denali. We would, though, like the one I reserved by phone."

The young man proved to be efficient. Within a short time, he'd handled the necessary paper work and was able to provide them with clear directions to the Kodiak Hotel, as well as the headquarters of the International Seed Vault. All before turning them over to another employee, who conducted them out to the lot and the sturdy green Jeep that Chase had requested should they encounter challenging roads if their quest took them outside the city.

They had reached the open gate in the car rental lot when Chase halted the Jeep. A left turn out of the gate, Haley knew, would take them in the direction of the hotel. A right would...well, take them to any number of places.

Chase turned to her. "Would you mind if we didn't go straight to the hotel but instead head for the offices of the seed vault? We have to begin somewhere, and I can't imagine it wasn't one of the first places Josh visited. I want to make sure he isn't in real trouble."

She hesitated. Chase was clearly anxious to locate his brother, but had never said he feared Josh might be in some grave danger. After what had happened back in Portland, though, circumstances had changed.

Anchorage was a revelation to Haley. There were no

remains of its frontier days to be seen, at least not in the sections through which *they* drove. It was a modern city in every way, with shopping malls, high-rise buildings and streets humming with traffic. A city supported by military bases and a busy harbor. But the wilderness was never far away. And always the awesome mountains that dwarfed those she was used to in Portland.

Haley was the first to indicate the address of their downtown destination. "There," she said. "Over on the right. That office tower. Nowhere on the street to park, but it looks like a parking garage just ahead."

It was, and they found a space on one of its upper decks, took the elevator to street level and walked to the office tower. She had her jean jacket draped over her arm.

"It's funny to be hot in Alaska, isn't it?" she observed, having removed the jacket when they'd traded the Jeep for the heat of the outdoors. "Summer or not, you don't expect it."

"What were you expecting?" he teased her. "Igloos and polar bears?"

"Not quite that extreme, at least not in this part of Alaska."

"I guess being in the service as I was and posted in so many different places, I got used to surprises. People and places are never what you think they're going to be. Here we are."

The office suites that occupied the building were listed at the side of a bank of elevators.

"There it is," Chase said, indicating what they were looking for. *Headquarters for the International Seed Vault. Twelfth Floor.*

"This is something else that throws me," Haley remarked as they rode up in the elevator. "The headquarters for this seed vault being located in the heart of a bustling city instead of somewhere far away from any major population center."

Chase didn't respond to her. His mind seemed to be occupied elsewhere, maybe thinking Josh had ridden this same elevator not so long ago.

They didn't have to wonder whether to turn left or right when the elevator doors rolled back on the twelfth floor. The office suite they wanted was directly ahead of them, its title clearly printed on the door.

They entered a reception area, where an attractive woman with red hair and freckles was busy on the telephone. While they waited, a curious Haley tried to get a peek at the photograph on her desk. Unless she had the nerve to reach out and turn it around facing her, that wasn't possible. Or necessary. The redhead caught her being interested and, with an obliging smile, turned it herself.

Haley found herself looking at the photograph of a rawboned man in uniform holding a little boy in his arms, whose red hair and freckles unmistakably identified him as the son of the receptionist. Haley also found her face hot with guilt. She had been caught, so to speak, with her hand in the cookie jar.

"Sorry," she apologized when the receptionist ended her call. "I have this bad habit of being nosy when it comes to other people's pictures."

"Me, too, only I go one step further. I always want to know who all those faces are in the photos. The guy in mine is my husband. He's stationed here at Elmendorf Air Force Base. The kid with the missing front tooth is my pride and joy. And I'm Donna. So," she moved on cheerfully, "how can I help you folks?"

Chase answered for them. "Is it possible to see the director? Or if—" He broke off. "I'm sorry. Is it he or she?"

"Our current director is Dr. Greta Hansen."

Chase thanked her and went on. "Or if she's not available, to make an appointment for tomorrow?"

"I'll check with her. If she asks, can I tell her the nature of your business?"

"It's—" he hesitated "—a little complicated."

Donna understood. Rising from her desk, she left them in reception and headed into the interior of the office suite.

Chase turned to Haley when they were alone with a solemn, "You know you're shameless, don't you? Trying to sneak glimpses of people's private photo collections."

"Remind me to ask you your shameless habits, McKinley."

"Anytime, Adams. Anytime."

They didn't have to wait long for the receptionist's return. "Dr. Hansen is free to see you."

She conducted them to a spacious private office where a middle-aged, stocky woman with an intelligent-looking face was waiting for them. Chase gave her their names. She shook their hands and invited them to sit down in the two chairs facing her desk before seating herself in her own chair behind the desk. Haley heard a slight accent in her speech. Scandinavian, she thought. No surprise since this operation was international.

"You're very welcome," she greeted them. "We don't often get visitors. Are you scientists, perhaps?"

Chase leaned forward. "We're neither that nor tourists, Doctor. But we are here for a serious purpose."

The director's eyes widened. Chase's earnest reply seemed to startle her. "Yes? And that would be what?"

Chapter 8

Chase took a deep breath and exhaled slowly before stating their problem. "My brother is missing, and we hope you can help us to find him."

He watched Dr. Hansen's face and saw her eyes blink several times before she cleared her throat to respond to him. "I—I'm afraid I don't understand you, Mr. McKinley."

The poor woman is wondering just what kind of nutcase she invited into her office, Chase thought. Realizing he'd begun badly, he tried to clarify. "I'm sorry, Doctor. I need to explain myself. I should have started by telling you that my brother is actually my half brother, which is why we have different surnames. He's Josh Matthews."

Her gaze shifted to Haley. "And Ms. Adams?"

Haley hastened to explain her own connection and the reason for her presence. "I'm a close friend of Josh who's also very concerned about his disappearance."

The director nodded slowly as if the problem was clear to her now. Chase knew it couldn't be and that she needed to be supplied with more pieces if she were to make any sense of the puzzle. He made that effort.

"Josh Matthews," he repeated with emphasis. "Do you remember the name? I think he must have visited you not long ago."

"Did he?" She frowned, thinking about it for a moment. She held up one finger. "I ought to remember, and I do. That's right, Josh Matthews. A young man wildly enthusiastic about a story he was preparing for publication. It concerned our seed vault. He asked me a great many questions, mostly to do with the security of the vault. I wondered why that was a particular issue for him, but he just smiled and denied that it was."

"The vault isn't here in Anchorage, though, is it?" Haley asked.

"That's correct." Dr. Hansen got to her feet and turned to a large framed map that hung on the wall behind her. It featured the Aleutians, a long necklace of islands that stretched out from the western coast of Alaska. She pointed to the outermost island of the chain. "Moa," she said. "That's where you'll find the vault."

"Is the island inhabited?" Haley wanted to know.

"Oh, no, Moa is much too isolated and frigid for that. Very rugged terrain, but perfect for the vault buried deep in the side of a cliff. The weather there is so cold for most of the year that it supports permafrost, which is ideal for preserving the seeds if a power failure should ever occur."

"Not even a station there with staff to take care of the vault?"

"It isn't necessary. The vault is served by state-of-the-art equipment and protected by thick concrete walls and steel doors. That's not to say it isn't visited periodically to deposit new seed samples and to make certain everything is functioning properly."

Professor Rostov had already told them some of this, but Chase felt it didn't hurt for Haley and him to hear it again, along with learning what else the director had to tell them.

Dr. Hansen seated herself again at her desk. "As I already mentioned, Mr. McKinley, your brother was particularly interested in the vault's security. I think he would have asked even more questions, but by then I had another appointment waiting. I told him I was sorry we couldn't continue talking but that he was welcome to come back again. He said he would do that, but I never saw him again. That was several weeks ago, and now you say he's missing. That has to be very distressing for both of you. And you haven't heard at all from him?"

Chase glanced at Haley. She must have realized what he was silently asking her. Her almost imperceptible nod granted him the permission he sought to share what he felt Dr. Hansen ought to know.

"Actually, we did each have a communication from Josh, if you can call it that. He sent us separate packets of seeds accompanied by brief notes telling us they were valuable and asking us to place them in our bank deposit boxes for safekeeping. There was nothing to identify the seeds or to let us know where he acquired them. I don't suppose…"

The director understood him and answered with a swift "Your brother didn't get them from us, Mr. McKinley. We never release any seeds from the vault except to the original depositors who placed them with us. I can't imagine where he would have obtained them or why."

"I think Haley and I might have been ready to believe

it was some kind of joke, except…" Chase didn't want to alarm Dr. Hansen with what had resulted from those deliveries, but he'd decided she needed to be alerted. He went on to inform her that both packets had been stolen and under what circumstances, omitting only the murder of Professor Rostov. The woman didn't need to hear of that brutal event.

"I can see why you're so concerned about your brother, Mr. McKinley, and that both he and you wondered about the security of our vault. I do appreciate your telling me of the thefts, but there has been no threat of that kind here. Nor with our high-tech security measures can anything like that happen to our seeds."

She was probably right, Chase thought. "I wonder, though, Doctor. Did Josh happen to say where he was going when he left here?"

"He said nothing about his plans. I can only hope he makes contact with you soon."

The director got to her feet, a sign she had no more to tell them. They also stood, allowing her to walk them out. She was parting from them in reception when a sudden memory seemed to occur to her.

"There is something else. I'm not sure it will be of any use to you, but for what it's worth…"

"Please."

"Just before he left, your Josh asked me if I knew George Fellows, a local man he learned about online. I do happen to know of him. Reputedly, he has a vast knowledge of seeds. Or did have. He's very elderly now, and I hear his faculties are questionable." She turned to the receptionist at her desk. "Donna, didn't you tell me that you and your husband ran into George Fellows a while back?"

"Not exactly. Ray and I were out walking in the hills

above Elmendorf with a friend. He was the one who knew George Fellows and pointed him out roaring down the road in his old pickup. He lives alone, practically a recluse, in a log house back in the woods."

"Any chance you can give us directions to the road in there?" Chase wanted to know.

"I can do better than that. I can show you on a map."

"I'll leave you in Donna's capable hands." Dr. Hansen shook their hands and returned to her office.

Chase fixed his attention on the redhead digging through one of her desk drawers. "Ah, I knew I had it." She came up with a road map she spread open on the surface of the desk. "Bought it that day we went walking there."

Chase leaned over, watching her trace the route with a red pen. "I don't have an exact location of this log cabin, but it's somewhere in here." She drew a circle where the back lane ended. "At least, that's what our friend said."

"I'd better get some of this down. Could I trouble you for a pencil and paper?"

"Not necessary." The receptionist folded up the map and handed it to Chase. "Here, you can have it."

"Won't you want it again?"

"I can always get another one."

Chase took the map. "I've learned one thing."

"What's that?"

"People in Alaska are friendly. And generous. Thank you."

They were out on the street again and headed for the parking garage when Haley said to him, "It's getting late. You're not going to try to visit this George Fellows today, are you?"

"How do you know I want to visit him at all?"

"Josh asked about him, didn't he? I'd say that's a pretty strong indication of your intention."

"He may be the key to picking up Josh's trail. And no, tomorrow is soon enough."

Haley didn't say anything at first. She wanted to see if Chase was simply dealing with the rush hour traffic in an unfamiliar city while driving an equally unfamiliar vehicle or if he had a better reason for constantly checking both his rearview mirror and his side mirrors.

She, too, began to steal quick glances behind them until, sure of herself, she addressed her companion behind the wheel. "There isn't, you know."

He turned his head to look at her. "What are you talking about?"

"A particular car following us."

"Who said there was?"

"You did."

"I never—"

"Your actions did. You keep looking behind us for any suspicious vehicles. And, by the way, you've been so busy being preoccupied with that, you just missed the turning to Sitka Avenue."

"Huh?"

"The way to Kodiak Hotel. Car rental attendant. Directions he gave us. Remember?"

"You might have told me," he grumbled.

"I just did. Turn around. Sitka is two blocks back."

He cursed under his breath as he corrected his error. Haley had the urge to tease him for being a crank but decided he was in no mood.

Chase waited until they were on the right route before he defended himself. "Okay, so maybe I am being just a little paranoid hunting for bad guys on our tail.

But after what happened in Seattle and Portland, isn't it only smart to be on the lookout up here for threats in the place where this whole odd mystery seems to have originated?"

"You do have a point," she conceded.

If he was right, that could mean whoever stole their seed packets and murdered Professor Rostov was now in Alaska. A frightening possibility, maybe even a certainty. Or, just as chilling, other members of a wide, dangerous network based here in Anchorage. But if there was any truth to that, then who was behind it, and what did it all mean? And how was Josh connected?

"We're here," Chase announced.

"What?"

"Kodiak Hotel. Now who's being preoccupied?"

He was right. They had arrived at the front entrance of a substantial building located on the waterfront of Cook Inlet and the Port of Anchorage.

Haley and Chase were pleased with the suite they were conducted to on the third floor. It consisted of two bedrooms with baths separated by a sitting room, its front windows looking out on a variety of vessels below.

Chase didn't need any further reminder he was in Alaska when he and Haley went to their separate beds that night. The sky outside at this late hour should have been dark, not still light as day. That was mid-June for you at this latitude.

He blamed the twilit sky for his wakefulness. It was a poor excuse. The truth was, he'd slept so many hours on the plane that he was no longer tired.

And why had he needed those long hours? There was a reason for that, too. At Haley's invitation, Chase had spent last night, his second night at her home, in her guest room. He'd felt the need to stick close to her for her safety.

That being decided, he'd promised himself that unlike the previous night, he was going to behave himself. No more lying awake picturing her in the next room wearing thin nightwear that revealed the shape of her provocative body, then invading her room and being welcomed into her bed.

He had ultimately resisted making love to her that night. But last night, although there had been no second visit to her room, he hadn't managed to prevent being assaulted again by a lengthy session of seductive images.

There were going to be no more nights like those. Here in Alaska, with Josh somewhere within reach, Chase was going to win the battle. Keep himself from stealing the woman his brother loved.

He was not going to tell himself he was susceptible again tonight because of the sky. If that was keeping him awake, all he had to do was close the drapes and shut out the light.

But even after he did close the drapes and go back to bed, Chase could feel himself losing the fight. He could picture Haley in that other bedroom. The images of her in there, with only a sitting room between them, were even stronger than before. And the lust that triggered them wasn't cooling. It was hotter than ever.

Haley was unable to sleep. Not liking what she was thinking about herself probably had something to do with that. She had convinced herself she'd accompanied Chase to Alaska solely for the purpose of helping him find Josh. That wasn't true. Or at least not totally so.

Nor was she here to benefit from Chase McKinley's protection. Much as she appreciated his broad shoulders to lean on, she'd always been able to take care of herself, thank you.

The selfish truth was that Haley had come to Alaska to try to determine who, when all was said and done, really mattered to her—Josh or his brother. Both men had their share of fine qualities. Josh was easygoing, fun to be with and ambitious about his career. She admired that. And Chase? Well, he was harder to define, with a temperament subject to swift changes of mood. One minute pleasant, the next hotheaded. But always, whatever the mood, sexy as hell.

Except, Haley told herself, this was not a very mature reason to base her judgment on. Admittedly, an exciting, even important one, but in the end not what counted. There had to be more than that. Didn't there?

So, Adams, is that what's keeping you awake? The guilt of desire?

Somewhere along the way, Haley did manage to doze off. It couldn't have been anything like a deep sleep. Seconds later she sensed another person's presence in the room, and light despite the blackout curtains.

There was a tall, solid figure in the doorway. No way to make out his face. Not when the light came from behind him, making him no more than a silhouette. As he came slowly, silently toward her, her pulse accelerated. It wasn't because of fear. She knew who he was.

When he reached her, she made room for him on the bed.

She couldn't see his face, but she could feel the heat of his body. Smell the male aroma of him as he leaned toward her, some mixture of the soap he used and the faint but identifiable primal animal smell intended by nature to attract his mate. Haley trembled, finding it intimidating and exciting at the same time.

It wasn't until then that he spoke in a deep, husky voice with a volume so low she had to strain to hear the words.

"I tried to keep away from you, tried not to want you, but it was no use. I had to come to you."

"Yes," she whispered. "It was the right thing to do. The *only* thing. We were meant for this, Chase."

Whether he agreed with that or not, she didn't know. Wasn't going to let herself care. Her yearning for him was all that mattered. Was it something tangible, something that finally compelled him to reach out for her, gather her up from the pillows and hold her tightly against him?

He wasn't wearing any kind of top. His chest was bare, his skin warm and firm with muscle. She pressed her hand there and felt the beat of his heart.

"When I looked up and saw you in the doorway like that," she said, "I thought maybe you were checking on me to make sure I wasn't having another bad dream, like that night back in Portland. Then when you went on standing there without moving, saying nothing, I wondered if maybe you were sleepwalking and that this time you were the one having the dream. Do you sleepwalk, Chase?"

"Does this feel like the action of a sleepwalker to you?"

His rugged face moved toward hers, millimeter by excruciatingly slow millimeter, his glittering dark eyes searching hers. What did he find in her gaze? Before she could begin to determine that, his parted lips were on hers, his mouth moving across hers from side to side, the tip of his tongue leaving a moist trail.

"Verdict?" he demanded, lifting his mouth from hers.

"Hard to say," she managed to tell him with some difficulty. "I've never been kissed by a sleepwalker before."

"Then, by all means, let me provide you with another demonstration."

His mouth fastened on hers again. This time it was more than just the tip of his tongue performing his magic. Before she invited it or even knew it was happening, his tongue was deep inside her mouth. There was nothing gentle about it. His hungry exploration had a rough possessiveness about it.

Haley could have objected to this kind of treatment. He would have released her, but the truth was that something wild in her relished his unrestrained kiss. She could hear the low growls in his throat, the echo of her own moans.

She felt deprived, cheated when he drew away from her. A disappointment she registered with a series of little whimpers.

"And now?" he wanted to know.

"Not a sleepwalker," she whispered. "Definitely not a sleepwalker."

"Damn right. No sleepwalker ever had a need like this."

His hands burrowed under the light blanket that covered her from the waist down, found the hem of her nightshirt and dragged it over her head, stripping her of all but her panties.

"Or this."

While his hand softly kneaded one of her breasts, that hungry mouth of his descended to her other breast, taking it into his mouth, suckling strongly on the nipple that had hardened with his first kiss. The matching nipple was waiting eagerly for its turn. Chase did not disappoint it, giving it equal attention when he moved on to that breast.

The pleasure she felt was so exquisite that her emotions built on it, expanding to such a degree that they had her writhing wildly on the bed, unable to express herself.

"What do you need, Haley? Tell me what you need."

"I want—"

"What?"

"Everything. That's what I want. *Everything*."

"Then let's start here, baby."

He peeled away what was left of the blanket covering her. His hand was hot when it made contact with her panties, exploring what the lighter-than-light silk barely covered.

The silk was no barrier. His fingers were easily able to seduce her sensitive flesh underneath. They circled and pressed, working all the while toward his goal. Haley bucked when he reached that vulnerable prize.

"That's right," he coaxed her, rubbing her groin, his other hand supporting her by the hip.

She was so ready that it took only a few strokes for her to reach a climax. In no mood to wait after that, he rolled her panties down and away from her, leaving her entirely open to him. He wasted no time in ridding himself of his briefs. There was nothing between them now, nothing to interfere.

"Touch me," he commanded her.

Sensing just where he wanted to be touched and how, Haley grasped the rigid shaft of flesh that rose from his loins. The heat from it was incredible. It took only her touch to have him sharply sucking in air.

"That's right, baby," he groaned. "That feels just right."

Her fingers began to squeeze and pump. He endured

the action for a moment, then gripped her hand, stopping her.

"Any more of this," he complained, "and I won't have anything left for you."

"That I wouldn't like. I wouldn't like it at all."

"Then let's see exactly what you do like."

Grabbing her legs with a rough urgency, he dragged her away from the pillows and down flat on the mattress, where he fitted himself close beside her on his side. Haley could feel the hair on his muscular legs tickling her thighs. The pleasant sensation had her squirming. Chase used that opportunity to reach down and, with a kind of raw fury, insert two of his fingers deep inside her.

"You're tight," he said, the fingers working to gain him passage. "Tight and wet. Already ready for me, aren't you?"

She didn't answer him. Didn't seem to have any oxygen left to answer him. He apparently didn't need an answer. He was that sure of himself as he ripped open a condom package he'd had nearby and nudged it over his erection.

Elevating himself over her, his knee nudged her thighs apart. Without guidance or hesitation, he plunged inside her, thrusting deep. There was no pause before his long strokes began. She responded with her own rhythms.

Why, she thought, didn't she mind his absolute certainty about her, his lack of gentleness? They matched the face above her, dark and tough with that scar. It was part of the ruggedness that was so much a part of him. But before she could pronounce any negative judgment in that direction, he changed suddenly, surprising her just as he had so often before.

This time it was Chase's lovemaking going from

fierce to tender. As if he was not one man but two different men. She could see the tenderness in his eyes gazing down at her.

"My God, but you're beautiful," he praised her softly.

That tenderness remained, strong and searing, for the rest of their joining. When it culminated, it did so with an intensity that consumed both of them.

She came down from her release to feel him kissing her slowly before he rolled away with a long, contented sigh. There was no need for them to speak. They lay there side by side in an easy silence.

Haley thought about it and decided here was one thing she had learned tonight. Josh was probably the better man for her, but it was Chase who made her burn.

Chapter 9

Chase was so quiet that Haley wondered if he had fallen asleep. If that was the case, the only way for her to verify it without disturbing him was to prop herself on one elbow and gaze down at him.

That was how she discovered he wasn't asleep. Flat on his back, with brawny arms folded behind his head, hands linked, he stared up at the ceiling. The expression in his eyes was a revelation.

There was no question what he was feeling. Guilt. A naked, raw guilt.

Not all guilt was the same. It existed for different reasons, took different forms. Haley knew this, just as she knew she was the motive for this particular guilt.

It was because of Josh, of course. Chase's realization that he'd just slept with the woman he'd convinced himself belonged to his brother was tearing him apart. Would he never understand that Josh had no claim on her?

Probably, Haley thought, she should be turning to

him now, sympathetically telling him it was all right and that she understood. Even offering to share his guilt.

The hell she would. It wasn't all right. What they had shared was pure and satisfying, and she was angry that Chase was spoiling it. Why did he have to darken it with blame just because she had gone out with his brother, enjoyed Josh's company for a few weeks?

Feeling in her present mood that she had to put space between Chase and her, she got off the bed, wrapped herself in a lightweight summer robe and went to the window. She parted the blackout drape. There was still light outside, a gray, late-night light that softened the quiet inlet waters.

Haley sensed rather than heard him leave the bed and move toward her. She could feel him when he stopped just behind her, but she didn't turn around. She kept looking out at the inlet.

"Are you okay?" he asked.

She didn't answer him.

"Not okay." He waited for a few seconds. "I think maybe I'd better go back to my own room."

"I think that might be a good idea."

She heard the door shut behind him and wondered if he was feeling as miserable in this moment as she now was.

There was one thing Chase had learned about Haley back in Portland. She didn't hold grudges. She had a cheerful good-morning for him when she came down to the sunlit dining room for breakfast.

"You didn't wait for me," she said, seating herself across from him.

"I came to see if you wanted to join me, but your

bathroom door was locked, and you didn't answer my knock."

"Some bodyguard you are. I'm surprised you didn't break the door down, thinking I was a victim of foul play."

"Not when I could hear you singing and the water in the shower running."

Which had left him relieved. Not because he feared she was being threatened. The only entrance to the suite was the hall door to the sitting room, and that they kept locked. This relief had come from the knowledge she couldn't still be angry after last night. Or so he hoped.

Chase had already ordered. The waiter came to their table to take Haley's order, provide her with coffee and refill Chase's cup. She noticed Chase's smartphone on the table when the waiter left.

"Who have you been calling?"

"The people I should have been contacting the minute we landed instead of thinking I'd find the answers at the seed vault's office."

"The police and hospitals?" Haley guessed.

"That's right. The cops were nice about it. They were willing to make an exception and waive the usual waiting period here for missing persons. Instead, they would accept Josh as missing starting from when we last heard from him in Oregon. I could make it official if I would stop by central police headquarters and file a report."

"And the hospitals?"

Chase shook his head. "No one by that name or description was checked in to any of them."

"What now?"

"We can't count on the police or the hospitals alone. We have to rely on ourselves and go hunting on our own."

"George Fellows next?"

"George Fellows."

Their breakfasts arrived, and while they ate, Chase thought about the guilt that had haunted him last night after making love to Haley. He'd been unable to shake it, and since then it had been joined by a second, separate guilt. This one he was being careful not to reveal. It was the guilt he felt for having hurt Haley by spoiling something special. She didn't deserve that pain. Hell, *he* didn't deserve *her.*

They were on the road when Chase, at the wheel in the rental Jeep, suggested stopping at the central police station on their way out of town.

"The sooner I file that report, the sooner they can get busy on a search for Josh."

Haley agreed it was a good idea.

The officer who met with them was Native American. People in the lower continental states tended to think that all native Alaskans were Eskimos, but Haley knew that wasn't true. There were many different tribes in Alaska, and this man could be a member of any one of them.

Whatever his origin, Sergeant Blackfeather was friendly, cheerful and efficient. He helped Chase fill out the necessary information, cautioning him, "We do our best to locate missing persons, issuing bulletins, asking questions, but there are always obstacles. For instance, Alaska isn't divided into counties like other states but boroughs, large ones. The subject could have moved on to any one of them, making the search difficult. Or he could have moved out of the state altogether."

"I understand," Chase said, "but we'll hope for the best and be grateful for your efforts."

Leaving the police station, Haley remembered what

Chase had said back at the hotel. They couldn't count on the police, who could have any number of missing persons to track down. They had to try to find Josh themselves, and that might be an impossible undertaking.

George Fellows might provide them with a lead, of course, but what if he couldn't? Where could they go next? The outlook was dismal. Even worse was the bleak possibility that Josh was no longer alive. If their search led to that eventuality, could she learn to accept it, be prepared to go home without him?

She knew that Chase couldn't. That he'd never give up until…

Come on, Haley, don't think like that, she ordered herself. *Be positive, and keep on being positive until you have to be otherwise.*

That determined, she broke out the map the receptionist at the seed vault headquarters had given them yesterday. She had it unfolded and awkwardly spread open on her knees, ready to direct Chase to their destination, when he sidetracked her.

"You remember yesterday when I was imagining we were being followed?"

She looked up from the map. "Yes."

"Well, I'm not imagining it today. We have a burgundy SUV on our tail."

Haley started to turn around.

"You do that," he said, "and you're just going to tell him we're onto him."

She stopped halfway around, using the action instead to look at Chase. "Are you sure we're being followed?"

"It's one hell of a coincidence if we aren't. I've been doing some twists and turns up and down streets that aren't on our route out of the city to make certain. He's managed to stick with us every time. Use your side mirror and see for yourself."

Haley did just that. He was right. There was a burgundy SUV back there, sometimes only a car length or so behind them, at other times putting another vehicle between them to keep from being obvious, but never entirely losing them. And never getting close enough for her to distinguish the driver, other than to know it was a man.

"I think the two of you are a couple of boys playing a game," she decided. "You warn me not to turn around and look because that would tell the driver back there we're onto him. Then you let me know the elaborate efforts you went through to ditch him. Unless the guy is a complete fool, he knows what you were doing and why, so that makes the two of you aware of what each other is doing."

Which meant it wouldn't have made a difference if she had turned around and looked directly through the rear window. But game or not, the presence of that SUV made her uneasy.

"Why in the world is it back there, anyway?"

"I think," Chase decided, "someone has assigned a shadow to keep track of us and to let whoever that someone is know where we go and who we see."

"Whatever the explanation, I don't like it. It isn't a game. It's threatening. What are we going to do?"

"We're going to see George Fellows."

"You're just going to let the SUV follow us there?"

"Not this trip."

He seems very certain of that, she thought. She didn't oppose him. She waited to see just what he was going to do. It didn't take him very long to achieve his intention. They rolled along for several blocks at a deceptively easy speed. Then, just as a traffic light was changing, Chase punched the accelerator to the floor. The Jeep obeyed, leaping through the intersection, leaving the SUV caught at the red light behind them.

He wore a smile on his bold mouth.

"Pleased with yourself, aren't you?" she asked drily, but actually she was pleased, too, to no longer have that sinister SUV behind them.

Haley had discovered by now that Anchorage, if measured strictly by population, was not one of America's bigger cities.

In terms of the land it occupied, however, it was extensive.

Thankfully, there was no further sign of the burgundy SUV, permitting her to direct Chase north out of the city without interruption. The suburbs here were a sprawl of shopping malls, more trailer parks than Haley could ever remember having seen before and the vastness of Elmendorf Air Force Base, merged in recent years with Fort Richardson Military Reservation to the east.

Dwarfing all of it, and always looming there in the background, were the mountains, massive in their grandeur.

That civilization could be left behind so abruptly and completely didn't seem possible. One minute there were traffic and buildings. The next they were in the wilderness.

The forest seemed to close around them, thick and tall. Sitka spruce, black spruce, white spruce, birch, cottonwoods, hemlocks. The route narrowed, the pavement uneven until, finally, there was no pavement at all, just gravel and a road that seemed to become rougher with each mile.

"Are you sure we're on the right track?" Chase asked.

"According to Donna's map, we're headed where we're supposed to be headed."

"Not anymore we're not," he announced after another mile or so when the lane had dwindled to a dirt track not much wider than a path and a challenge even for a Jeep. "I'm pulling off here. It may be the only spot wide enough for us to turn around when we're ready to go back."

"Suits me. We can walk from here."

They had scarcely exited the Jeep when Chase was attacked from all sides. "Holy jeez!" She watched him slapping and swatting at every square inch of bare flesh and some areas that weren't exposed.

"I should have warned you back at the hotel," she said. "Apparently you haven't been reading your guidebook or you would have known that mosquitoes are Alaska's most dangerous form of wildlife."

"And I thought it was wolves and mean bears. Ravenous little buggers, these dive-bombers are. Only they aren't so little, are they?"

Taking pity on him, she tossed him a tube of repellant she extracted from her shoulder bag. "Here, slather yourself with this. I used it back at the hotel, and it seems to be effective."

She watched him apply the lotion, then exhale with relief as the army of mosquitoes retreated. "I'd rather face a grizzly than those devils."

"No, you wouldn't," she said, taking the tube back from him.

"Then let's hope we don't meet any. Anything else you forgot to warn me about?"

"Don't think so."

"So let's see if we can find George Fellows."

They set off up the trail. If there was wildlife in the dense forest on either side, it didn't choose to appear. The only company they had were the croaking ravens in the treetops. According to what Haley had read, they were revered by the natives and common almost everywhere in Alaska.

The trail ended for them when they rounded a bend, where they were confronted by a crude wooden gate barely wide enough to accommodate the passage of a car. When it was opened, that is. At the moment it was closed and secured by a padlock and chain. If the land was private on the other side of the gate, and it must be, there were no signs posted to indicate this.

"George Fellows," Haley surmised.

"I suppose so, but I don't see any board with his name on it."

Nor was there any glimpse of a log cabin in there, Haley thought. Nothing but the heavy growth on either side of the narrow lane that continued up a long slope on the other side of the gate.

"Doesn't look like there are any Keep Out signs posted, either," Chase observed.

"And no fence. Just the gate. We shouldn't have any trouble squeezing around that."

"We don't have a choice if we're going to find that cabin and Fellows. Let me go first."

Haley stood aside and watched him slip sideways through the left opening between the gate post and an impassable willow thicket. She was about to follow when she was startled to a halt by the blast of what sounded like a shotgun. It was very loud and very close.

The profanity that Chase roared after he'd checked to make certain she hadn't been hit was equally loud and very explicit. She could only assume by the anger driving it that he hadn't been struck, either.

"Hey, you up there," he yelled, "wherever you are, stop shooting! There are people down here! You wanna kill someone?"

A gravelly voice shouted back, "I didn't even come close. If I'd wanted t'clip ya, I woulda clipped ya. This here is my land, an' I don't allow no trespassin'."

"Then it should be posted No Trespassing!"

Haley decided that if this was George Fellows and they expected to speak to him, then someone had better make peace. And it looked like it would be she.

"Mr. Fellows," she called politely, "if that's you, you might want to know that it was Dr. Greta Hansen, the director of the International Seed Vault, who sent us to see you. She said you were something of an expert about seeds, and we hoped you'd be willing to talk to us."

There was a long pause. She wished she could see him. Carrying on any conversation was difficult since he was well hidden in the woods, although he obviously had some kind of decent view of them. Or maybe his boast about his marksmanship was an exaggeration, and they had been in some danger. His response when it finally came had her gulping nervously.

"How many of ya down there?"

So he hadn't had any safe target. "Two. Just the two of us."

There was another silence and then a reluctant acceptance. "All right, come ahead. I'll wait for ya here at the top of the rise."

Haley cleared the gate, and they started up the slope. They were halfway to the top when they heard a menacing growl that had them halting again.

"Behave yourself, Wolfie," commanded his owner waiting for them somewhere up ahead.

Chase issued another curse. "Oh, great, he's got a canine of some kind. Sounds like a nasty one, too. Like something out of a Jack London tale."

"Let's hope he has control of *Wolfie*, or I'm climbing the nearest tree."

They approached their objective cautiously, with Haley wondering just how wild this dog was. It wasn't until they rounded a wooded bend that they could view George Fellows and his dog.

She and Chase looked at each other and voiced their disbelief at the same time. *"Chihuahua?"*

Even for an eccentric, it seemed just a bit out of character for someone to have an animal like this in the wilderness of Alaska. And there was no question George Fellows was an eccentric.

Haley judged he was somewhere in his eighties, scrawny with patches of whiskers he'd missed scraping off the last time he'd shaved, clothes that hung on him like a scarecrow's and a thatch of handsome white hair that looked as if the only barber it had seen had been its owner, who had chopped it off unevenly.

The yapping Wolfie in Fellows's arm was squirming furiously to be put down. "Thinks he's a vicious guard dog," the old man cackled.

Since he was cradling the shotgun in his other arm, George was unable to hang on to the Chihuahua. The second it was released it raced toward them, a snarling enemy.

"Don't worry. He don't bite."

No, Haley thought, but it turned out he did like to nip at ankles. To Chase's credit, he courageously managed to scoop up Wolfie, snuggle him firmly in one arm and with his free hand stroke the dog while speaking to him soothingly. Amazingly, Wolfie stopped trying to nip Chase's fingers and switched to licking them.

George seemed pleased with Chase's success charming his dog. When they reached him, he asked their names and shook their hands before turning around and leading the way to the rustic log cabin just ahead of them.

This man was a expert on seeds? *Never judge books by their covers, Haley*, she reminded herself as they climbed the porch that stretched across the face of the cabin.

George turned his head at the door to address Chase. "You can let Wolfie down here. He likes to sit on the porch and watch for the squirrels. Has himself this big desire to catch one, but he never will. Come on in, folks."

Chase deposited the Chihuahua on the porch floor as instructed, and George deposited the shotgun in a wall rack just inside the front door.

"Got coffee fresh made and hot on the stove. Sit yourselves down at the table there while I pour, and we'll have us that talk."

Haley gazed around at her surroundings. She found herself in one long, open room, with a sitting area and stone fireplace at the other end and a combination kitchen and dining area at this end. The archway in the rear wall hinted at other rooms in the back. The cabin with its primitive furnishings was rustic but pleasantly comfortable.

When they were settled across from one another at the round table and sipping coffee, George was ready to answer their questions.

"So, folks, what can I tell you 'bout seeds that you couldn't learn at the seed vault headquarters?"

"Actually," Chase said, "it's more than that."

The old man scowled as if he had just learned he'd been deceived into seeing them with a bogus reason and wasn't happy about it. "Oh, yeah? And just what would it be?"

"I have a half brother whose surname is different from mine. Matthews. Josh Matthews."

George didn't react to that as Haley expected. He gave them a flat "So?"

"Dr. Hansen told us that Josh planned to visit you. I'm worried about my brother, Mr. Fellows. We haven't heard from him in weeks. That's why we've come to Alaska. He seems to have disappeared, and we're trying to trace his movements in an effort to locate him."

George continued to look suspicious. This time he was looking not at Chase but at Haley. "You ain't a brother. Sister?"

She shook her head. "A close friend. Josh and I dated back in Portland. I promise you, Mr. Fellows, we are legitimate."

George considered this for a moment and then nodded, accepting them. "He visited me all right. Stayed for quite a piece. I have to say I was impressed by his research on seeds and the vault. He was aimin' to do a story on that."

"That's right," Chase said.

"I give him quite a bit on what he didn't already know."

"Did you suggest another source for him to investigate when he left here?"

"I think he had that already fixed in his mind, but he didn't share it. Said he might come back when he had it all put together, but he never did."

"And that was it?" Chase pressed.

"Exceptin' for the seed packets I give 'im. He seemed real touched by the gift. Said he would see to it they stayed safe."

Haley and Chase exchanged swift glances. She knew he was thinking the same thing she was. That those seed packets had to be the ones Josh sent to them to be put into their safe deposit boxes for safekeeping. This, then, was their origin and Josh's reason for valuing them.

She hoped Chase would understand the plea in her gaze. It would be wrong to tell the old man the seed packets had been stolen. Why hurt him with something like that?

Chase's slight nod was all she needed to let her know he did understand and agreed with her.

George apparently hadn't missed their silent communication but chose to misread it. "I know what the two of you are thinkin'. You're wonderin' how an old, un-educated fool like me comes to have an interest in seeds o'all things, never mind this big knowledge about 'em."

"That is unique," Haley conceded.

"Well, the truth is I can't tell you. Ain't a secret. I just plain don't know. It seems growing things was al-ways there from the time I can remember. Started as a youngster plantin' seeds of all kinds in gardens, pots, window boxes, you name it. Got fascinated with them seeds and any and all others and read everything about them I could get my hands on. Still do."

He stopped there. Haley had a feeling he had more to tell them, but for a long moment he was silent, as if making up his mind. Then slowly, with a sly look on his face, he confessed, "I got me a seed collection of my own I built up through the years. Nothing like the seed vault, a'course, but it ain't bad for one man." He hesitated be-fore asking, "You interested in seein' it?"

Haley was touched by his offer. For a man with his pride, this was a real trust. "I think we'd both love to see it."

Chase agreed with her. "I'd consider it an honor. Am I right in thinking you showed it to Josh?"

"He asked, and I obliged."

"Well, if my brother saw it, I have to see it. I never let Josh get the best of me if I can help it."

"Then we'd better do something about that." Chuckling, George got to his feet and beckoned them to follow him.

Haley assumed they were going outside and was surprised when he ignored the front door and led them to the other end of the long room near the fireplace. There was a worn throw rug here on the plank floor, its once colorful pattern faded from age.

The old man knelt at its edge and peeled half of it back, revealing a stout metal ring embedded in the wood and the outline of a trapdoor. Both had been concealed by the rug.

Grasping the ring, George raised the door and lifted it back.

Haley and Chase peered into the yawning blackness.

"Smart place to hide your collection," Chase observed.

"Oh, it's not to hide the seeds that they're down there, it's to preserve 'em. You'll see." He turned to Haley. "It's pretty cold. You want I should get you one o' my heavy sweaters to wear?"

"Thanks, but I think the coolness will feel good after all that summer heat we walked through to get here."

George looked like he had another opinion, but he didn't argue with her. "I'll go ahead and get the lights.

You be careful on them stairs. They're steep, and they're long."

He disappeared into the darkness. Within seconds, bright lights bloomed from below, along with an invitation. "Come on down."

Chase preceded her on the flight. As they'd been cautioned, it was steep and long but safe enough with a handrail to cling to. George was waiting for them at the bottom.

Blinking at the powerful lights as she looked around her, Haley felt she had arrived in Aladdin's cave. The riches it contained were stored on rows of shelves in labeled, clear plastic boxes.

The overhead fans blew down continual streams of cool air. George explained their presence as Haley shivered.

"Seeds has got to have two conditions to last for any time. If they get those regularly, they can be good to sprout for years, even centuries. One is the coolness. We don't have permafrost in this part of Alaska, and that's why I got the deep cellar. Just as good as refrigeration, you see."

"And what's the other thing?" Chase wanted to know.

"Dry air. That's even more important than the temperature. Seeds got to be kept dry to last."

"Which explains the fans."

"And the tightly sealed boxes. Nothing like all the high-tech apparatus the seed vault has got, but stuff that's good enough for my collection."

Haley sauntered slowly down the rows, looking at the contents of the various boxes. Some of them were familiar enough that she was able to identify them without consulting the labels. The majority of them she didn't recognize and could name only with the help of the labels. She did enjoy gardening in her backyard at home, but she wasn't much of a botanist.

Chase did better in that department. He had just enough knowledge about plants that he was able to keep up a lively conversation with George on the subject. Haley went on looking at the boxes. She was ambling along the last row when her attention was fixed on a certain box.

"Chase," she called, "come over here. There's something you need to see."

Accompanied by Fellows, he joined her where she waited. She pointed to the box in question.

"Aren't those seeds the same kind Josh sent to me?"

"They look like it."

George settled the matter for them. "They are one of the kind of seeds I give to Josh. Legumes of the bean family. Highly nutritious and in their day widely grown. That was long ago, and since then many other varieties have been developed and replaced them. Beans whose fruits are larger, more dependable and more appetizing."

"So are you saying nobody grows these beans anymore?" Chase asked.

"Ain't very likely when the modern strains are so much more available."

"Then does that make these seeds rare and valuable?"

"Well…uncommon, anyway. But I wouldn't say worth a lot of money, even to collectors, or I wouldn't have parted with any of them."

But Josh somehow got the impression they were precious, Haley thought, maybe even priceless, or the notes he'd accompanied with the seed packets wouldn't have indicated as much. And whoever had stolen those packets must have agreed with him.

"That's not to say there aren't rare seeds that exist,"

George instructed them. "They've been found in sealed pottery jars in ancient tombs by the people who do that kind of thing in places like Egypt and them there dead cultures down in Central America. And would you believe those seeds is still viable after all those centuries?"

"Meaning they could be planted today and actually grow?" Haley asked.

"Sure could. It's been tested."

"And what would they produce?" Chase wanted to know.

"Grains. That's what those ancient folks counted on for their foods. Wheat in lands like Egypt, corn in America. But not the kind of wheat and corn we know today. Those ancient crops died out long ago. Got replaced by better ones."

"Which would make the ancient seeds, if they still existed somewhere and were available, extremely valuable, especially as people look for different food supplies," Chase surmised.

"For sure," George agreed. "But not for collectors like me. I hear tell the International Seed Vault does have them."

The old man's face screwed up into a frown. "Funny thing, though. Josh and me was talking about this very thing when he went and got this funny little smile on his mouth. 'What?' I ask him. That's when he says, all secretlike, 'There's this megal—'" George struggled with the word "'—megalomaniac who would go to any lengths to get his hands on such seeds.'"

"Did he name him?" Chase asked.

George shook his head. "Clammed up on the subject. I got the feeling it was something he mighta been saving for his story. After that, he left with the seeds I gave him."

Chapter 10

"Nice guy once you get past his defenses," Chase remarked when they'd thanked George, said goodbye to him and were heading down the drive.

"After seeing his seed collection," Haley said, "I can understand why he'd meet strangers with a shotgun and an unfriendly attitude."

"Not to mention a vicious dog helping to protect that collection."

"Uh-huh," she agreed drily. "Why, Wolfie would have torn us to pieces if he hadn't fallen in love with you."

"Lucky thing I have such a powerful charisma."

"With canines it seems you do. Where the rest of the animal population is concerned, I wouldn't be so sure of that."

Chase favored her with a perfectly executed sour look that had her grinning.

Haley waited until they were past the gate and on their

way back to the Jeep to raise a different matter, this one without any note of levity.

"Megalomaniac?"

"Yeah, I've been thinking about that, too. Wondering who on earth Josh could have been talking about, and why he matters."

"Do you suppose," Haley speculated, "that whoever this man is, he's connected with the seed thefts and Professor Rostov's murder? Maybe even ordered them?"

"The head of a criminal network? Anything is possible, I guess. There's one certainty. If Josh mentioned his existence, you can bet he counts him as a major player in this story he's chasing."

And dangerous, a threat to Josh, she thought. But she couldn't bring herself to say that when Chase was already so worried about his brother.

What she did say with a shake of her head was, "But *seeds*. I still can't bring myself to understand how something so innocent could set off a chain reaction as it did. One that's *still* going, it seems."

Though Chase was silent, she could imagine him thinking: *With Josh caught in the middle of it.*

Chase remained quiet until they were on their way back into the city. Then, his tone offhand when she knew that underneath he was anything but casual, he voiced a proposal. "I'm considering stopping by the central police station. Asking whether they've made any progress locating our boy. What do you think?"

She turned to look at him behind the wheel. "Chase, it was only this morning that you let them know Josh is missing. You can't seriously expect them to have some answers for us when they've barely had time to work on the case."

"I guess you're right. We can't expect them to deliver miracles. Maybe I'll check with them tomorrow."

That would be too soon, also, she thought. She understood how anxious he was. That it was making him unreasonable. She feared he'd reached the same conclusion she had:

If Josh had failed to attempt any return visits to either the offices of the seed vault or George Fellows, as he'd indicated he would, then he must have been prevented from doing so.

How could Chase not reach that logical conclusion? And possibly something worse beyond that?

At least the burgundy SUV was no longer shadowing them. Was that also the work of Josh's megalomaniac?

They ate out that evening in a downtown Italian restaurant that featured authentic Tuscan fare. It was a romantic setting, with the soft glow of candlelight and a strolling violinist who played traditional Italian street songs.

It should have put them in an equally romantic mood. It didn't. Chase was quiet. Haley made an effort to encourage conversation, but it fell flat.

The one subject we could always talk about, she thought, *and did talk about perpetually, was Josh's disappearance. That's the trouble. We've exhausted it. There's nothing more to say.*

It seemed unfeeling, maybe, but she'd hoped that for one evening they could put Josh aside. Talk about something else. Even if it didn't involve the kind of emotion that seemed appropriate for an Italian restaurant.

Chase did try when she asked him about his years as an army ranger. He told her about the rigorous training required to be a ranger. Though he never mentioned his brother's name, she could tell that's where his thoughts lay.

With nothing else to take them in a fresh direction where their search was concerned, they went back to their suite in the Kodiak Hotel, where Haley worked on her laptop and Chase watched the news on television.

Was he hoping for some report that would provide a clue to what had consumed them even before their arrival in Alaska? He didn't say, and she didn't ask him.

Haley went to bed early, leaving him in the sitting room. He didn't join her. She decided it was just as well. How could their lovemaking mean anything with the shadow of Josh always there between them?

Haley must have slept as poorly as he had. It registered in the shadows under her eyes. Her mood was also an indication when they met in the sitting room.

Other women in the same situation might have been silent, worn expressions of unhappiness. Haley's behavior was the polar opposite—a chatty cheerfulness. Chase knew her well enough by now to understand it wasn't genuine but a forced attitude.

Since they had lingered in their separate beds, resisting efforts to get up, their breakfast out on the dining terrace was a late one. Conversation, what there was any of it across the table, was scant and awkward.

He realized she wasn't pleased with him. After the passion he had demonstrated on earlier occasions, she must have been disappointed that he hadn't come to her last night. He had hurt her, and she deserved an explanation. An apology at least. But he wasn't expressing either one.

What the hell was the matter with him? He was crazy about her but afraid to admit it even to himself. There was only one explanation that made any sense to him. He was suffering from two paths of conflicted guilt.

A guilt because he seemed incapable of telling Haley how he felt about her. And she needed that if they were going to go on from here, forge any meaningful relationship. But the other guilt prevented that. The guilt that constantly whispered to him: *Even if he doesn't know it yet, you're hurting someone else at the same time you're hurting Haley.*

She was gazing out over the terrace railing at the waters of the inlet. Beautiful as always with that raven hair and those deep blue eyes, even with her ivory skin looking more pale than usual this morning. Maybe because she hadn't bothered with makeup. Or maybe because a sadness had crept over her.

We shouldn't be just sitting here like this, Chase told himself. *We should be talking, a safe, practical subject. Like planning something for the day, even if it isn't connected with our search.* A change would be good. Maybe a tour of the local sights.

Before Chase could propose anything, a familiar figure appeared on the terrace, looking dashing in his police uniform. He looked in both directions, spotted them at their table and strode toward them.

Excited by the arrival of Sergeant Blackfeather, Chase got to his feet to greet the officer.

"Sergeant, you're a welcome sight. Please, join us. We've got a pot of coffee here still hot. I can ask the server for another cup."

The officer shook his head. "Thanks for the offer, but I can't stay. I will sit for a minute, though." Settling himself in one of the chairs, he acknowledged Haley's presence.

Chase leaned eagerly toward him from his own seat.

"Since you've tracked us down out here, I'm thinking you must have some word to report."

"I do. I wish I could tell you we've found your brother. We haven't, but we do have evidence of him." He explained how the department operated when they tackled cases of missing persons. "When it's visitors to Anchorage we're dealing with, it's standard procedure for us to check with the hospitals and hotels. You told us, Mr. McKinley, that you'd already called the hospitals, but sometimes they'll give us what they won't give even a family member. We came up empty there, and he hadn't been registered in any of the hotels. That was yesterday. We had better luck this morning."

"How's that?"

Sergeant Blackfeather went on to tell them, "Next we try the rooming houses. It was at one of them on the other side of town that your brother was staying. The landlady couldn't tell our officer anything useful about her lodger. Just that he left his things in his room and didn't come back for them."

Chase was disappointed. "When was that?"

"Almost three weeks back. I wish she'd reported it, but these rooming houses aren't always reliable about that kind of thing. Reluctant to get involved, it seems."

"Where are his things now?" Haley asked.

"Landlady packed them up in his two suitcases and kept them. She turned them over to us. I brought them along for you, Mr. McKinley. The desk clerk is watching over them."

They accompanied the sergeant out to the lobby, where he asked Chase to identify the old-fashioned, hard-style cases.

"Yes, those are Josh's suitcases all right."

"I wish I could have produced your brother himself,

but don't let his abandoned luggage and their contents have you assuming the worst. We've had nothing to make us believe he isn't still out there somewhere. As for his things… Well, there could be all kinds of reasons to explain why he left them behind."

"I'll try to remember that."

"One more thing. We had a look through those contents and found nothing but the usual clothes and toiletries. I'm guessing you'll want to go through them yourself. If you find anything at all worthwhile that might help us, let me know."

Chase promised he would, thanked him and told him he would be in touch if something turned up.

Sergeant Blackfeather was climbing into the squad car waiting for him out front when Haley placed a hand on Chase's arm in an effort to comfort him.

"He's right, you know," she said in a soft voice. "The luggage Josh left behind doesn't mean something terrible happened to him."

"I'm in perfect agreement with both of you. He is out there, possibly in hiding, possibly even restrained but still alive, and I'm going to find him. Maybe not until the mess is all sorted out and made clear, but I *will* find him."

There was a look of mingled surprise and admiration in Haley's eyes. She must have expected something else from him, a low mood, maybe even defeat. If so, she didn't know rangers with their strong-willed self-promises never to surrender, but she was finding out.

"What now?" she asked.

"Let's carry these cases upstairs and, if necessary, take them apart piece by piece. There's got to be something to learn from at least one of them that will help us."

Five minutes later they were in the sitting room of

their suite with the door locked behind them. Chase had the larger of the two matching cases open on the sofa and was removing the garments piece by piece, closely examining each one and placing it on the sofa cushions.

Haley was doing the same with the smaller case on the table across the room.

"I have nothing but clothes in mine and two pairs of shoes," he reported. "What do you have in yours?"

"Socks, underwear, several summer polo shirts, a shaving kit with an electric razor, deodorant, soap. Things like that."

Her tone suggested there was nothing interesting. He wanted to urge her not to overlook anything, to open any drugstore bottle or can to make certain they contained what their labels indicated. He could trust her to know that, though, so he kept his advice to himself.

He emptied his suitcase, having discovered nothing of use in it, not so much as a discarded gum wrapper in any of the pants or shirt pockets he examined.

"I've struck out with mine," he called to her. "You having any luck with yours?" She didn't answer him. "Haley," he persisted, "what's up over there?"

"I—I'm not sure. I'm thinking there might be something behind the lining on this side of the case I folded back on the table. I can't see anything on the surface of the lining, but it feels like there's a very slight bulge there."

Chase was across the room and by her side in three swift seconds. She was right. The pattern of the lining was busy enough to hide any swell underneath, but the palm of his hand could detect it.

"It's rectangular and thin," he said. "Like a magazine."

"Something Josh hid behind there?"

"Maybe."

He was afraid to speculate out loud about this possible discovery, but he was growing more hopeful of its potential by the second. He ran his fingers along the edges of the lining on all four sides.

"There's no zipper, no snaps, nothing like that. It wasn't meant to open for any storage. It seems like Josh must have somehow gotten under it, slid whatever he wanted to conceal under there and then probably glued it back down to look permanent. We'll have to cut it open."

He found his small jackknife in his pocket, opened it and ran the point along three sides of the lining, careful not to damage what was underneath. Haley watched him free the lining and fold it down to reveal not a magazine but a notebook.

Chase knew by its soft blue cover that it wasn't an ordinary notebook. "That's a journal," he said. "The kind of journal Josh always used when he was working up notes for a story."

"But why did he conceal it back there?"

"I don't know. Maybe what's in it is dynamite, and he was afraid of it falling into the wrong hands."

"That's certainly a possibility. Don't just stand there, Chase. Take it out, and let's see what's in it."

He removed it gently from its hiding place, as if it was created from a precious, fragile material instead of ordinary paper. As far as he was concerned, it was precious, more valuable than gold if somewhere within its covers it told them where Josh was going after he left the rooming house and why.

Haley had been thinking along the same lines. "If he found what he was after, what was going to make his story sensational, and the journal records it, then it could tell us where he went to verify it."

"Exactly." *And what am I waiting for?* he thought. *Am I afraid to know? The hell with that.* He turned over the cover to the first page.

"What?" Haley demanded.

"It's in longhand. He used a pencil. No surprise there. Josh objected to laptops and anything else that was electronic and portable when he was building his stories. He said carrying them around just hindered him. Only when he decided the story was ready did he turn to a computer."

Chase flipped through the pages in the journal. "There's a lot in here. And wouldn't you know, it's in that illegible scrawl of his. It's going to take me forever to get through it."

Haley had an idea. "Look, why don't I spread out here on the table with my laptop? Then as you make sense of the passages, you can read them back to me, and I'll take them down on the laptop. That way we'll have a readable copy."

They cleared the table, returning Josh's things to the smaller suitcase and placing it with the other case on the sofa. Haley seated herself with the laptop in front of her. Chase settled across from her with the journal. His earlier idea of planning a day visiting the local sights had gone out of his head as he attacked his brother's sloppy handwriting.

Haley's fingers were poised above the keys, ready to record what he read to her. A moment later he, too, was ready. "All right, here we go. In Josh's words:

"This story begins in a Detroit slum forty some years ago with a boy who lived with his family in three crowded rooms of a tenement house. If there had ever been a father, he was

long gone. The mother worked odd jobs wher-
ever she could. When she was sober, that is."

Chase paused here, struggling to make out the next paragraph. Haley waited patiently until he was ready to go on.

"Although the boy was intelligent, highly so
in fact, he seldom went to school. He spent
his time on the streets, where he learned to
survive by being tougher and meaner than the
other boys.

"Now this next fact is one you need to
know. The boy was always hungry. There was
never much food on the table, and what there
was was never very appetizing. How could
there be with a family of five to feed? You're
probably thinking, 'What's so unusual about
that? A lot of kids don't have enough to eat.'
I know that shouldn't be true in America, but
sadly, it is.

"Here's the thing, though. You wouldn't
have known it to look at him, because the boy
wasn't much different from the other boys
on that Detroit street. You wouldn't have
guessed back then he was going to be special."

Chase stopped there. "How am I doing?" he asked Haley. "Going too fast for you now? Or still too slow?"

"Don't worry about it. I'm getting it all down. He has an interesting way of writing, doesn't he? Talking to the reader like that."

"That's Josh for you. Then before you know it, he'll switch to talking to himself. That's the way he works in his notebooks and journals. He's not consistent until he's ready to sit down at his computer."

Chase's gaze cut to the minibar on the other side of the sitting room. "I need a bottle of cold water. I'm getting parched with all this reading aloud. You want anything?"

She shook her head as he got to his feet. When he came back from the minibar, uncapped bottle in hand and several thirsty swallows later, he was ready to continue. Seating himself, he bent over the journal, studied where he'd left off for a minute and then pushed on.

"By the way, the boy's name was Victor Kandinsky. Still is. By learning about his childhood, mostly from bits and pieces on the internet (Victor never liked any form of exposure about himself, even as a kid) and later on by consulting what the media reported, because by then he couldn't avoid the publicity, my knowledge of him deepened."

Chase hesitated long enough for another swallow of water.

"Now where was I? Oh, yeah, got it.

"Victor's education on the streets served him well. He learned the value of wealth. Because if you had money, lots of money, you never needed to starve. Drugs were the best way to make it. As he grew toward adulthood, he built a successful drug operation. In time he became a crime lord worth billions. But he never stopped being hungry. Never stopped remembering the food he was denied as a child. He could afford to eat whatever he wanted now,

and he ate prodigiously. His size grew along with his fortune.

"Because Victor had always been cunning, he was aware that his vast wealth, being earned illegally as it was, made him vulnerable. He'd managed so far to avoid prison, but with enemies all around him, how long could that last? So this is what he did. He left America and settled in the Maldives Islands. Why the Maldives? Because he was safe there. The country had no extradition law. He couldn't be sent back to the United States to be prosecuted. Even better, his empire went with him. He could buy political favor, and he did. He became important in those tropical islands, and that fed his enormous ego.

"Now here's something, folks, I should have been telling you. Something that developed along with the rest of Victor Kandinsky's history, and this is it."

Chase broke off there, leaning back in his chair, his hand massaging the back of his stiff neck.

"Is that it?" Haley wanted to know. "It ends there?"

"No, there's plenty more, but I need a break, and I'm hungry." He consulted his watch. "It's almost noon. How about we order room service?"

She agreed to that, and a half hour later, sandwiches and fruit were delivered to their suite. While they ate, they discussed the material Chase had haltingly read and Haley had copied on the laptop.

"This Kandinsky character Josh is writing about," Chase said. "He might be a rotten human being, but Josh makes him fascinating."

"The megalomaniac," Haley murmured.

"My brain must be tired. I'm not following you."

"Don't you remember what George Fellows told us back at his cabin? That just before Josh left, he mentioned a megalomaniac who would love to get his hands on those ancient, priceless seeds in the International Seed Vault? But Josh never identified him. Now in his journal he talks about Victor Kandinsky's enormous ego."

"You're right. Kandinsky must be that megalomaniac."

The realization had Chase eager to get back to the journal. "You ready to go on?"

"I'm just as anxious as you are to know what comes next."

But that proved to be a frustrating challenge. Chase wasn't happy with his brother as he battled slowly to unlock what followed.

"Josh, Josh, your penmanship is really lousy. Always was, bro, but I think it's gotten even worse with the years. Like this sentence, for instance: 'Victor Kandinsky became interested in pants.' What's that supposed to mean? That his wardrobe became important to him?"

Haley left her laptop and came around to Chase's side of the table, leaning over his shoulder to try to make out the sentence herself. He was conscious of her warm breath on his nape, her subtle fragrance that had him thinking of an activity conducted in a soft bed and not at the side of a hard table. He was relieved when she drew back and he could breathe again.

"Not *pants*," she corrected him. "The word is *plants*. The L got smudged."

"Yeah, that makes better sense. 'Victor Kandinsky became interested in plants.' Thanks for translating."

Haley went back to her laptop, enabling him to recover his self-control. Damn, but she was a bewitching distraction.

He resumed work on the journal, strengthening his efforts to unlock its puzzles, resolved this time to avoid involving the seductive help of the woman seated safely across from him now. Having that hot body lean over him was just too much of a temptation. Her mere presence made it more difficult, with awkward delays when he wavered and faltered, but he always managed to recover and soldier on.

"All right, let's try it again. I think I've got it this time.

"Victory Kandinsky became interested in plants. Their history as well as their future. He realized from research it was plants that made all the foods he'd yearned for as a child possible. There could be no meat or dairy products from the animals that provided them without grasses for the animals to feed on. And no grains or fruits or vegetables or nuts for mankind to—

"What's this word, Josh? 'Supplement?' Yeah, 'supplement.'

"—supplement their diets.
"It all depends on seeds, of course. Victor saw that. Because if somehow the seeds weren't available, there could be no essential plants. Victor read about the International Seed Vault and was jealous of its existence. He understood that whoever controlled the world's supply of seeds could conceivably rule all mankind. But he could have a seed vault of his own. He had that kind of power and wealth.

"*Victor bought an uninhabited island that belonged to the Maldives but was of no use to them. It was located in the far southern region of the Indian Ocean near the Antarctic waters with the kind of frigid climate ideal for preserving seeds. Victor built his vault there and stocked it with seeds collected from around the world.*

"*Now, folks, here's where I do a bit of rum—*"

Chase stopped and tried again, pronouncing the word carefully.

"*—ruminating. Because it occurs to me that if my audience is still there and hasn't stopped paying attention long ago, they might want to know how you learned all this stuff.*

"*It began back in Seattle. There was that blind date you got talked into. Remember? Big mistake, like most blind dates are. Except for one thing. The girl recommended this book she'd been reading about the International Seed Vault. You were on the lookout for a new story, and this one sounded promising. You checked it out of the library, and she was right. It was a solid subject. Only it needed a lot of fleshing out for the kind of investigative journalism I do.*"

Chase paused for a few more swallows of water before he continued.

"*Did a lot of research, both online and in the library. That's where I learned about Victor Kandinsky. And Dr. Anton Rostov, too.*

Anton is one of the good guys, and he knows all about plants. I went down to Portland to meet him where he teaches at the university. I met someone else there, too. A woman who blew me away. Her name is Ha—"

Chase could have smacked himself in the head for choking on the word. There were a few seconds of silence, and then Haley asking quietly, "You want to take another break?"

He feared his "no" was too curt. He amended it with a politer "I'm ready to go on."

Going on meant maintaining his composure, which he managed.

"This journal isn't about her, though. Actually, she deserves a journal of her own, and one day... Come on, Josh, back to the subject. It was about then I saw some chatter online I didn't like. It wasn't anything definite, but enough to convince me I needed to go to Alaska where the International Seed Vault and its headquarters are located.

"I asked a lot of questions here in Anchorage, but I wasn't satisfied with the answers. And I met George Fellows, who had a miniature seed vault of his own. George taught me quite a bit, and when we parted, he gave me some of his rarer seeds.

"Folks, you already know Victor Kandinsky is not a man with scruples and is so bloated, both physically and emotionally, that he regards himself above the law. All right, maybe he can't step onto American soil himself without being arrested, but I suspect he has a

wide network of thugs to do his dirty work for him, very possibly some of them right here in Alaska. I didn't trust myself to keep George's gift safe while I'm in Anchorage, so I divided the seeds and mailed half of them to my brother in Seattle and the other half to Haley in Portland."

Haley stopped tapping keys to whisper, "Sorry, Josh, we couldn't protect them for you. But how were you to know the bad guys were in Seattle and Portland, too?"

Chase gazed at her, wondering how affected she was by all of this. He waited for her to tell him she needed a break of her own, but she signaled with a nod she was ready to go on.

"You know what, folks? I keep having this feeling that something big is up. Not just from that chatter online, but from something I feel right here in Alaska. Something that comes through Kandinsky. I swear I can feel his people watching me, and it makes me damn nervous. But whatever it is and no matter how it worries me, I don't think I can just stand by and let them get away with it. Heck, I know I can't."

Chase looked up, meeting Haley's gaze.
"What comes next?" she asked, ready to resume typing.
"Nothing. The journal ends there."

Chapter 11

"You're sure of that?" Haley asked. "That there isn't more about his intention? Like where he was going next? Anything?"

Chase shook his head.

She realized it had been foolish of her to press him. If the journal had revealed any further information, any details whatever, he would have shared them with her.

She didn't know what to say now. She gazed at him solemnly, feeling awful. His disappointment was plain on his face. He had expected so much from the journal. They both had.

And it wasn't there. No revelations about what might have happened to Josh.

It was worse than disappointing. It was totally disheartening.

Where did they turn now? Haley wanted to offer a suggestion, an encouraging one, but nothing occurred to her.

It was Chase in the end who offered a solution. Not that it did solve their dilemma, but it was welcome just the same.

"I need to get out of this room," he said. "Get some air and exercise. You interested?"

She told him she was.

"What do we do with the journal? I don't want to leave it here unprotected."

"The hotel must have a safe for the valuables of its guests," she said. "We can stop at the desk on our way out and leave it with the clerk to be locked up. I'll have them keep my laptop, too. I can pick it up after dinner."

Having decided they both wanted a long walk, they exited the hotel by the outside dining terrace at the back. Below the terrace, a wide public walkway extended in both directions along the edge of the Cook Inlet port.

"Which way?" Chase asked when they reached that level.

"It doesn't matter. To the left I guess."

They set out with neither of them interested in conversation. There was enough to occupy them with watching the variety of boat traffic out on the water, as well as eyeing all the craft moored at the docks that stretched along the waterfront like teeth on a comb.

It was Chase who finally ended their silence with a deep, wistful, "There was such a promise there. You know?"

She did know. He was referring to the journal and its failure to hint at Josh's destination when, after hiding his work from anyone who might end up searching his belongings, he left the rooming house and disappeared.

Where was he going? Somewhere definite? And if he got there, what did he find? The sensational something he'd referred to back in Portland that he needed to make his story?

The *something* that had brought him to Alaska in search of it?

She and Chase freely discussed all of this, especially Josh's enlightening information about the mysterious and dangerous Victor Kandinsky. There were, however, two subjects they carefully avoided.

Neither one of them suggested by any word or glance that what Josh feared, but was bravely, perhaps foolishly, determined to confront, in the end killed him. Considering everything, it was a logical outcome for a man whom no one could find and who had communicated with no one after he'd vanished. But Haley couldn't bear the thought of what Chase would suffer at such a conclusion.

And the other forbidden subject they had agreed by a kind of unspoken, mutual consent not to mention? Josh's private revelation in the journal of his feelings for Haley. No question of those feelings now when they had been written down. That had troubled both Chase and her, leaving Haley wondering if they would ever openly discuss it.

They had turned around and were headed back to the hotel when Chase introduced a concern that did need to be addressed.

"Our friend Sergeant Blackfeather asked to be notified if we came up with anything useful when we examined Josh's things. What do you think? Should I turn the journal over to him?"

Haley thought about it for a minute. "There isn't anything useful in the journal that would help the police find Josh. How do you feel about it?"

"Honestly? That I'd like to hang on to the journal for a while longer. Maybe go over it again before I hand it in."

"There's your answer, then."

* * *

They had dinner in the hotel dining room that evening, then decided to call it an early night. Haley watched the news with Chase in the sitting room of their suite before excusing herself to turn in.

Stripping, she put on her nightshirt, drew the blackout curtains at the window and switched on the lamp on her bedside table. Her only companion when she climbed into bed was the book she planned to read for a while before turning out the light.

After what Josh had revealed in the journal regarding his feelings for her, she knew that Chase wasn't likely to show up at her bedroom door.

So she was surprised when later, as she sat up in bed with the book open in her lap, a soft knock sounded on her door. She was puzzled for a silent moment before answering with a hesitant, "Yes?"

The only sound was the whisper of the door opening. *Chase.* She knew he wasn't here just to speak to her briefly and then retreat. Otherwise, he wouldn't have closed the blackout curtains behind him in the sitting room and left just a single night-light burning.

She could see just enough of him standing there in the doorway to make her breath quicken. He was naked except for a pair of briefs, a warrior with a body that was all sleek, hard muscle. He had earned just enough scars in battle on that body to have any woman lucky enough to see it appreciate the man he was.

When he finally spoke, it was in a husky voice impossible to resist. "Can I join you?"

Haley's mouth went so dry that all she could manage was to nod her head, close her book and move over to the other side of the bed to make room for him. He was with her before she could register his action of crossing the room to the bed, lifting the cover and sliding in beside her.

"I know I shouldn't be here," he rasped. "I know how wrong it is, but I couldn't help myself."

"No," she insisted, "it's right. I promise you it's right."

Whether he believed her or not, that was all he needed to reach for her. Those powerful arms of his went around her like strong metal bands, clasping her to his hard chest.

He seemed fiercely possessive at first, but a mouth that was nothing but gentle descended on hers, coaxing from her lips a sweet, lengthy kiss that affected her like a prize wine.

When he drew back an inch or so, it was to plead, "Open your mouth for me, sweetheart."

She couldn't have done anything else. When her lips parted, his tongue followed, slipping smoothly into her mouth to find and fondle her own tongue. He tasted of mint, and at the same time she found herself inhaling a citrusy fragrance on his skin. Oddly, it made an unusual but pleasing blend of flavor and scent, something she'd never experienced before.

That gifted tongue of his wasn't through with her when, to her dismay, he withdrew it from her mouth. He applied it to her cheeks instead, working it around wetly and warmly to each ear in turn. Its tip probed the contours before he sucked on the lobes. Then he moved on to her throat.

It was as if his mission was to miss no portion of her. He confirmed that when he murmured an impatient "I can't get where I want to go. We need to remove that shirt of yours."

He didn't wait for her to help him. Yanking away what remained of the bed cover, his hands closed on the hem of her nightshirt and peeled it over her head, throwing it away as well.

"Beautiful," he breathed, taking in the sight of her breasts.

"Chase…"

"What?" he demanded. "What do you want?"

"Nothing. Just you, Chase."

"I know what you want," he insisted. "This is what you want, isn't it?"

She knew he was right when his amazing hands captured her breasts, squeezing and stroking, turning her nipples into hard, yearning peaks.

"And this, too."

He took one of her buds deep into his mouth, suckling on it strongly. She arched her back and whimpered as he traveled to her other nipple, where he treated her to the same pleasure. Hands planted on either side of her, he pushed himself slowly downward, dragging her flat on the mattress beneath him. All the while that swirling tongue of his was busy with the area between her breasts and her thighs.

She could hear a long, lusty growl from him when he reached her groin, burying his nose in the nest of curls there.

"You know what I want here, don't you?" he muttered like a threat. "You know because you want it, too."

"Yes," she gasped, "I want it, too."

"Like this, sweetheart?" he said, parting the folds at the opening of her waiting vessel, inserting one finger, then a second finger, slowly stretching the channel before plunging the length of his two fingers inside.

All she managed in response was to moan. She assumed he translated it as her approval since that miraculous mouth of his replaced his fingers, finding and fastening on the nub just inside the core of her womanhood.

Once he settled there, he nibbled and licked and sucked, while her head twisted wildly from side to side in an action that begged for release. Chase was in no hurry, taking his time to build her to the peak that, once it was reached, sent her crashing down the other side with a joyous cry.

Haley collapsed, lying there while he elevated himself on his elbow, the forefinger of his other hand stroking the tender flesh of her stomach. It seemed to her in that lazy moment, although it wasn't true, of course, as if this was the first time they had ever made love together, possibly just because he was a man of original talent. Certainly one of new invention. He demonstrated that by suddenly flipping over on his back and carrying her with him.

He was now pinned beneath her, and she was stretched lengthwise on top of him.

"Scoot down," he commanded her, "until you can sit up straddling my hips."

"Satisfied?" she asked when she'd accomplished the position.

"Oh, yeah," he said, exhaling a long breath.

Haley looked behind her and down, making herself conscious of his full, upright erection. At some point she'd been unaware of, he had managed to rid himself of his briefs. "We'll have to do something about that," she said.

"What did you have in mind?"

"I don't suppose you brought—"

"A condom with me? Right here on the table."

Another unexpected appearance. Snatching it up, he handed it to her with a cheerful, "Here, you do the honors."

"My pleasure."

And she meant that literally.

Slitting the foil and extracting the condom, she wriggled back until she was positioned directly over his shaft. Unable to resist the target below her, she wrapped her free hand around it, surprised by its velvet heat. Then, her fingers squeezing its circumference, she pumped the column vigorously.

"Careful, sweetheart. I want to be there for the finish."

"Let me arrange that."

Which she did by rolling the condom down over his pulsing length until it was snug at the base. He was breathing fast by then, telling her he was ready for her. Sinking slowly, she guided the tip of his erection inside her before pausing.

Chase could apparently take only so much before urgency kicked in. A powerful urgency that had him lifting his hips, surging upward until he had filled her channel before expelling his breath with satisfaction, leaving her in charge for the rest of the journey.

Haley didn't hesitate to seize that control, hair whipping as she tossed her head from side to side, riding him with strong, even rhythms that he strove to match. She loved the way he looked beneath her, cords standing out on his neck as he strained up to meet her.

Between them, they constructed a pinnacle of ultimate intimacy. With a final, furious surge of his hips, Chase sent her into paradise before following her there with a shout of victory.

He didn't give either one of them more than a moment of rest before, his arms locking around her, he rolled her over on her back, covering her with his body along with a deep, sensual kiss.

"That was sensational," he whispered. "*You* were sensational."

She could have chosen three different words for him, but this wasn't the time. Maybe it never would be. Not for either one of them. For now being satisfied was enough.

He tucked her close beside him. They drifted off to sleep with the kind of sighs that brought contentment.

Haley found herself on her own when she woke sometime later. Chase had covered her before leaving her, but the blanket did nothing to soften a chill loneliness.

She was aware of light but not of its source. Only when she sat up in bed did she detect the partly open door to the sitting room and what it revealed in there.

A lamp burned on the table where Chase was seated hunched over the laptop she had reclaimed from the front desk after dinner. She didn't have to wonder what he was studying so intently. It had to be the copy of Josh's journal that was far more readable than the original, which remained in the hotel safe. Nothing else on the laptop could possibly interest him.

There was just enough of a glow from the sitting room for Haley to make out her travel clock on the bedside table. A little after three o'clock. What would make Chase desert her at this ungodly hour to pore over a document whose content must still be fresh in his mind? She could guess that, too. From what she now knew about him and Josh, it was fairly evident.

Guilt. His lust for her earlier had been strong enough that he'd been able to silence that maddening guilt where his brother was concerned. But when his desire had been satisfied, the poison had crept in again, made worse by the feelings Josh had expressed for her in his journal. Chase hadn't been able to sleep then.

A restlessness had forced him to get up and go to the laptop. Why? Had he thought to soothe that eternal guilt by searching relentlessly all over again for a clue that would tell him where Josh had gone and how to find him? A clue that probably wasn't there?

This seemed the right explanation to Haley. But maybe she was all wrong. There was still so much she *didn't* know. But unlike Chase, she couldn't convince herself Josh was serious about her. Whatever he claimed in the journal, there had been nothing to indicate it when they'd been together in Portland. It had been a relationship of mutual respect and fondness, nothing more. At least that's what she'd felt at the time. She certainly wasn't in love with him.

And Chase? What did she feel for him? And what did he feel for her? She couldn't tell. They had never talked about it. It was a subject they purposefully avoided, possibly because they were afraid of it. There was only one thing Haley knew for sure. Sexually, they were compatible. Compatible? They were explosive together.

No more of this, she told herself. *You can't go on see-sawing about the emotions of three people. Emotions you don't understand, which are wearing you out.*

Willing herself to relax, she sank down again on her pillow and managed to go back to sleep.

The blackout curtains weren't tightly closed. There was morning daylight coming through them when Haley awakened again. She felt the warmth of a strong body pressed against her side.

Lifting her head in surprise, she looked down to find Chase had come back to bed at some point and was solidly asleep.

He didn't stir as she gazed at him for several long

minutes. She had never noticed it before, probably because she'd never taken the opportunity to observe him when he was peacefully asleep like this, but there was an endearing little boy quality in his face that brought a lump to her throat.

Maybe that quality was there because it was made possible by the long lashes on his closed eyelids. And those, too, she'd never taken the time to notice. Why would she when such features seemed totally out of character for a rugged man who'd earned himself a tough guy's wound that had just missed the corner of his eye? A wound prominent enough to have left a permanent scar.

In another minute, all this tenderness she was experiencing would have tears in her eyes. She had to get out of here, had to think about Chase and her, and she could only do that away from him. A walk. She needed a walk.

Managing to ease out of bed on her side without disturbing him, Haley collected some fresh clothes from the closet and closed herself in the bathroom to wash and dress. When she emerged, she was wearing slim jeans and a shaker-stitch A-line sweater.

Finding a pad and a pencil, she wrote a note for Chase: "I went for a walk. Don't worry. I won't go far, and I'll stay where it's safe. H."

Leaving the note on the bedside table on his side, where he would be sure not to miss it and worry if he woke up before she returned, she picked up her shoulder bag in the sitting room and let herself quietly out of the suite.

There was a light buffet in the lobby for those guests who didn't care to order a full breakfast in the dining room or on the dining terrace. Haley helped herself to a disposable cup of coffee from the urn at the end of the table and a bagel from a basket, which she split and spread with cream cheese. Bearing the only breakfast she wanted, she went out on the terrace, where she had her coffee and bagel standing at the rail.

Finishing her quick breakfast, Haley rid herself of the cup and paper napkin and returned to the lobby. The clerks who served the front desk made it their business to learn the names of the guests. The young man with the cheerful smile and a head of flaming hair was no exception when she stopped at his station.

"Good morning, Ms. Adams. What can I do for you?"

His name tag read Andrew. "Hi, Andrew. I'm in the mood for a walk, somewhere close to the hotel but not out back. It's too cool along the waterfront. You have anything to recommend?"

"Have you visited Heritage Trail yet?" She shook her head. "Then you're in for a treat."

"Why is that?"

"They've moved a number of Alaska's historic landmarks there, nearly all of them original, and erected them along a heritage trail in a pleasant wooded section. You get both history and nature and all for free."

"Sounds good. How do I find this Heritage Trail?"

"That's the easy part. You cross the street out front, turn left and head down the sidewalk. It's less than a half block along, and you'll see it marked. There's a post there at the entrance with a box attached. They keep it filled with leaflets that name and describe each of the landmarks on the trail."

She thanked the clerk and left the hotel. Following his directions, she reached the prominently marked arch that served as the gateway to Heritage Trail within minutes. And there was the box of leaflets mounted on a post. Lifting its lid, Haley helped herself to each one of the various leaflets.

There was a small gift shop just inside the entrance. It was built in the rustic style, like something that belonged on the old Alaskan frontier. She was to learn as she toured through the park that almost all of the structures fell into that category.

The gift shop wasn't yet open for the day. In fact, there seemed to be no other person but her currently in the park. It was apparently too early for sightseeing.

Haley didn't mind. She had no wish to be distracted by crowds as she strolled along a gently winding flagstone walkway. Or her own thoughts. As it turned out, though, she had plenty of these whenever and wherever she stopped to view the exhibits.

The first of these was a collection of totem poles erected in a grassy clearing just to her left. The leaflet informed her that they had been moved here from their original locations in far southern Alaska, where the long arm of the archipelago was bordered by the Pacific on one side and Canada's British Columbia on the other.

The totems, each of them unique, had been carved and painted by Indians of different tribes. The pigments were weathered away in some places and in others still bright.

Chase and Josh. Josh and Chase. Her mind had been occupied now not by totem poles but by the images of those two men and the emotions they had raised in a triangle of their own creation. A triangle, and she was unwillingly one of its sides.

Being brothers in a situation like this was tricky enough. Unfortunately, their mother and Josh's father, concerned that Chase would be jealous of Josh's arrival after he'd had their sole attention all those years, had deposited the new baby in Chase's arms. It had worked. Had their parents realized, however, that Chase would never shake off the responsibility of looking out for his brother, even going to the extreme of leaving the army behind in order to come home to be there for Josh, they might have reconsidered their actions. But now…

Come on, she told herself, *it's time to move on to the next exhibit.* That was situated on the right side of the trail. Just to the left, however, on the other side of a safety railing, was a deep, sheer-sided ravine, the result of a cataclysmic earthquake in March 1964.

The next exhibit was a delight. Russia had been the first to claim and occupy Alaska before selling it to the United States in the nineteenth century. This building, constructed of logs, was an onion-domed Russian Orthodox church that, according to the leaflet, had been moved from a Russian settlement along the coast. Haley was consulting the leaflet for further details when her mind took over again in another direction.

She stood there without moving, her head lifting from the leaflet, eyes staring straight ahead at nothing in particular, as if she were in a trance. But she wasn't in a trance. She was in a state of sudden revelation. Why it should occur now, she didn't know. All that mattered was the realization itself.

She was in love with Chase McKinley. No more denials. No more indecision. She was in love with him and probably had been for some time, maybe even as far back as Portland. In love and prepared to fight for him if she had to.

Coming back to earth, she noticed a padlock on the church door. She remembered the leaflet mentioning there were Russian icons in there, many of them very old and no doubt valuable enough to keep the church locked. Seeing the interior would be pleasant, but it wasn't worth lingering until the guide came to open it.

Still in a giddy condition, Haley moved on to the next exhibit. This one was also a church. Or more properly, a small chapel. The leaflet for it referred to it as a *stavkirke* rescued from an abandoned Norwegian fishing village. She was surprised to learn that a colony of Norwegians had once settled in Alaska, bringing with them the peasant crafts that had built this charming wooden structure, its high roof topped with a belfry, the eaves decorated with carved dragon heads.

This building was locked, too. Feeling like Snow White peering in the windows of the dwarves' cottage, Haley snooped through the panes. She refused to feel guilty about it. There was a wealth of carvings and murals in there, along with a cupboard covered in rosemaling.

It was when she backed away from the glass with a sigh of contentment that her mercurial mind switched channels on her again. Chase. She was forgetting about his feelings. It was one thing for her to be in love with him without reservation, but he had never indicated he returned that love. And perhaps never would.

Like a wall between them, there was the issue of Josh. Always Josh, with Chase seeming incapable of convincing himself that he wouldn't be injuring his brother if he acknowledged a love for Haley.

It was with a feeling of bleakness that she continued on to the next exhibit, a gold panning shack and its equipment from the Yukon River. It was time, she decided, she had a serious talk with Chase about this thing that was tearing him up inside. That was hurting both of them. And if he wasn't ready to listen to reason…then it might be time for her to think about leaving, returning home. But she hated the idea of abandoning him and their quest.

It was these troublesome thoughts, along with her visits to the exhibits, that had Haley so occupied that she was unaware of the man who had been following her.

Chapter 12

Chase returned slowly to awareness with a sense that something was missing. It wasn't until his hand reached out to his side, groping for what wasn't there, that he realized what was wrong. Haley. She wasn't where she was supposed to be.

Not until he came fully awake, opening his eyes and turning his head, was he was ready to accept her absence. He was sorry about that. He liked sharing a bed with her.

Stretching, he sat up against the headboard, not bothering to cover his yawn. So, where was she? He looked in the direction of the bathroom, but the door was open, and there was no light inside. The connecting door to the sitting room was also wide-open, admitting daylight, which meant she had to have opened the blackout curtains in there.

"Hey," he called, "anybody home?"

No answer. It was when he turned on the bedside lamp and swung his legs over the side of the bed, prepared to go look for her, that he discovered the note on the night table.

Until this moment, he'd been nothing but lonesome without Haley, and maybe just a little concerned. Reading her note, however, made a difference. He was now genuinely worried.

Chase was immediately off the bed and on his way to the other bedroom where his own clothes were. He had meant to occupy that bedroom during their stay here, but who had he been kidding? He hadn't been able to stay away from Haley, whatever it cost him emotionally.

Now he was ready to wring her neck. What had she been thinking to go off blithely for a walk on her own? After all that had happened in Portland, then their getting followed here in the city the other day, not to mention Josh's disappearance, she should have thought of the risk.

He kept up a stream of curses in an effort to allay his fears as he dressed in jeans, one of his knit polo shirts and a pair of loafers. Slapping his wallet into his back pocket, he left the suite, locking the door behind him.

When he arrived in the lobby, Chase realized it could be a problem catching up with Haley. He had no idea where she'd gone. Out the back to the waterfront? Then in what direction? Left? Right? Or maybe out the front, in which case the same problem of direction applied.

The desk clerk might know. Chase was relieved when he approached him to hear that he did.

"She was headed to Heritage Trail, Mr. McKinley. It's a short walk just up the street on the right with a…"

Chase was out the front door while the young man

was still talking, glad to know Haley was within reach. He was more than ready to put his anxiety to rest.

That all changed when he reached the entrance to the trail and discovered the vehicle parked there at the side of the street. It was an SUV. A *burgundy* SUV. He didn't stop to wonder if it was the same burgundy SUV that had tailed them the other day. He *knew* it had to be the one.

Chase's heart dropped to the bottom of his stomach like a rock as he raced into the park and tore along the flagstone pathway.

He was sick with the thought of losing her. That couldn't happen. He wouldn't *let* it happen. She was much, much too important to him. If he hadn't understood that before, he understood it now. All right, maybe he wasn't ready to name what he was feeling, but that didn't matter. It could wait.

Chase went some distance before he spotted a figure ahead of him. Having seen no other person in the place, he felt this had to be Haley's shadow. There was a furtive manner about the way he moved that seemed to verify this.

But where was Haley herself? He'd caught no glimpse of her. If he was too late, if something had already happened to her...

He was approaching a blind curve when the apprehension seized him. His target had already rounded the bend. Fearing he might lose him, Chase hurried to catch up. He'd just cleared the thick shrubbery that made the sharp curve necessary when he sighted them not far ahead of him. Haley out in front and apparently oblivious to the tail behind her.

His heart now back in place where it belonged, Chase closed the distance between himself and Haley's stalker.

Whoever the guy was, he must have sensed someone behind him. He stopped and turned around.

This was not Chase's idea of a tough thug. Short, paunchy and balding, he wore a look of sudden alarm on his round face. That look was all it took to confirm for Chase this was no innocent visitor to the park but someone startled to discover he and the woman he was following weren't alone.

Chase hailed him when he started to move quickly away. "Not so fast, my friend! You and I have got some business to discuss!"

The sound of Chase's voice had Haley alerted and whipping around on the path. "Chase? What on earth are you doing here? And who is that you're talking to?"

"He's the guy who was stalking you."

"I don't know what you're talking about," the little man defended himself nervously. He had turned off the walkway and was backing slowly away toward the safety railing that edged the lip of the gorge, apparently fearing he was about to get trapped between Chase and Haley, who were closing the distance from both sides. "I don't know either one of you."

"Sure you do. You were following us in the city the other day in your SUV."

"That's not true. I'm just here walking through the park, and you have no right to intimidate me like this."

"Chase, are you out of your mind? Let that poor man alone."

"Haley, there's only one car parked out there by the entrance. A burgundy SUV. Wanna bet it's his?"

There was a different expression on her face now, one of realization, as she looked from Chase to the little man who had reached the railing and, with his back pinned against it, could go no farther.

Time for me *to play stalker now*, Chase told himself, eyes narrowed, as he moved slowly toward his prey, whose nose was twitching like a cornered rabbit facing an armed hunter.

"You'd better stay away from me."

"Or you'll do what?"

"You—you'd just better."

"Chase," Haley appealed to him, "come away and let him alone. Can't you see you're terrifying him?"

Chase's gaze held the other man's. "Haley, this is our chance to learn some of the information we've been wanting. I'm just going to ask him some questions, and you're going to answer them, aren't you— Hey, what's your name? If we're going to be buddies here, we ought to know each other's names. You've already heard mine. Come on now, no stalling. I wouldn't want to have to hurt you to get your name."

"R-Ronnie," he squeaked.

"Hear that, Haley? His name is Ronnie. Nice name, huh?"

"Chase, stop threatening him. Let the police handle it."

"And miss this opportunity?"

The little man made an effort, summoning a modicum of courage. "I don't have to answer your questions. You can't make me."

"Now, Ronnie, that's where you're wrong. See, I was an army ranger. They taught us a lot of useful techniques in the rangers. One of them was how to interrogate the enemy. What we did was sometimes pretty extreme, but it got results."

"You—you wouldn't."

"Hear that, Haley? He thinks I wouldn't hurt him." In reality, Chase had no intention of harming the guy. Not unless he made it absolutely necessary, but he did need to convince both him and Haley that he meant business.

"I'm not going to stand here and witness this."

"Actually, that's probably a good idea. I think I see the corner of a bench up there. Should be enough out of the way not to hear or see anything unpleasant that might be happening here."

Haley left him with a look of disbelief. He sent her off with a smile and then turned to the man he had physically squeezed against the railing.

"So, Ron, want to tell me why you've been following us?"

Chase got no answer, unless you counted a pair of very frightened eyes and a bobbing Adam's apple.

"No? Okay, we'll play it your way. Suppose you look over your shoulder and get a look at the bottom of this gorge here. Wouldn't you say it's a long way down and an awfully rocky landing when you get there?"

"That—that would be murder."

"Oh, no, Ronnie, that would be just an unfortunate accident."

"Please, I—I can't answer your questions. If he found out, I would be in very serious trouble."

"Looks like you already are. And since I'm here on the spot, and this mysterious *he* isn't..."

Chase's captive made a hasty decision. "All right, I'll answer your questions."

"Smart choice. This is a chance to kill two birds with one stone, as they say. Why have you been following us, and who is this man you're working for?"

Ronnie hesitated briefly, eyes closed before taking what Chase guessed was probably a big risk for him. "His name is Victor Kandinsky."

Now why is that no surprise to me? Chase thought. "And he's instructed you to follow us?"

"That's right. I'm to learn everywhere you go and, if I can, why."

"For what reason?"

"I don't know." Chase must have looked threatening again, because Ronnie vigorously shook his head. "It's the truth, I swear."

"Hasn't Kandinsky told you anything at all about what he does with the information that you provide him?"

"I've never met him. He isn't here in Anchorage. I report to one of his trusted people who passes it on. He has them everywhere."

After what he and Haley had experienced back home, he knew that to be the truth. "It sounds like you're not very happy working for Kandinsky. Why do you do it?"

"I don't have a choice."

"Why not?"

"He knows something about me. A couple of years ago, I struck a boy on his bicycle with my car. I'd been drinking. Thank God he didn't die, but he was injured and spent time in the hospital."

"A hit-and-run, Ron?" Ronnie's silence told him how miserable this ugly truth made him. "So, Kandinsky is blackmailing you, and you give him what he wants to maintain his silence. Wonder how many others work for him under arrangements like this?"

Ronnie's shake of his head signified he didn't know.

"I have one more question for you, Ronnie. It's vital that I know the answer. Are you listening?"

"Yes."

"I have a brother. His name is Josh Matthews. He's an investigative journalist. Josh came to Alaska chasing a story. He disappeared several weeks ago. Ms. Adams and I came here to find him. The story concerns Victor Kandinsky. I want to know where my brother is, Ronnie, and I want you to tell me."

"I'm sorry, but I can't tell you that."

Chase's hand flattened against Ronnie's chest, his face thrust into the other man's. "It wouldn't take much to tip you over this rail if you hold out on me."

"I swear I'm not holding out on you," he pleaded. "I've never heard his name. Besides, if your brother is after such a story and the people close to Victor know of it, I would never be trusted with such information. I don't count when it comes to anything important."

"But you know Kandinsky isn't here in Anchorage. You know that much."

"Only by chance when I once asked the man I report to if I could speak directly to Victor, and he told me he was never here."

Kandinsky's nonpresence in Anchorage, or for that matter anywhere else in the United States, wasn't news to Chase. Josh had explained that in his journal, how Kandinsky had to avoid being arrested for his crimes by living in the Maldives, from where he couldn't be extradited.

Chase relaxed his hand, drawing back from Ronnie. There was a movement over to his right. Glancing that way, he discovered Haley close by. Knowing her even the short span of time he had, he could read her. He felt that close to her. And what he read on her face was her realization that, after seeing and hearing what she could from the bench of his exchange with Ronnie, he'd never been serious about hurting the little guy. That's when Haley drifted back.

Chase could see a warm look of sympathy for him

on her face that made him want to take her in his arms in gratitude. She understood how deeply disappointed he was to have learned nothing about Josh.

"So," he appealed to her, "what are we going to do with our friend here now that we know everything he knows that matters?"

"Excuse me," Ronnie interrupted him, "but you *don't* know everything that matters."

Chase gazed at him suspiciously. "What are you trying to tell us, Ronnie?"

"That there is one important thing I do know I haven't shared with you."

"Hold on here. A minute ago you said you weren't trusted by any of Kandinsky's key people with important information."

"That's right. And I'm not supposed to know this, either. I learned strictly by accident a few nights ago when I was told to report for new directions to one of the men who control me. I was expected at six-thirty that night in this empty warehouse office where we meet. See, I didn't think it would matter if I turned up a bit ahead of time. That way, if we finished early enough, I wouldn't have to miss my AA meeting. Only it turned out when I got there, the door was hanging open a bit. I could hear him inside talking on the phone to someone and decided I would wait outside until he was through. But when I heard enough to understand what they were talking about, I didn't try to hang around. I figured what I was hearing was bad enough that I'd better not get caught listening. I should come back at the right time."

Chase was skeptical about what Ronnie was trying to sell him but just intrigued enough to learn whether it was genuine or not. "All right, Ron, let's hear this major news."

The little man looked suddenly sly. "Not until you agree to what I want."

"Just what are you trying to pull? If it's money—"

"It isn't money," he maintained stubbornly. "But you have to promise."

Chase and Haley traded puzzled glances. She had moved in close enough now not to miss a word of what was transpiring. Her only communication with Chase was a shrug. She was leaving it up to him.

"Just exactly what is it you do want, Ron? Because I'm not going to promise you anything until I hear it."

Ronnie drew a deep breath, as if filling his lungs with courage, and then released it. "Look, I know you and your friend aren't going to just walk off and forget me. You're going to call the cops and have me arrested. That's right, isn't it?"

"No one's decided anything here yet."

"I have," the little man insisted. "I've decided I *want* you to call the cops and have me picked up. Yeah, I know that sounds crazy, but it's just what I want."

"You have to admit, Ron, this is a little screwy when not that many minutes ago all you wanted was to get the hell out of here as fast as you could."

"That's right, but I've been thinking since then. Asking myself what I've been doing all these months living under Victor Kandinsky's threats, always afraid if I made the wrong step or failed to obey an order that one of his people would see to it the police got the truth about the hit-and-run. Well, I'm sick of it. I won't do it anymore. I'd rather face a judge and take my punishment."

"If that's all you want me to promise…"

"That's only one half of it. There's another half. If I shouldn't get a sentence, if I'm out on the street again and Kandinsky and his thugs learn that I heard the phone conversation and blew the whistle on them, my life won't be worth anything. So you also have to promise me I'll get police protection."

"Ron, I can't promise that. It's strictly up to the police, but I will promise to speak up for it."

Ronnie considered this briefly before agreeing. "Fair enough."

"Okay, what have you got?"

"Do you know about the International Seed Vault? It's on the island of Moa in the Aleutians."

"It's connected somehow with the story my brother came to Alaska to get."

"Then you'll want to hear what I overheard in that warehouse. Victor Kandinsky has ordered an attack on the seed vault."

Chase's gaze met Haley's. *Is she asking herself the same thing I am?* he wondered. *Can this be real?*

Ronnie must have sensed their doubt. "It's true, I swear. He has this little army of mercenaries, and he pays them big money to do what he wants. In this case, he wants them to raid the seed vault."

This time it was Haley who spoke up. "For what reason?"

"They didn't mention anything about that. So I don't know the why, but I do know the *when*. I got the impression that this thing has been in the works for sometime, and that just a few days ago it was being firmed up."

"No good without the actual date of the attack, Ron."

"I do know. It's the end of this week on Friday. That's all I can tell you."

For now, Chase thought, it would have to be enough. "Haley, you got your cell phone with you?"

"Here in my purse."

"Call Sergeant Blackfeather, will you? Ask him to

meet us here and bring whatever and whoever he needs to make an arrest."

While she made the call, Chase turned to the little man who stood there patiently. "Ronnie, it occurs to me we never asked your surname, and it might be a good thing for us to know it before Sergeant Blackfeather gets here."

"Peters. It's Peters. Do you mind if I go up and wait on the bench Ms. Adams sat on? My legs are tired. You can trust me to stay there. I don't have any intention of going anywhere."

Chase nodded his permission. He and Haley, who had finished her call to police headquarters, gazed after Ronnie.

"You know," Chase said, "this may sound funny, but right now I think I admire that guy for finally having the guts to stand up for himself."

Haley agreed. What followed was a silence between them before she voiced what she was thinking.

"We heard from more than one person that Josh said he wasn't after just another story about the seed vault. That this one had to be special for someone to want to publish it. That he already had a lead on it, and if it was what he hoped for, it was going to be sensational."

"I haven't forgotten. And if Josh managed to verify what we just learned, we have something to back up Ronnie's story. And I think we're going to need that backup to get more than just the cops to take this thing seriously."

Haley and Chase waited in the corner of the hotel lobby for Sergeant Blackfeather to return after seeing Ronnie Peters booked at police headquarters.

They hadn't spoken since they'd settled down here

in a pair of easy chairs. Haley was afraid to ask Chase what he might be thinking about. It could, of course, be the very thing that was haunting her, but knowing how Chase felt about his brother, she doubted it. In any case, she wasn't going to be the one to mention it.

The plain truth was, however, that if Josh had somehow managed to learn about the vault attack, and Kandinsky's people had discovered this, they could have eliminated him. Otherwise, wouldn't he have informed the authorities who could prevent the raid? There was always the chance, of course, he was somewhere in hiding.

Haley knew this last explanation was exactly the kind of thing Chase would build a story around in defense of the argument that Josh was alive. Obstinate to the end, he would never entertain the merest suggestion that Josh was dead.

The thing was, she wanted to believe herself that Josh was still alive somewhere, though it wasn't very realistic to think that way about it. And if the worst should occur, she knew she would hurt very deeply for Chase.

Sergeant Blackfeather entered the hotel at that moment, immediately sighted them and crossed the lobby to the corner where they were situated. The officer, waving Chase down when he started to stand, pulled a chair around for himself and joined them.

"Sorry I'm late, but I had to see our prisoner processed and settled before I could drive over."

"How is he?" Chase asked.

"I don't think in my whole career I've seen a man so relieved to be behind bars."

"Well, like we explained to you back at the trail, he's afraid that if he isn't protected, he'll end up dead."

"Let's hope that before we have to release him, this attack he swears is going to happen on Friday is over with and the people responsible for it are under lock and key themselves. Whether Ronnie Peters is granted further protection after that is something to be decided by someone other than me. Could be he'll get it as the prosecution's main witness. And if he continues to be cooperative, he could get a deal that would forgive his past sins."

"Will the police here be involved in defending the seed vault?" Haley wanted to know.

The officer shook his head. "The Anchorage law enforcement has no authority to operate outside the city. Since to my knowledge the seed vault has never been under any threat before, I'm not sure who's responsible for its defense. Could be one or both of our military bases here. Maybe even the FBI and the coast guard. But it will take some solid convincing before they act."

"You didn't buy Ronnie Peters's story yourself?" Chase wondered.

"Oh, I bought it, but like I say, I'm not the one it has to be sold to. And, frankly, there's not a lot of time."

"Which is why," Haley said, holding up her two printouts of Josh's journal, "I brought these along to the meeting."

"And I brought this," Chase said, waving the original.

They took turns explaining its contents. "We thought," Chase said, "that what my brother says here in his last entry about something big going to happen… that reading this in his own words would support Ronnie's story."

"But if, as you say, he went off to prove it, he seems never to have gotten that proof. Otherwise…"

He's going to suggest there's a reason why Josh didn't return, Haley thought in a panic. *He's going to say Josh couldn't return because he was murdered for what he knew.*

Her gaze managed to catch Sergeant Blackfeather's with a silent pleading. To her relief, he seemed to understand her, ending what he'd been about to say with a rapid "But as I already said, I'm not the one who has to be convinced."

Haley was bewildered. "Then you're not yourself…"

"Going to do this convincing? I have no authority that applies to something like that outside of Anchorage, remember? I will report this to the higher-ups, but something like this—if true—is a different beast. You've got to be involved. And I suggest that the director of the seed bank is the person to start with." He got to his feet. "But, listen, if you need some backup, phone me, and I'll be happy to provide it. I know Dr. Hansen, and she's dedicated to her vault. She won't want to see anything happen to it. And take those journals with you, where they'll do the most good. Gotta go now. Good luck. And, oh, we'll still be looking for Josh out there."

Chapter 13

Chase was silent at the wheel as they headed in the Jeep toward the offices of the International Seed Vault in downtown Anchorage. That he was deep in thought was apparent. The somber expression on his face told Haley that.

"What's bothering you?" she asked him.

"It's more a question of what's not bothering me."

It never failed that, sooner or later, he would take a subject and make a puzzle of it. "I think you enjoy frustrating me. All right, what's *not* bothering you?"

"What people are thinking about Josh."

"And what's that?"

"That he's dead," Chase said with a bluntness that surprised her. "And I'll tell you what else they're thinking. That I'm not facing the truth. Oh, I know they don't say it. They don't have the heart to spoil my conviction because they have to consider that, after all, there might be a chance—a slim one, mind you, but still a chance—that he could still be alive. But I'm not as blind as they think I am. I happen to have a reasonable argument for my claim."

"And that is?"

"Haley, think about it. If Josh *did* learn the truth about this intended attack, he probably realized the knowledge made him vulnerable. So he decided not to go back to his rooming house, to protect himself by hiding out somewhere safe until it's absolutely necessary to tell the right people what he knows."

Which should have been by now, she thought, but she wasn't about to raise that problem in his theory. "Chase, if you believe this so strongly, then why haven't you said so?"

"Because they'd just pick holes in it."

As she just had in her mind, Haley told herself. Did Chase think *she* was one of those people? Possibly, but on the other hand, he'd just trusted her with his theory.

"Why bother," he added, "when it will prove itself in the end?"

He had more faith than anyone she knew. And, wrong or right, she loved him for it.

Donna, the redheaded receptionist at the offices of the seed vault, greeted them without surprise.

"Well, hello, you two. It's good to see you back here again."

"That cheerful welcome almost sounds like you were expecting us," Haley said.

"Actually, we were. Sergeant Blackfeather at police headquarters beat you to it. He phoned to tell us you were on your way. Dr. Hansen is waiting for you."

Donna ushered them down a hallway with closed office doors on both sides to the main office of the director. The receptionist must have buzzed the director to alert her of their arrival, because Dr. Greta Hansen was on her feet, hand extended, when they entered the office.

"I understand you have something to tell me," she said, shaking each of their hands in turn.

"We do," Chase said.

Dr. Hansen nodded to her receptionist to gain her attention. "Close the door on your way out, will you, Donna? And, please, no interruptions."

The receptionist obliged her, leaving the three of them alone. "Please, sit," she invited them, indicating the same two chairs Haley and Chase had occupied on their last visit. She sat behind her desk, facing them.

The director's whole manner was a sober one, suggesting to Haley that Sergeant Blackfeather must have already informed her of the nature of their business. Haley didn't comment on this, but Chase didn't hesitate to put it into words.

"It sounds like Sergeant Blackfeather explained why we've come."

"Not at all. He simply made me aware it was a matter the police department had no authority to deal with beyond what they have so far, and from here on out it would be my responsibility. I think," she went on slowly, "the sergeant was trying to tell me as nicely as possible that I would want to listen seriously to what you had to tell me. And, of course, I would in any case. It seems that, whatever this is about, the sergeant is on your side."

He's enlisted himself as our ally, Haley thought. *Ready to support us if we need his help to convince Dr. Hansen of his belief in this impending attack.*

"But before we go there," the director continued, "I would like to inquire, Mr. McKinley, if you and Ms.

Adams have had any luck in locating your missing brother."

Kind of her to ask, Haley thought.

"I'm afraid not," Chase said. "But we've made some progress by finding this." He held up the journal. "It's my brother's handwritten journal."

"And this," Haley said, holding up her copy of the journal, "is a computer version of the document for easy reading."

"Which we're not going to trouble you with now. We only brought them because they have a connection with the reason we're here."

"And what is that reason?"

Haley and Chase alternatingly told their story. Since they had already related the Oregon events to Dr. Hansen on their first visit, they only briefly reviewed them before summarizing their efforts to find Josh here in Alaska. This included what they had learned from George Fellows at his cabin, their contacts with Sergeant Blackfeather and, because it was so important to understanding the need for this current visit, a more detailed account of Victor Kandinsky's history in Josh's journal.

Even though the director tried out of courtesy to hide a growing restlessness, Haley could see she was wondering what this was all about and how it could possibly involve her.

Haley could tell Chase saw it, too, which was why he ended their story with a quick apology. "I'm sorry, Dr. Hansen, that we had to be so long-winded about the background, but you'll understand when you hear the rest."

Since it was Chase who had confronted Ronnie Peters in the park, Haley verbally stepped aside and let him tell that part. He did it with a note of urgency in his voice that had Dr. Hansen's face growing more grave with each passing second.

We have her complete attention now, Haley thought, but to be certain of that, Haley contributed something of her own. "We think Josh caught some rumor of this attack, and that's why he came to Alaska. He wanted to track it down, try to verify it for his story."

Since there was nothing more at the moment for either her or Chase to add, they were silent, allowing Dr. Hansen to consider what she had just heard.

"Because I am the director of the global vault," she finally said, "I'm responsible for its welfare. I must take every threat to its safety seriously. I must also question the truth of that threat."

She isn't buying the attack, Haley feared.

"You might remember," the doctor went on, "that I told you when you were here before that the vault was built into a cliff with thick concrete walls, steel doors and state-of-the-art security. To achieve any successful attack on it would be extremely difficult."

"But not impossible, Doctor," Chase quietly said. "Not if you have explosives that could blow it wide-open."

"This is true," she admitted. "But this information of an attack has no real evidence to support it, and if I'm going to act…"

"You want that evidence," Haley said. "But that's the trouble. There's no time to try to gather it."

"And," Chase pointed out, "if you don't believe in the reality of this attack on the strength of the information we've brought you…if you fail to take steps to deal with it…"

"Then I may well regret my decision for the rest of my days. Yes, I realize that." She sat back in her chair, buried for a long moment in deep thought before telling them, "I won't risk the vault, but I want support for my decision. We have a defense at our disposal for such a crisis. I'm going to phone the army officer at Fort Richardson in charge of this kind of operation. Colonel Micelli is a very intelligent man. I'll ask him to meet us here so we can get his opinion. Then, if he's in agreement, we'll need to make plans."

Dr. Hansen reached for the phone and, without needing to look it up, dialed the number. There must have been an arrangement between her and the colonel that any phone call from her should be considered a priority, because in a matter of seconds, he was on the line.

Their conversation was only long enough for the director to explain the essentials. She turned to Haley and Chase when she hung up. "Colonel Micelli will be here in an hour. Meanwhile, although it's a bit early for it, I suggest we have some lunch. There's a sandwich shop off the lobby on the first floor with a very good selection. We have menus here. All we have to do is order, and they'll deliver to us up here."

That seemed to be a very good idea to Haley, since her only breakfast had been coffee and a bagel at the hotel. Chase, who'd had nothing, readily agreed. Dr. Hansen summoned Donna and asked her to bring in the menus. The receptionist arrived promptly and took their orders.

"Donna," the director instructed her before the redhead left the office, "Colonel Micelli will be here in less than an hour. Show him into the conference room when he arrives, will you? We'll meet there. And again, no interruptions."

The receptionist nodded her understanding, but Haley could see she realized something important was underway and couldn't wait to hear what it was.

The conference room was even more spacious and comfortable than Dr. Hansen's office. While they waited for Colonel Micelli, ate their sandwiches and drank their beverages, the director asked to discuss certain particulars.

"I know we have no specifics about this attack," she said, "but I think if the colonel is going to be on the same page with us, he might want to find us prepared when he shows up."

"In what way?" Haley wanted to know.

"Being able to name the reason or reasons why the attack is in the works."

"We can only guess about that," Chase said, "but I think I have a good handle on it."

For the next forty minutes, they shared their speculations, with Chase leading the way. "George Fellows and Josh's journal have told us what we need to know. That Victor Kandinski is a megalomaniac who had the money to build his own seed vault. But that's not enough for a man like him. He'd want the *only* seed vault in existence."

"Which would mean," Haley said, "destroying the International Seed Vault here, and that would put him in control of the world's vital seed supplies."

She couldn't help noticing Dr. Hansen actually shuddering at the very concept of such a scenario. "But I can't believe he has them all," she objected. "Not the rarest ones we have here."

"That would be another reason to mount an attack," Chase added soberly. "Maybe not to destroy your vault at all but to break it open and rob it of its most valuable seeds, which would still put him in the lead."

"Or," Haley added, "he could ransom the seeds like a kidnap victim for an immense sum."

And so it went, with the three of them trading possibilities, although none as strong as the first two, until Colonel Micelli arrived.

He was purely military in manner. He had a rigidly erect bearing and an immaculate uniform with creases so sharp, Haley could have cut herself on them. She wouldn't have been surprised if he had expected them to salute when they were introduced.

Nor was it surprising that the colonel had no patience for delay. He joined them at the table without invitation and immediately requested a concise but complete explanation of the situation. Dr. Hansen was apparently used to handling the officer. Haley and Chase let her do the talking.

She built a strong argument, but when she was through, Micelli leaned back and shook his head. "As you know, Doctor, I'm sworn to protect Moa and that vault from any assault. But quite frankly, on the strength of what you have, which strikes me as more hearsay than actual evidence, I don't know that I'm ready to commit my soldiers to this operation."

We're losing him without even having had him, Haley thought woefully. She could see, too, how frustrated Chase was. If his cell phone hadn't rung a few minutes later in his shirt pocket, with the colonel and the director still arguing, the whole thing might have been abandoned.

Muttering an apology, Chase got to his feet and took the call on the far side of the room, where he wouldn't disturb their conversation at the table. Not wanting to miss anything, Haley tried to listen to Micelli and the director while keeping an eye on Chase.

She finally managed to catch his attention, mouthing a silent "Josh?"

He shook his head, indicating Josh was not the subject of his conversation, mouthing back a fast "Blackfeather."

Haley could hear only Chase's one-sided low murmurs from that corner, and now that she knew the caller was Sergeant Blackfeather, she was eager to learn why he'd phoned. It must be important, she thought, if he was willing to risk interrupting the meeting he knew they'd intended to have with Dr. Hansen directly after he left them at the hotel. Was this to do with the backup he'd offered if they needed it?

Chase himself was ready to interrupt the conversation at the table the second he ended the call and came back to them, earning him a frown of disapproval from Dr. Hansen. The frown vanished when he launched into an explanation.

"Excuse me, Doctor, Colonel, but I think you'll agree with me this is what we've been needing to hear. The call was from Sergeant Blackfeather at police headquarters. You probably already know this, but if you don't, the sergeant informed me that the coast guard works with the police departments in Alaska."

"And this has bearing, how?" Micelli demanded.

"It's one of the duties of coast guard planes and ships regularly to patrol the waters both along and away from the Alaskan coast. Just before the sergeant phoned me, he had contact from a crew member acquaintance on one of those planes who wanted to report a sighting of a suspicious foreign vessel."

"Suspicious, how?" the colonel asked.

"Didn't radio its presence with its identity. Not that it had to, since it wasn't in American waters, but it's customary when vessels registered in other countries are anywhere at all in the neighborhood. A closer look with some high-powered glasses revealed it was a particularly large seagoing yacht. Her name is the *Sultana*."

Haley already had a flash of insight about where this was going.

"That close look," Chase continued, "also disclosed a few figures on deck. Apparently, there was one of them you couldn't mistake. Carried an enormous weight." He looked around the table. "Anyone care to make a guess?"

"I think we get the who and the why here, McKinley," the colonel growled, "without needing to make a game of it."

Dr. Hansen exhaled what, from the sound of it, must have been a deep breath she'd been holding. "Victor Kandinsky. He must be on his way to Moa and the vault."

"I don't think that's likely," Haley said. "From all accounts, the man is too cunning ever to come near American territorial waters, much less land on American soil and risk arrest."

"Right," Chase agreed, "but you can bet he wouldn't sail halfway around the world without a purpose. He has to keep his distance from Moa, but he can anchor close enough in neutral waters to gloat over a success when his mercenary army goes ashore for what they probably plan to be a quick, easy strike."

There didn't seem to be any more to be determined. Three questioning gazes around the table turned to the fourth figure in uniform.

Colonel Micelli spoke to Haley. "Ms. Adams, I would appreciate having one of those copies of the journal to take back with me to the base. I'd like to read it tonight."

And that was all he needed to say to tell them he'd made his decision with no further misgivings. Haley passed him the copy he requested.

"I may not find anything beyond what I've already

heard from you, but I believe in being thoroughly prepared for any operation. And that's what I intend to be when I lead my men in there come Friday."

Haley was surprised. "I didn't think high-ranking officers led their men into battle."

"As Dr. Hansen here knows, I've visited and am familiar with both the island and the vault. My men aren't, and I don't have a lot of time to train and familiarize them. This will have to take place here on the base. And that's only after I plan the operation. Don't worry. By the time I brief them on Thursday, they'll be ready. We'll save your vault, Doctor."

Chase had been silent during these last exchanges. Haley hadn't bothered to wonder why and was as startled as the other two when he suddenly, decisively spoke up.

"I want to be there with you, *one* of you when you land on that island."

Colonel Micelli stared at him as if he'd taken leave of his senses. "Don't be absurd, man. I have no intention of taking a civilian into anything resembling a battle."

"I'm not a civilian. I'm a US army ranger, and I want to go. Sir."

"What is this?"

"It's all there in my army record if you want to check. Second Lieutenant Chase McKinley. You understand how it works when you join the army, sir. You sign a contract for eight years. You spend four of those years in active service. I trained as a ranger for most of two of them after basic, was in combat for the next two, and requested the last four to be on reserve because I needed to be home for my family. As you know, if you're needed for any emergency situation, you're called back in. I consider this an emergency situation, so I'm volunteering."

The colonel looked at him thoughtfully. Haley could tell he was seriously considering Chase's offer. "The men I'll be taking in there with me are all solid, but none of them have experience in actual combat, and none of them are rangers. I could use someone qualified in both areas. It may be against my better judgment, Lieutenant, but I'm going to include you in the operation. Don't let me down."

"Thank you, sir."

The colonel got to his feet, journal in hand. "Be there at the base on Thursday, McKinley. I may need you to help me run some last drills. You'll also need to be in on a final briefing, as well as be issued your combat gear and weapon."

"Understood, sir." Chase stood and saluted him smartly.

Colonel Micelli tossed back a salute of his own and strode from the conference room, accompanied by Dr. Hansen. Haley and Chase were left alone. They didn't speak. All she could do was gaze at him numbly, sick at the thought of him going into battle with the risk of being wounded, maybe even worse. How could he do that to her? To both of them?

But she had no knowledge of his ever thinking of them in those terms. He had never once referred to them as either *both* or a *couple*. Was he still reserving that for his brother and her? Didn't he have any idea what he did to her emotionally? How he made her ache for him?

He certainly didn't fail to read the accusation in her eyes at this moment. He must have understood what it asked, if not the reason behind it.

"I have to go, Haley," he told her softly. "I have to be there for Josh."

Always Josh, she thought bitterly. Always fighting the battles for his brother whenever he couldn't be there to fight them for himself. Maddening.

Chapter 14

They had just walked into the lobby of the Kodiak Hotel and were headed to the elevator when the desk clerk, holding out a phone, called to Chase.

"Call for you, Mr. McKinley. Would you like to take it here, or shall I switch it up to your suite?"

Chase hesitated for a second, looking puzzled, before he decided. "I'll take it here."

He's wondering who could be calling, Haley thought. The only possibility was Sergeant Blackfeather, and he had Chase's cell number. Dr. Hansen? But she had his cell number, too.

She waited by the elevator, watching Chase take the instrument from the clerk's hand and announce his identity into the phone. Whatever the caller replied must have satisfied Chase, because the puzzled expression cleared from his face. Haley's curiosity, however, remained.

The call lasted for a couple of minutes before Chase

returned to her side with an explanation. "It was Colonel Micelli. Something occurred to him on his way back to base that he felt couldn't wait."

"A problem?"

Chase shook his head. "A change in plans that makes sense. He wants me to come to base first thing tomorrow."

"Wednesday, not Thursday? Why a day ahead?"

"He feels we should be delivered to Moa and in position on Thursday, not wait for Friday. There's no telling how early on Friday the enemy will show up there. We need to be ready for them."

Haley nodded. "Yes, that does make sense. But it leaves only the rest of today for him to pick his men and plan his strategy."

"He'll manage it. He wouldn't be a colonel otherwise."

They spent the rest of the afternoon in the sitting room of their suite. Haley worked on her laptop, sending emails to her clients in Portland. It was important for her to remain in contact with the people who kept her business a healthy one. Where personal relationships were concerned, that was also true. Her closest friends deserved emails of their own and got them.

Chase kept busy with his own phone connections to Seattle, checking with the bail bond company he worked for and the mail service store that was holding his mail for him.

It was after they ate dinner and watched a newscast that he said to her, "I think we should make it an early night."

"Well, *you* should if you're going to be up and out to Fort Richardson first thing in the morning."

"We both should. I'm taking you with me. After what

happened to you in the park, I don't want you here alone all day."

"And won't Colonel Micelli like that."

"I think I can convince him of the wisdom of it. You'll be safe on the base."

And how would he make sure she was safe on Thursday and Friday when he was on Moa? He didn't mention it, and she didn't bring it up.

Although Haley was capable of taking care of herself, it was touching how he wanted to protect her. But was that more for Josh's sake than his own? Because she believed Chase was anything but certain about his feelings for her, whereas hers for him were sure and defined.

If she was concerned about anything regarding his absence, it was the loneliness that would mark their separation. Absurd to already mind this when they would be apart only a matter of two days. Anyway, they still had tomorrow and tomorrow night to be together before he had to leave.

As for tonight…well, for her it turned out to be unexpected.

She and Chase had gone to their bedrooms. She'd had a quick shower in her bathroom and was standing now at her bedroom window in her robe, enjoying a last view of the inlet waters before turning in for the night.

She never heard Chase behind her. The man had the ability to sneak up like some great, sleek cat. But she *felt* him there even before his broad hands rested on her shoulders. She always seemed to sense his presence somehow, even as far back as Portland.

They were both silent for a moment. Then he spoke softly at her ear. "Like magic, isn't it, the way the light is all gold on those waters?"

He was the one who was magic, the way his touch

made her shiver and his very breath excited her. He must have washed his hair in his own shower. She could smell his shampoo.

"Haley, I was thinking…"

"What?"

"We've still got tomorrow night together, but I don't think either one of us is going to be in any mood for intimacy. Not when we've got only a few hours until we have to part. And I don't want anything rushed for us." Before she realized it, he spun her around and they were face to face. "Do you understand what I'm saying? What I'm asking?"

"You want to be with me tonight. Here in my room. In my bed."

Her answer was to put her hands on either side of his head and bring his face down to hers. His mouth was slightly parted, ready for hers, when she kissed him, a long, sweet kiss that involved the tip of her tongue licking along his lips. The raspy sound that rose from low in his throat when she entered his mouth seemed to be telling her he was enjoying her attention. Enjoying it immensely.

At what point he took possession of the kiss, making himself the commander of it, she couldn't say. She just knew that it became *his* tongue in *her* mouth. She could taste him then, the by-now-familiar flavor of his minty toothpaste.

And she could feel him. His hands, in no hurry, played with the ends of the sash that tied her robe together at her waist. One of those hands slid inside the robe where it overlapped, searching until it found a full, plump breast, stroking and squeezing gently before it moved on to the second breast for a similar sensual treatment.

Chase lost control of the kiss then, his tongue retreating from her mouth to permit his forehead to rest weakly against her brow. His hand withdrew from her breast to join his other hand in closing around her arms to steady her. She seemed to be swaying. She was conscious that he maintained balance for both of them.

"It ought to be illegal, what you do to a man just by coming into contact with him," he said gruffly.

Was that a complaint or an invitation? Haley wondered. Because he was wearing a robe of his own, not floor-length like hers but knee-length, she decided to define it as an invitation.

If he felt entitled to explore hidden places, why couldn't she boldly do the same?

She heard him suck in a mouthful of air when her hands crept inside his robe, brushing against bare flesh as they stole around behind him. "Where are you going?" he demanded.

"Here," she said, her fingertips pressing into the firm, rounded, fleshy cheeks of that male backside she'd admired from the first time his tall figure had struck out in front of her. She thought his backside felt even better than it looked.

The air he'd inhaled rushed out of him. "You're not just illegal," he said. "You're dangerous. Let's level the playing field."

His idea of that was to move his hands up her arms and around the curves of her shoulders. The loose sash dropped away from her waist as he tugged at both sides of the robe's collar, drawing the garment off her shoulders and down her arms until it was ready for Chase to release it. It dropped to the floor, where the shimmering folds pooled at her feet. Haley stood naked above it.

"Join me," she whispered.

He didn't hesitate. Peeling off his own robe, he tossed

it to the floor. He was naked now himself, a brawny body that backed her toward the bed until she found herself toppled over and tumbled across its width with Chase stretched out beside her.

"Now we're fair and ready for the game," he announced.

The action that followed consisted of a series of intimacies that ranged from the tender to the robust. It began with Chase trailing slow kisses from her mouth, along the side of her neck and down to her breasts, which he took in turn in his mouth, sucking strongly until she was bucking wildly under him on the bed. He progressed from there to her waist, where his tongue swirled around her navel before he licked his way to her thighs.

Along the way, Haley became aware of several things—his pulse beating hypnotically in the hollow of his throat; the muscles he'd developed over the years in his arms, chest and legs; and most prominently, the rigid column that sprang from his groin.

"It needs your attention, sweetheart," he begged. "This kind."

Leaning over the side of the bed, he scooped a condom out of the pocket in his robe where it lay on the floor and pressed it into her hand. She understood his need and his wish to have her clad that proud shaft.

"It will be my pleasure," she promised him.

"I was hoping it would be mine, too."

And that's what the two of them strove to achieve in the exhilarating moments that followed. There was no question of it. Chase was a dynamic lover, starting with his sensitive preparation to receive him and proceeding to his slow, exquisite penetration and the energetic strokes that followed. Their lovemaking ended in powerful climaxes for both of them.

Considering the early hour they would need to get up in the morning and the long day ahead of them, it would have been understandable, probably even sensible after their bout of lovemaking, to fall asleep in each other's arms and stay that way until the wake-up call Chase had requested from the desk.

Sensible, but not what either of them wanted. What they wanted, and managed between brief periods of rest, was more sex in a variety of positions.

She could only suppose their greed was connected with Thursday when Chase would be gone to Moa. Neither of them discussed it, and Haley could hardly bear to think of it, but there was always the possibility that this would be their last session of lovemaking, and they needed to make it count. Because if Chase didn't come back…

Maybe that was why, during one of their intervals of rest, Haley found herself trailing her finger over the scar near his eye—caressing it, actually—and unable to prevent herself from asking him, "Result of an enemy bullet in Afghanistan?"

"Uh-uh. A Taliban knife in hand-to-hand combat."

What on earth was wrong with her, introducing such a subject when she feared for his life on Moa? He was almost casual about it, but she shuddered at the very mention of combat.

As if to compensate for her thoughtlessness, she was particularly passionate during their lovemaking that followed. He must have appreciated her extra effort, because in return he lavished endearments on her.

She heard it all whispered into her ear, words and expressions she cherished. Everything but the ones she longed to hear. And those precious words of commitment she still feared Chase was incapable of speaking.

Haley fell asleep on that sad realization. When she

woke up, she was alone in her bed, and it was Wednesday morning. One more day, and Chase would be gone to Moa.

One more day, and she couldn't shake the thought that haunted her. It was stronger than ever. It accompanied her down to breakfast, insisting on a recognition that until now she had thrust into the back of her mind. She could no longer silence it.

If Josh was somewhere out there, still active…if he had managed to learn about the attack, then surely by now he would have warned Dr. Hansen. Or if not the director, then someone with authority to act. He would have done something to save the vault.

Was Chase, sitting across the breakfast table from her, permitting himself to consider all this? He had to be thinking it, and she refused to let him go on keeping it to himself any longer. As usual, he had several reasonable arguments supporting his brother's survival.

"We lucked into finding out about the attack and its planned timing, Haley. Josh could be out there keeping low but still looking for what was only a rumor for him and having no way yet to know it's a reality. Or maybe— and I hate to think this—he has the facts and is unable to report them, because Victor Kandinsky's thugs here are holding him somewhere."

There's another explanation, Chase. A very likely one, but even if you considered it, you would refuse to hear it vocally expressed.

Haley, however, was beyond that. Even if she couldn't bring herself to hurt Chase by saying it aloud, she said it to herself. *Josh was no longer alive.*

After driving on to Fort Richardson and being admitted, they drove on to training ground that was still empty. Chase parked the forest-green Jeep in an adjoining lot before reporting to a building where he would be issued his gear while Haley took her laptop and settled in an open shelter.

The training field remained deserted until a solitary figure in civilian dress ambled in her direction. "Would you object if I join you?" he asked her.

He had fair, thinning hair, eyes almost as blue as her own and a friendly smile. He was also so tall he had to duck his head to enter the shelter.

"Are you waiting for your army buddies?"

"Oh, no, I am not in the service. You are Haley Adams, I think?"

"And how did you know that?"

"Dr. Hansen described you to me. She said it would be possible I should meet you here."

"And how do you know Dr. Han—" Haley interrupted herself. "Look, you'd better sit down before you bump your head." *And put a cramp in my neck looking up at you*, she thought.

He took her advice and parked himself on a bench. "Dr. Hansen and I work together at the seed vault headquarters. I have advanced training in the field, too, but in a junior capacity. I am Dr. Rolf Schneider."

He stretched out a long-fingered, bony hand for her to shake. Schneider, huh? She'd thought there was a bit of German accent in his formal speech, like there was Norwegian in the director's.

"Did you come out to the base today to visit?" Haley wondered.

"Nothing of that kind. Dr. Hansen sent me. She thought it might be useful for me to observe the maneuvers." Schneider could obviously see her puzzled look. "I know. It is not like I am going to be needing them, even if I am going to Moa tomorrow with the troops. It is a precaution, you see. I will be the only one in the company who knows the code to unlock the vault and can identify its most valuable deposits."

"Will there be a reason to do that?"

"I cannot imagine there should be. Will you be going, Ms. Adams?"

"No, I'll be staying here in Anchorage. I'm just here today with a friend who will be going with you."

And where is he? Haley asked herself. It looked like most of the soldiers had already assembled on the field, but she didn't see Chase among them. That, she discovered when she searched again, was because she hadn't recognized him at first.

He was a stranger wearing combat boots, a camouflage field uniform and matching cap, and equipped with an assault rifle.

The colonel, whistle strung around his neck, was there, too. He was an officer who missed nothing—not only carefully watching his men to make sure they were alert, but also managing to spot Haley's presence in the shelter. She received a brief nod of acknowledgment from him. She felt as if she should be returning it with a salute of her own but hoped he would accept a nod back.

It seemed after that moment everything went into action and stayed that way. Micelli bid the men to stand at ease and briefed them about their operation tomorrow before introducing Chase and his role as a special ranger. Chase was chosen to lead some rigorous drills.

While these were being run, a board on wheeled legs was rolled into place and a map pinned to it. It was a map sizable enough to be seen easily by the men grouped in front of it on the ground when they came off the drills in need of a break.

Dr. Schneider leaned over to inform Haley in a low, confidential voice, "That is a detailed map of Moa."

The two of them weren't close enough to hear, nor were they meant to, as they watched the colonel at the board with a pointer indicating what few landmarks there were on the island and the positions the troops would assume.

The map session was followed by a series of maneuvers, after which the troops were dismissed for the midday meal in mess. Haley and Dr. Schneider were the guests of the army at chow, the eager gazes of the young men following her through the tray line and across the hall to a table at the side, where Dr. Schneider joined her.

She was surprised when she looked up to find that Chase had arrived with his own tray. "I kind of had the impression you'd be much too busy to take time for me today."

"That was my intention," he said with a mock grimness, "until I noticed about a hundred slavering guys around us ready to riot."

"That bad, huh?"

"Yeah, that bad. Hello, Dr. Schneider."

"And here I was going to introduce you," she said.

The doctor filled her in. "We have already met. The second lieutenant knows I will also be going to Moa tomorrow."

Haley was silent, letting the two men talk about the training that was being conducted here today, although she noticed that Chase's years in active service must have taught him to be careful what he said when it came to preparing for combat.

Haley and her new friend were still eating the army's version of pizza—among the best she'd ever tasted—when Chase got to his feet. "Excuse me. I need to see the colonel for a couple of minutes before we go back to the training ground."

Her gaze followed him to the tray return, then on to another table across the hall, where he joined Colonel Micelli in an earnest conversation that had elements of mystery about it. At one point she caught the colonel turning her way with a severe glance.

Now what, she asked herself, *is that all about?* And she wondered if Chase would tell her if she asked him about it.

When Haley and Dr. Schneider returned to the shelter, her attention was drawn to the far end of the field. It was a direction she hadn't paid any particular notice to before this. But the men were all gathering there now, which she supposed was why she discovered the wall.

It was an unusual wall, maybe one hundred fifty yards or so in length, made out of wood, with a fairly wide walkway all along the top and a ladder at each end mounted to the walkway.

"It looks like a timber cliff," she said.

"It was built to resemble just that," the doctor said.

"What for?"

"You will see."

It didn't seem fair that everyone seemed to know these mysteries all the time but her, she thought as they turned their benches to face the new scene of action.

Colonel Micelli didn't hesitate to put the maneuver under way the moment he appeared. The men were divided, roughly one half of them remaining on the ground, the other half sent scrambling up the ladders. Rifles strapped to their backs, they were ordered to spread out at intervals along the walkway and seize ropes attached to the back of the wall.

Chase had been appointed to demonstrate this ranger technique, and within minutes, the soldiers were correctly wrapping the ropes over and around themselves. At a signal, they dropped together over the side. Rappelling as swiftly as they could down the side of the wall, they detached themselves at the bottom and fell flat on the ground with their rifles in hand.

"Ah, I understand," Haley said. "The vault is built into the side of a cliff. The men here are going to surprise Kandinsky's little army of mercenaries by dropping in on them over that cliff."

Dr. Schneider nodded. "I believe in this case that must be the intention."

The other men took their turns learning the technique. Haley watched for a while. But when all of them needed to practice it under Chase's watchful eye until it was familiar to them, she grew bored and opened her laptop, turning to the projects she'd brought with her from Portland.

It was a long day for all of them, particularly the men. Dr. Schneider returned to his office at the seed vault headquarters at midafternoon. Chase wasn't able to leave until the training was done much later. She could see how tired he was when they walked to their Jeep, carting the gear he would need for Moa.

"I'll drive us back to the hotel," she insisted.

He didn't argue with her, proof of his fatigue.

"I think Micelli was satisfied with the way it all went," he said when they were underway.

"Does that include the conversation you had with him about me at lunch?"

"How did you know about that?"

She was thankful he wasn't trying to deny it. It made

it easier. "I caught him looking at me when you were talking to him."

"I was planning to tell you back at the hotel."

"Tell me now."

"You won't like it."

"Why don't you let *me* decide that?"

Chapter 15

"It won't matter, Haley, because whatever you decide, I'm not going to change my mind about it."

"Oh? And who put you in charge?"

"About this specific subject? I put myself in charge."

"All right, let's not argue about it. Just tell me."

"Maybe you'd better pull over and let me drive."

"Why? Because when I hear what it is, I'll turn hysterical—like, naturally, all women do when they're upset—and have an accident?"

"No, of course I don't think that. But you have to admit there was that time when you snatched the keys from the ignition and threw them out the open window."

"Not the same thing, McKinley. Come on, spill."

"It's about tomorrow and Friday. I don't intend to leave you on your own. I've arranged for someone to stay with you."

"Seeing as how you insisted I spend today with you

at the base and not be left alone, I was wondering when you'd get around to this. But a bodyguard really isn't necessary, Chase. I promise to stay in the suite with the door locked, have all my meals delivered by room service in the sitting room and, if I feel like exercise, use the hotel pool. See, no hysteria. Handled calmly."

"You can't think I'm going to settle for that," he said stubbornly.

Keeping her attention on the traffic, Haley opened her mouth and issued a scream so long and high-pitched it could have damaged her passenger's hearing.

She could feel him shrinking away from her with a startled "Holy crap!"

Haley couldn't help it. She began to laugh. The poor man probably didn't know what to make of her reactions at this point. When she finally got her laughter under control, she spoke to him with a reasonable level of sanity.

"I'm sorry. None of this talk about the next two days is at all funny. But, Chase, you can't think I'm in any danger at this point. I'm past that. It's you who'll be risking yourself at Moa."

"I wish that was the case," he said solemnly, "but it isn't. Think about it, Haley. After what you've seen and learned all along, especially today, you have enough information for the enemy to grab you. We know Kandinsky has agents all over the place, and by now some of them have got to be aware that Ronnie Peters turned informer. With all this, why do you suppose Colonel Micelli agreed to assign one of his soldiers to stay with you at the hotel until all of this is over?"

This put an entirely different perspective on it, Haley realized. Her own safety was one thing, but she had no right to take chances with the men who were going to defend the vault.

"You win. I accept the company of this soldier the colonel is posting. Just one thing. Is he cute?" She only needed a single quick sidelong glance at Chase's face to know that if she went on like this, she was going to be in trouble. Remembering that Chase would be leaving her within hours definitely put her out of the mood for any more flippant humor. Back at the hotel, neither one of them wanted to make this last night funereal. They didn't have many hours together in any case, not after the long day they'd had and with Chase needing to get to bed early.

They were awkward with each other at dinner, neither of them knowing what to say to the other. Over coffee, Chase finally reached across the table, covering her hand with his.

"Haley, I'm not immune," he said solemnly.

She waited for him to explain himself.

"I mean, about certain feelings you might think I ought to be having and should be expressing, especially during and after our lovemaking. And maybe you have them, too."

Her reply was a guarded one. "Maybe."

"This is hard, because I don't want to go off tomorrow having you suppose I'm not aware we need to talk about these things I've been avoiding. We do have to talk about them. You, me and, yeah, where Josh might fit in, too. But not now, not tonight."

"Then why did you bring the subject up?"

"It was for a selfish reason, I admit it. Because if something should happen to me on Friday—not that it will, but it could—I wanted you to know that I wasn't just using you whenever I went to bed with you."

"And that's it?"

"No. I also wanted you to know that one of the first things we have to do when I get back, and we have all the time we need, is to sit down and have that talk."

"But not tonight?"

"Not tonight."

Haley didn't push him. Not that she could have, anyway, since shortly after that, he went off to his own bedroom to pack what he would need for tomorrow. He spent the night in his own room, possibly because that way he would get the sleep he needed, which mightn't have been the case sharing her bed.

She certainly wasn't able to go to sleep in that bed. Not for some time, anyway. It didn't matter. It gave her the chance to try to understand what Chase had been trying to tell her over the dinner table. He hadn't been very clear about any of it.

After lying there for a while, though, she thought she had Chase's code figured out. He'd made what he wanted to say sound complicated when it was really pretty simple: *Don't go off to battle having tried to dump strong emotions on whoever you're leaving behind. Because whether the feelings are negative or positive, you need to save them. Then, when you come back, your mind clear, you'll be able to deal with them.*

On the other hand, if you were the one left behind waiting and wondering—and that was her—how could that be better? You'd have all those questions about the serious talk going around in your head and making you crazy. Did he love you, or was he going to hurt you?

In the end, Haley managed to put it away and go to sleep.

She was annoyed with herself when she emerged from her room the next morning. She'd planned to be up and in the sitting room, cheerful and encouraging, when

Chase appeared. But he was already there with his gear by the door.

He wasn't alone. There was another soldier with him. Her bodyguard, she supposed. And, yes, he was cute. How could he not be with those dimples bracketing his mouth in a boyish face? He would be perfect for her younger sister. That is, if she had a sister, younger or otherwise.

"Haley, this is Corporal Greg Goldman. He's going to look out for you until I'm back."

She went forward to shake his hand. "Corporal."

"Ma'am."

"Have you had a chance to get settled yet, Corporal?"

Chase answered for him. "We've put his things in my room, including his sidearm locked in a drawer of the bureau."

Haley wasn't happy about the gun, even though he was a soldier guarding her. It all still struck her as unnecessary.

The phone rang. Chase answered it. He spoke briefly, rang off and turned to her. "That was downstairs. They're here to take me out to Elmendorf."

"You're not going by boat?"

"Too long and too slow. The army here partners with the air force. They'll be flying us to Moa with choppers." He took her into his arms and kissed her hurriedly.

"Be safe," she whispered fiercely.

"You, too. Corporal, take good care of her."

"The best, Lieutenant, I promise."

Before she knew it, Chase was gone, and she was already missing him deeply.

Haley, on the line with room service, held her hand over the receiver and asked Corporal Goldman if he'd like her to order breakfast for both of them.

"No, thank you, ma'am, I already had mine before I left base, but you go right ahead."

The corporal seemed to have no trouble passing the morning hours. He was easily entertained lounging on the sofa and watching TV. Haley, on the other hand, found herself after breakfast less able to concentrate on her current laptop project.

Her mind was with Chase more than it was with the work on her screen. She would stop and wonder what he was doing at that particular moment. What he might be thinking. Whether they had arrived yet on Moa.

Restless, she called across the room to her bodyguard. "Corporal, you must be wishing you're on one of those choppers with your buddies instead of stuck here with me."

"No, ma'am, this is fine."

"You're just being nice. You've got to be bored."

"Honestly, ma'am, I'm not. I do what I'm ordered to do and try to like it whatever it is, whether it's preparing for action or taking charge of a security detail like yourself."

Easy to please, aren't you, Greg Goldman?

Haley found him more open, and herself better entertained by his company, when he joined her at the table for lunch with another meal delivered by room service.

"Where's home for you, Corporal?"

"Wisconsin, ma'am. My folks operate a stock farm there. Sheep, goats, Angus cattle, even some bison."

"So, Corporal, have you got a girl back there?"

"I do, ma'am." He grinned, displaying his dimples to full advantage. "We're going to be married on my next leave."

They went back to their separate pursuits after lunch. The corporal traded the TV for a handheld electronic game he'd brought with him, and Haley returned to her work on the laptop. But as the afternoon advanced, her mind drifted back to Chase.

They have to have reached Moa by now, she thought. *Must be making preparations for tomorrow and just how and where they'll spend tonight. Does Chase have time for nothing but that, or is he thinking of other things? Like that serious talk he's planning for us to have when he gets back...*

Josh. He intended Josh to be one of the subjects of that talk. But Josh was dead. There. Even if she had yet to speak the word itself aloud, she had used it internally. Dead. A terrible, tragic admission, but what other explanation was there?

As she had told herself the other day, if Josh had learned of Kandinsky's intention to attack the vault, as he very well might have, then it should have been he who had reported it, not she and Chase. But he hadn't. Why? Because, sadly, he was gone.

The Aleutians, particularly the outermost ones, were frequently described as remote and rugged. Chase would have added *lonely* to the list.

He was feeling that now as he huddled in the shallow hollow that was meant to shield him and the men who had been assigned to him from the perpetual wind that blew in from the sea. And didn't shield them at all since even this basin was exposed to the elements. Other than some stunted trees and the waving grasses, there was very little cover on the island.

Why Chase should be feeling lonely didn't make sense. On the other hand, there were two good explanations for his state of mind. Moa was a damned forlorn place with nothing here but the vault and the sea birds.

An even better reason than that was the inactivity of both him and the other soldiers. It was late Thursday afternoon, not yet time to think about an evening meal, and they'd completed all their preparations for tomorrow morning's anticipated attack. They had set up the lines of their counter action, Chase with his force down here and Colonel Micelli with his on the flats above the vault.

They had even made their camp arrangements for the night, so now with nothing else to do but wait through the long hours, why wouldn't it feel lonely?

That all amounts to a lot of bull, McKinley, he finally admitted to himself. *There's only one good reason why you're lonely. You're missing Haley. Wondering how she's managing and what she's doing. You keep picturing her with that mass of dark hair and milky, smooth skin, those blue eyes and that little cleft in her chin that right now you'd like to be kissing.*

He hadn't told her that somewhere along the way, he had fallen in love with her. He was saving that for the talk they would have when he got back. But he feared that declaration of love.

Not for the usual guy reasons. No, Chase had a brother he believed was still out there somewhere. A brother who had given a strong indication he was in love with Haley. And even if Haley didn't love Josh—if somehow she loved him instead—Chase was bound to hurt someone. Either Josh by stealing his girl or Haley if he felt he couldn't do anything but step aside for his brother.

His mind raced. Yeah, all this waiting was a damn lonely time, all right.

Haley had thought Thursday was difficult to get through. But it was nothing compared to Friday. The morning alone was endless. She never even opened her laptop, knowing she wouldn't be able to concentrate on the work. Her thoughts were nowhere else but Moa.

Had Victor Kandinsky's mercenaries arrived? Was the anticipated battle raging? And, most vital of all, was Chase all right?

Please, God, keep him safe.

What worried Haley here and now was Corporal Goldman. Yesterday he had been nothing but calm and casual. This morning he was restless, interested in neither TV nor his handheld electronic game. He, too, had to be thinking about Moa and the men there he cared about.

"Ma'am," he finally suggested, "would you care to play some cards? Might help to take our minds off what's happening on that island."

So they sat down at the table, and the corporal dealt the cards for their first game of gin rummy. She was able to get through several games before tension caught up with her and, unable to go on, she laid down her hand.

"Did anyone indicate to you they would contact us when they knew anything definite?"

"No, ma'am, and I didn't think to ask."

"I didn't, either. I just thought we'd hear."

"To tell you the truth, ma'am, I don't think they could contact us, not by personal cell phone anyway. I don't think there's any tower there equipped for that. What I heard is there's protected electronic stuff up there sending out signals that get monitored down here by people at the seed vault."

"Yes," Haley said, "we were told they regularly check the readings to be sure everything is working properly."

"But listen, ma'am, the colonel wouldn't be up there without being able to communicate with the base. He's sure to have a powerful radio with him, and sooner or later we're bound to hear."

Sooner or later. That was the trouble, she thought. That it would be later rather than sooner, and by then she'd be a wreck.

Fog was common in the Aleutians. Chase was told not to be surprised if it occurred. And that was what happened Friday morning. It was a slow, gradual thing, no more than a mist at first crawling in from the open sea.

Lying low in the hollow, he tried to decide if the weather was an advantage or not. Probably both. If it thickened, and it looked like it was doing just that, they would have trouble seeing the arrival of the enemy. Problem was, they didn't know if they were coming by air or by water.

Another negative was the temperature. Even in midsummer like this, the Aleutians were raw. A fog would make them even colder.

On the plus side, any fog, even a mist, would help to conceal them from an enemy who had no idea soldiers of the US Army were here waiting for them.

The hollow was deep enough on the side that faced the vault to prevent Chase and his force from seeing the approach to its entrance. But the water side of the hollow was lower, permitting Chase, who had stationed himself there with raised head, to look out to sea.

Where were the mercenaries? he wondered. Unless they'd been warned somehow that they would be met by a defending fire and called off the attack, they should have been here by now.

And that was when Chase saw them before he heard them. A small fleet of flat-bottomed open crafts materializing like ghosts out of the fog bank, their engines muffled by the fog.

He slid himself down the slope to alert the men he was commanding of the enemy's arrival. It seemed they were already learning of it. One of the soldiers had been equipped with a two-way radio and was now in touch with another two-way up above the vault.

It figured they would have a better view from up there, must have spotted the fleet some minutes before Chase had and were now passing the word. Making certain all his men were ready for action and would understand his signal when it came, he crawled back to his watch at the top of the slope.

This time he heard the low throb of the engines as they approached the island. He knew that these flat-bottomed crafts, even with their shallow drafts, couldn't make any landing on the shingle beach here. The waters of the cove that fronted the beach were so shallow near shore that the boats with their human cargoes would scrape bottom.

At a shouted signal, the mercenaries aboard the crafts clambered over the low sides and waded toward the shelving beach. Lightened of their loads, the landing crafts backed off toward the open sea and were swallowed again by the fog.

Hell, they were ghosts all right, Chase thought. Like something out of World War II. But the men who had been aboard them were very real as they swarmed ashore and headed up the beach, rifles slung by straps over their shoulders and explosives strapped to their backs.

Chase, unseen by any except the men behind him in the hollow, lifted his arm, ready to give his own signal. *But not yet, guys. Not yet.*

That arm of his couldn't drop until the action commenced on top of the cliff. It waited until the mercenaries began to stream toward the vault. It was then Colonel Micelli gave the command that rained gunfire down on the other army as a cover for his soldiers rappelling down the face of the cliff. Then, as had been arranged, Chase dropped his arm.

With his own men behind him, his M4 carbine and theirs raised and ready, he led them out of the hollow. Their position permitted them to come at the mercenaries from the rear, cutting them off from any possible retreat.

With weapons blazing at them from both front and back, more as a demand for their surrender than anything else, the bewildered, yelling enemy didn't know what hit them.

Haley was relieved when the desk rang up shortly after lunch to tell her there was a phone call for her, and would she take it?

Would she take it? She'd been waiting all morning to hear something, hadn't she? Not that this was necessarily news about Moa, but what else could it be?

"Yes," she responded breathlessly, "of course I'll take it."

A few seconds later, a male voice inquired, "Ms. Adams?"

"Yes. Who am I speaking to, please?"

He seemed a little surprised. "This is Colonel Micelli."

"Oh, I'm sorry, Colonel. I guess I didn't recognize your voice. It seems even deeper than I remembered and at the same time a little faint."

"Understandable. I'm speaking on radio from Moa to the base, and they're patching this through to you."

"Is—is everything all right there?"

"We've done what we came here to do. The other side has surrendered and given up their weapons."

"That's wonderful news!" Corporal Goldman, as anxious as she was to hear the outcome of the fight, was hovering nearby. She nodded to him just to be sure he understood what she'd been told. "And Chase—Second Lieutenant McKinley—is he okay?"

"He's fine and asked me to relay that to you. I'd let him speak to you himself, but he's pretty wrapped up now directing our men. There's always a mop-up after a fight. We probably won't be able to clear out of here until later tomorrow, but there is an opportunity for you to see him before then."

"How is that possible?"

"I'm issuing you an invitation to visit us. Several of our boys, as well as some of the enemy, were wounded. The more serious ones are being air transported right now back to Anchorage for treatment. They could be landing any minute, and shortly after they off-load they'll be turning around and coming back for the others. You could be on that return flight. I think you'd enjoy seeing the island. Dr. Schneider is here with us. He's checking the vault and is willing to give you and the lieutenant an inside view. Are you interested, Ms. Adams?"

Haley didn't hesitate. "Absolutely. There's just one thing. Corporal Goldman is here with me. Does that invitation include him?"

"Corporal Goldman?"

"My bodyguard."

"Yes, I'd forgotten him. Sorry about that." There was a brief silence of consideration on the other end. "Yes, I suppose he should stay with you. I'll have someone from the plane pick you up. It would probably help if you'd both be waiting out front at the hotel."

It wasn't until they'd collected a few essentials and were waiting out front as directed that Haley noticed the corporal was a bit quieter than usual.

"Did I assume something?"

"Ma'am?"

"It occurs to me that I should have asked you first if you wanted to go along. It's okay, Corporal, if you'd rather stay behind. I'll be perfectly safe when the ride comes along."

"Oh, no, ma'am, I want to go all right."

"That's good. You weren't talking, so I wondered if something might be bothering you."

"Not really. I was thinking, is all."

"Oh? About what?"

"Well, you said the colonel told you someone from the plane is picking us up. That's right, isn't it, ma'am?"

"Yes. Anything wrong with that?"

"It's just that one of the guys was saying after the briefing at the base on Wednesday that the air force boys from Elmendorf would be taking them out to Moa by chopper and bringing them back that way."

Come to think of it, Haley thought, Chase had mentioned something like that himself. "It doesn't really matter either way, does it, Corporal?"

"I guess not, except…"

"What?"

"They told us there's no landing field on Moa, just a couple of chopper pads."

"I'm sure there's an explanation, Corporal."

And Haley meant to ask for it as soon as their ride arrived, which happened less than two minutes later when a service Jeep raced to a stop in front of the Kodiak front entrance. The lank, lantern-jawed driver, wearing an air force flying suit, hurried out from behind the wheel, made certain they were his pickups and quickly introduced himself.

"First Lieutenant Wallace. I'll be your copilot. Our pilot, Captain Delgado, is with the plane."

"Uh, about that, Lieutenant. We understand there's no landing field on the island, just chopper pads."

"That's correct, ma'am, which is why you'll be flying there by seaplane. We can not only transport more wounded that way but also fly them out a lot faster." He glanced at his watch. "We need to be in the air as soon as possible to get back for the second group, so if you'll just pile in…"

Haley sought out Corporal Goldman's gaze, hoping he was as satisfied by First Lieutenant Wallace's explanation as she was. She wasn't entirely certain, although he nodded at her with a little smile.

The Jeep tore through a network of less traveled streets, delivering them to some out-of-the-way harbor on Cook Inlet where a sizable two-engine seaplane waited for them. The first lieutenant wasted no time in getting them on board.

There were only a few seats in the passenger portion of the plane. The rest of the space was taken up with stacked racks that Haley assumed held stretchers for the wounded when pulled down. She could see why the plane could transport more patients than choppers could.

They had no glimpse of the pilot up in the cockpit. The sharp-eyed First Lieutenant Wallace spoke to Greg Goldman.

"I'll have to lock up that sidearm you're carrying, Corporal. Standard rule. No firearms in evidence during the flight. You'll get it back after we land."

The corporal handed over his handgun without an argument, but Haley could see he wasn't happy about it. She had a feeling there would be no dimples in evidence this trip.

"Seat belts, folks. We'll be taking off here anytime. I'll be joining the captain up front now."

He left them, and a few minutes later, the engines roared to life. Haley had never flown in a seaplane before. Her best description for the experience was noisy and wet. Noisy when the plane, banging and bumping across the inlet, picked up speed. Wet when what seemed to be tons of water that was kicked up sloshed back over the body of the plane. That all dropped behind them, including Anchorage, when they rose into the air.

Haley's only feeling now that they were underway was a supreme gratitude. Chase was all right, safe and she would soon be with him. She leaned back, living with the happiness of that.

She was so wrapped up in the feeling that it took her a while to be aware of the corporal's return to silence beside her. His moody silence irritated her a bit, spoiling her enjoyment. Then she was sorry. It wasn't as if he were complaining. He was just frowning quietly.

"Does flying bother you, Corporal?"

"No, ma'am, I like flying just fine."

"But something is troubling you again, isn't it?"

"It's just that I'm responsible for you, and I keep thinking…"

"What is it now?"

"I just wish the colonel had asked to speak to me, too."

"He had no reason to."

"Understood, but I know his voice. I hear it often enough to be familiar with it."

"Meaning, I'm not." Micelli's voice *had* sounded deeper than she'd remembered, fainter, but he'd said the method of communication explained that. "Corporal, you're not trying to say it wasn't Colonel Micelli but somebody impersonating him?"

"I wouldn't say that, ma'am, but I wish Second Lieutenant McKinley had been available to speak to you, too."

"Uh-huh," she said drily. "Anything else on your mind, Corporal?"

"It's just…"

"Come on, spill it. I might as well hear it all."

"Well, ma'am, don't you think maybe it's a little funny that the colonel asked you to the island in the first place? You probably don't know, but it isn't like him. He'd consider it inconvenient and inappropriate."

Oh, great. Now he had *her* uneasy. "Corporal, I wish you'd told me all these things before we boarded this plane."

"I didn't think of them at the time, ma'am."

All right, she shouldn't blame him, because they were things they *both* should have been questioning then, not now when they were in the air and probably more than halfway to Moa. She hoped it was Moa they were headed to, anyway.

Like before, she made an effort to assure him that it all must be easily explainable. "You'll see. Everything will turn out the way it's supposed to."

"You're probably right, ma'am."

It seemed she had convinced him of that. The only thing was, she suddenly wasn't sure she'd convinced herself. She found herself sitting there worrying.

Suppose the two men flying this plane *weren't* legitimate. Then who were they, and where were they taking them, if not Moa? And why?

This was ridiculous. She couldn't go on sitting here like this. She needed answers. She had a right to answers.

Unsnapping her seat belt, she got to her feet, alarming Corporal Goldman. "Ma'am, where are you going?"

"Up to the cockpit to find out a few things."

"Ma'am, you can't do that! Second Lieutenant McKinley would skin me if I let you do that!"

"Then come with me."

He did just that and was close on her heels as he followed her up front to the cockpit. But the door was locked. She knocked on it and waited. There was no answer.

"Hey," she called loudly enough that they had to hear her, "open up, will you? I need to speak to you."

Again she got nothing. She raised her fist, prepared to pound on the door this time. The corporal caught her by the wrist.

"Come away, ma'am. It's plain they're not going to open up."

She knew he was right. There was no use standing here. She let him conduct her back to their seats, where they belted themselves in again. There was no verbal speculation from either of them this time.

Haley's concern was now bordering on fear. What was going on? Chase had wanted her protected, fearing if the enemy somehow heard of the army's plan to defend the vault against their attack, they could kidnap her for her knowledge.

But it didn't make sense to snatch her at this late hour. Even if the phone call had been a bogus one and the conflict on Moa wasn't underway yet, everything was already in place there.

She could tell the other side nothing that would be in any way useful to them.

This waiting was absolutely unnerving. She hated it. She and the corporal tried gazing out the window. But there seemed to be nothing below them to see but a blanket of fog.

Eventually, to Haley's relief, the cockpit door opened, and one of the pilots emerged. It was not First Lieutenant Wallace this time. This man was on the bulkier side and dark. Unless there was a third person in the cockpit, this had to be Captain Delgado.

"We're going to be landing in minutes," he told them in a voice Haley could only describe as dark. "Make sure you're belted in. The water can be rough."

She opened her mouth to question him, but he cut her off.

"I don't have anything to tell you. Not now." He was gone then, returning to the cockpit.

The *now* had sounded ominous to her, as if it implied that later she would learn things she wouldn't like.

"This is a little late to be asking it, Corporal, but being in the service yourself, have you happened to see either of those two men in the cockpit before?"

Goldman shook his head. "That doesn't mean anything, though. We don't mix much with the airmen at Elmendorf."

And maybe it did mean something, she thought, deciding she'd been careless and too hasty when she had accepted this invitation. She should have asked some questions first. But all she'd been able to think about was being with Chase, and for that she might end up paying dearly.

Chapter 16

Within minutes, as the pilot had indicated, they started to descend. Haley and the corporal pressed toward the window, anxiously hoping to see open water below. At first, however, all they saw was that same bank of fog. But as the seaplane lost altitude, the fog thinned. That was when Corporal Goldman, the first to spot it, excitedly shared his discovery with her.

"That's land below, ma'am! Not just land, either, but an island! And can you make it out, the front of what has to be the vault? It's Moa, ma'am! It can't be anything else!"

Yes, it was Moa, and Haley went limp with a tremendous thankfulness. Nothing was wrong, as she and the corporal had feared. It was all turning out to be what it was supposed to be. She could even see a crowd of figures down there between the beach and the seed vault. It was possible Chase was among them, and very soon she would be with him.

Haley experienced a surge of joy as the plane banked and circled around for a landing. Joy, yes, but she still meant to get some answers to a few things that puzzled her about this flight. Just now, though, the men at the controls of the plane were bringing it down on a smooth sea where, after plowing through the waters, it rocked to a halt a few hundred feet off the beach.

The soldiers they had discovered below them before were now collected thickly along the shore, staring at the seaplane. Even from here Haley could see expressions of surprise on their faces.

The twin engines of the seaplane were shut down, and in the silence, Captain Delgado and First Lieutenant Wallace exited the cabin. Haley and the corporal took it as a signal to unfasten their seat belts.

"Lieutenant," the captain directed his copilot, "break out the raft, will you?" He unlatched the cabin door and spread it open before turning to his two passengers who were now on their feet.

"Sir," Corporal Goldman addressed the captain, "can I have my sidearm back now, please?"

Delgado ignored his request. "This is where you leave us, Corporal."

"What you mean," Haley said, "is that we *both* part from you here."

"I don't mean that at all. I meant just what I said. The corporal goes, and you remain with us."

The warmth of relief that Haley had experienced a few minutes before sank to a sudden chill. This was not turning out to be a happy ending, after all.

"Sir," the corporal stiffly challenged Delgado, "I've been ordered to stay with Ms. Adams until I'm relieved of that duty."

"Consider it done, then, Corporal."

Lieutenant Wallace returned from the rear of the plane bearing what he'd been asked to get—the raft currently in a flat, folded state. From beneath it, he produced a revolver, turning it over to the captain, who waved it first at Goldman and then in the direction of the open door.

"All right, Corporal, over the side with you."

"You haven't inflated the raft yet," an angry Haley said.

Delgado looked at her coldly. "The raft isn't for him."

"You're going to send him into that water without it? What if he can't swim?"

"Then I'm sure one of those warriors lined up on the beach out there will swim out to save him. Not that it will be necessary. The water doesn't look to be any deeper than his chest. He can wade from here to shore. No more arguments from either one of you now. Corporal, I have a message for you to deliver to Second Lieutenant McKinley. Tell him to wade out here halfway to the plane and no farther. He's to come alone."

Corporal Goldman wasn't to be persuaded by the sight of the gun. He stubbornly stood where he was.

"No heroics, Corporal," Haley insisted. "Remember that girl back home, and do what he says."

Nodding, the young man moved reluctantly to the open door, where he sat down on the floor, legs over the side. He looked back at her, apology on his boyish face.

"I'll be all right," she assured him. She was far from certain of that. Not only was she deeply bewildered, she was scared as hell and longing for Chase as she watched Corporal Goldman slide down into the water and strike out for the beach.

"All right, Lieutenant," the captain commanded him,

"it's clear out there. You can inflate the raft now. And make sure it's tied off tightly. We don't want to drift away."

Chase was with Colonel Micelli in the tent that served as a command post, where he was helping to interrogate those prisoners who'd been in charge of the other mercenaries. He and the colonel were getting very little out of these sorry excuses for officers. They either swore that they didn't have the answers to their questions, things like who had provided the landing crafts and what might have happened to them after they'd unloaded the attackers, or that they had been forbidden to discuss anything connected with Victor Kandinsky.

The session was stalled when they heard the noise of engines overhead. The colonel got to his feet. "That's not a copter coming in. That's a twin-engine plane. What in the—"

Shoving aside the flap in the tent, he shouted for two of his men to guard the prisoners, then signaled Chase to come with him.

The field that fronted the vault, which had been the scene for all of the earlier action, and the beach beyond it, were some distance from the command post. By the time Chase and Micelli reached the site, US soldiers were collected along the shore, watching the unfamiliar seaplane that had landed out in the water.

"What's going on here?" the colonel demanded, pushing through the soldiers with Chase close behind him. "What's that plane doing out there?"

But none of the men had answers for him. By the time they reached the shoreline, a figure from the plane was wading toward them. Chase recognized him almost at once.

"That's Corporal Goldman! What the hell is he doing *here*? He's supposed to be back at the hotel with Haley!" A sick fear gripped his gut. He'd go out of his mind if anything had happened to her.

The corporal, his field uniform soaked, struggled through the last of the shallows to reach them. Chase gave the poor guy no chance to catch his breath before he was on him.

"Haley! Where is she? Why did you leave her behind?"

"Sir, I didn't. I came with her. She's okay. But she's on the plane."

Chase's gaze cut to the plane, where a raft was being inflated just outside the open cabin door. When it was ready, attached to the plane so it couldn't float away, a dark-skinned man in a flight uniform, with bushy hair and eyebrows, lowered himself into it.

"Corporal," the colonel thundered, "you'd better have a damn good explanation for what's going on here!"

Goldman, his sleeve dripping though it was, managed to salute the senior officer. "Sir, I'm sorry, but there is no time for a detailed explanation. The quickest thing I can tell you is that Ms. Adams and I were tricked into coming here. I'm afraid she's being held hostage out there."

Chase fought the wild urge to throw back his head and howl in rage. The corporal had turned to him. "Sir, he ordered me ashore so I could give you his instructions."

"What instructions? Who are these people?"

"There are two of them. Claimed to be air force from Elmendorf. They call themselves First Lieutenant Wallace and Captain Delgado. He's the one on the raft who wants you to wade out halfway to the plane where you can hear each other."

"You don't go out there unarmed, Lieutenant," Micelli insisted.

The corporal was frantic. "Sir, he can't be armed. They'll shoot her if they think they're being threatened."

That was all it took to convince Chase to leave any firearm behind. That and the sight of Haley now on the raft with the character who called himself Delgado, a handgun in her side.

Chase was about to take off into the sea when the corporal stopped him. "Sir, remove your boots and leave them here with us. It doesn't matter that mine are all soaked, but you may need yours dry if there's an opportunity later for you to rescue Ms. Adams."

Chase was not happy about any delay, even a slight one, but he saw the wisdom in the corporal's advice. Sitting down on the shingle, he began to unlace the first of his combat boots. Corporal Goldman crouched down and took charge of the second boot. Within seconds, they had been tugged off. Chase stripped away his socks, stuffed them into the boots and left them in the corporal's care.

Colonel Micelli had an order for him as he rolled up his pant legs. "Now you listen to me, McKinley. I don't want you taking any fool risks out there in some wild effort to snatch your girlfriend. We'll get her back."

"Yes, sir."

Chase sprang to his feet and, without any further hesitation, waded into the water. The seabed wasn't kind to his bare soles, but he ignored that in his need to help Haley. The water grew deeper as he advanced, rising to his thighs, forcing him to battle his way forward toward the plane.

All the time he kept his sights on Haley, trapped there on the raft with a gun on her. He had never felt more desperate or more helpless.

"That's far enough," Delgado called out to him.

"What do you want?" Chase demanded, stopping where he was.

"Why, ransom, of course."

"How much? How much money?"

"Not that, Lieutenant. Something far more precious to the man who sent us here to arrange for it."

Chase saw the look of sudden realization on Haley's face, and even from here, he was able to recognize her awareness of his own realization. Kandinsky. It had to be Kandinsky responsible for this kidnapping.

"Others came here before us to get what's in that vault and then destroy it," Delgado explained, "but they failed to blast it open and make off with its most valuable treasure. You and your soldiers prevented that. We won't fail. Not if you want your lady here back."

Rage went through Chase's veins like a red-hot blast of heat. "If you so much as touch a hair on her head, I swear you won't live."

"You're in no position to threaten, Lieutenant. I suggest you listen to my instructions."

He could tell Haley was silently begging him to obey, not for her own sake as much as his. She was afraid for his safety if his temper got out of control. "All right, I'm listening."

"This is what you have to do. We know Dr. Schneider, one of the keepers of the vault, is there with you on the island. You will convince him to open the vault and take from it three ancient ceramic jars, which he is to give to you. One of them is from the tomb of an Egyptian pharaoh and is filled with grain that grew along the Nile nearly three thousand years ago. The other two came from Mayan tombs and contain corn."

"I'm not sure it's possible to convince Dr. Schneider to hand over something as valuable as that."

"I have every faith in you, Lieutenant, that you can persuade him just how vital it is for him to give you those three jars, especially when the vault itself and all the rest of its contents are safe now."

"It won't be easy, and it may take some time. You'll have to wait for them."

"Oh, we're not going to wait for the jars. As soon as I'm finished here with your instructions, we'll be taking off again. Ms. Adams goes with us. We'll be delivering her to the man who wants those rare seeds."

"No! Let her go! If it's a hostage he wants, he can have me! Someone else can arrange for the jars."

"This isn't discussable, Lieutenant. You get the jars, and you take them yourself alone by boat to the *Sultana*. And as long as the jars and their contents prove to be genuine, Ms. Adams will be returned to you."

"And how the hell am I supposed to manage something like that? I don't even—"

"Don't try to tell me, Lieutenant, that you don't know the *Sultana* is Victor Kandinsky's yacht. We don't have time for games. We know you know this. As capable as you are, you *will* manage it. Get the coast guard to provide you with a small boat and direct you to the spot where the *Sultana* is anchored. It may be in international waters, but I'm sure they can handle it."

"Are you crazy? They won't—"

"Oh, yes, they will when it involves the rescue of an American woman. And with their sophisticated tracking equipment, they *can* direct you, even in fog. Victor is no fool. He understands the coast guard has been monitoring his presence all along. Just as he realizes that as long as he remains in international waters, they can't board the *Sultana*, which is registered in a foreign country where he's now a citizen. No extradition, Lieutenant. But I bet you knew that already, too."

What Chase wouldn't give to wipe the smug expression off that bastard's face. Instead, he had to stand here groin-deep in seawater, helpless to do anything but listen.

"We're through here, Lieutenant. You have the essentials. Be smart and use them."

Chase could do nothing but watch Haley driven back inside the plane by Delgado, who followed her. The raft was raised, deflated and brought inside. By the time the door was closed, the seaplane's engines were rumbling.

He went on watching with clenched fists as the plane swung around, roared across the waters and lifted into the air.

His anguish intensified when moments later it disappeared into the low clouds with Haley aboard it. Only then did he force himself to turn around and make his way as rapidly as possible toward shore.

He had to find Dr. Schneider. He had to get Haley back.

One of the lifeboats from the *Sultana* was sent out to the seaplane to collect her—alone. It was little more than halfway back to the yacht when Haley heard the plane take off again. When she looked back, it was already gone. She doubted very much she would see the men who called themselves Captain Delgado and First Lieutenant Wallace ever again.

What was past didn't matter. What was ahead of her was what she had to worry about. And she saw that when she faced forward once more. The sleek white *Sultana* loomed in front of the lifeboat. Haley had no idea that yachts came in this size. But then when you had the kind of fabulous wealth Victor Kandinsky did, she supposed you could have anything you wanted.

Hand on the railing, Haley began to climb the gangway. No one spoke to her from the top. They didn't have to. She could sense a presence up there. Stopping midway, she looked up to find a lean man with a face like stone watching her.

Haley had no idea what the people of the Maldives, where Kandinsky made his headquarters now, looked like. Or even if the man waiting for her up there on the deck was a native of that island nation. He had dark coloring and wore a simple white-cotton tunic and matching cotton pants.

When she reached the head of the gangway, he stood aside to permit her to step through the open gate of the railing, onto the deck.

"Considering this is hardly the place where you would choose to be," he said in flawless English, "I won't be silly enough to welcome you aboard."

Familiar. The voice was both deep and familiar. She had heard it recently. It wasn't enough, though, to identify it. She needed to hear more. Then, just as if he'd read her mind, he accommodated her.

"Victor is waiting for you, Ms. Adams. This way."

She recognized the voice now. This was the voice over the phone at the hotel that had managed so ably to be Colonel Micelli.

Whoever he was, he led her briskly into the interior of the yacht and along a corridor with gleaming fixtures and paintings on the walls that oddly seemed to depict nothing but platters and bowls heaped with fruits and nuts and vegetables. But maybe that wasn't so odd when you took into account that Victor Kandinsky had a reputation as a serious glutton.

A vessel so large and luxurious would need a commensurate crew, but other than her guide, Haley saw no one in evidence. Were they expected to keep out of the way unless they were needed?

When they reached the end of the corridor, the guide turned to her. "I'll try not to be too familiar with you, but I'll need to pat you down to be certain you're not carrying a weapon. Victor is particular about that."

It wasn't unexpected considering a man with Kandinsky's history and brutal reputation must have left a trail of enemies. To his credit, the guide made quick and impersonal work of running his hands over her. Opening a door behind him, he preceded her into the room, announcing, "She's here, Victor."

Haley was surprised by the high-pitched voice that answered, not at all what she would have expected from one of the world's richest and most powerful mobsters.

"Let her come in, Jamil."

The servant called Jamil, if that's what he was, stepped aside, giving Haley her first view of Kandinsky. The voice might have been surprising. The figure it belonged to wasn't.

It was an enormous body. A pair of beady eyes buried in rolls of fat examined her. Refusing to be intimidated, she stared back at him.

"She clean, Jamil?"

"No weapon of any kind on her."

"You can go, then."

The departing Jamil's choice of conservative clothing was in direct contrast to how his employer dressed—a gaudy, voluminous shirt, flashy rings on his pudgy fingers. Her imagination formed a picture of those fingers running gold coins through them, their owner gloating over his hoard like King Midas. *Or jars of seeds.*

He was still gazing at her from the table behind which he sat, taking her measure. "Sit down," he said, motioning to the plushly upholstered chair across from him.

Haley didn't know whether it was an invitation or a command. She didn't want him to think she was afraid of him, even if she was, so she put on her best poker face, sauntered across the room and lowered herself on the chair. He had a silver bowl of candied fruit in front of him, which he slid across the table to her.

"No, thank you."

He could have been insulted by her refusal or indifferent. There was no expression on his face to indicate which. Dragging the bowl back to his side of the table, he plucked a maraschino cherry from it, popped it into his mouth and chewed with what she presumed was satisfaction.

"What do I refer to him as?" he asked her out of nowhere.

"Who?"

"McKinley. Do I call him your boyfriend? Sweetheart? Lover?"

"You'll have to ask him that."

"Suppose we just say your friend. Not that it matters. Whatever he is, you've both lost me a lot today."

"Yes, I suppose your army must have cost you a great deal to hire. And now they've been defeated and captured."

"It isn't the money. There's always more where that came from. I've always had what it takes to get it."

"And to buy people with it," she said. "Like the mercenaries you sent to Moa."

"Very true. And they were paid very well, only to fail me miserably."

He doesn't care about those mercenaries, Haley

thought. *The only thing callous men like him can feel about the people who serve him is that, loyal or not, they're ultimately expendable.* "Then what have you lost?"

"The victory itself, of course. To have that vault blown apart and the three treasures in it that matter belong to me after the rest is destroyed."

He's not only callous, Haley decided. *He's crazy. How can one man be willing to sacrifice others just for the sake of some seeds?* Josh had been right.

"It looks like you *are* going to get those treasures you want so badly, thanks to your two pilots," she said bitterly. "So you can't say all your mercenaries failed you."

"Yes, *they* were worth what they were paid. As well as the father and his sons who built the landing crafts for me. And they were smart, too—took the money and disappeared."

Haley was suddenly disgusted with the whole thing, this evil man and all he'd arranged to get what he wanted. What more was he capable of? She didn't want to know. All she cared about was leaving his presence.

Permission or not, she got to her feet. "If you don't mind, I'd like to get out of here."

There was malice in his gaze when he looked at her. His response was to lift his head and shout in that high, thin voice. "Jamil!"

The servant must have been waiting just outside for a summons. He came into the salon with a low, "Victor?"

"Our guest doesn't seem to be happy in my company. Take her away and lock her in one of the cabins."

On a yacht as splendid as the *Sultana*, there was bound to be more than one stateroom. This was not one of them. But although what Haley saw when the lock clicked behind her was small and plain, with a tiny adjoining bathroom, it was clean and comfortable, and that was all that mattered to her.

No, that wasn't true. What mattered was Chase. She thought about him when she stood by the cabin's single porthole and looked out on the expansive waters. There wasn't a boat or a scrap of land in sight. It was a lonely scene, made even sadder without Chase's company.

God, she missed him, longed for his touch.

The porthole was large enough for her to climb through, had she wanted to escape. But that would have been pointless with nothing out there but the ocean.

Somewhere across that vast stretch, Chase was working to effect her rescue. It wouldn't be a simple operation. Knowing him as she did, however, he wouldn't give up until it was accomplished. He would arrive here with those three containers of seeds. Not anytime today, though. It was already late, evening really.

She had to keep reminding herself this was mid-June in Alaska, where you couldn't measure the days and nights by the sun. You had to rely on your watch for that.

It would be sometime tomorrow morning before she could expect to see Chase.

Haley went on standing at the porthole, gazing out mindlessly at the sea until the cabin door was unlocked and opened. Jamil stood there in the doorway.

"I hope you didn't think we were going to starve you, Ms. Adams. I've brought you a supper tray."

He motioned behind him, stepping to one side to permit a crewman bearing a tray to enter the cabin. Haley remained at the porthole while the crewman snapped down legs folded into the bottom of the tray and placed it in front of a chair.

"Watching for whales, were you, Ms. Adams?" Jamil wanted to know.

"Maybe."

"They tell me they're out there at this season." The crewman retreated to the door. "Eno here will collect the tray when he brings you breakfast in the morning."

The cabin door was shut and locked again. *They know I can't run away*, Haley thought. *Locking me in is just Victor's method of humiliating me.*

She wasn't too proud to eat his food, though. She hadn't eaten a thing since lunch hours ago, and that was very little. Her concern about what was happening at the time on Moa had diminished her appetite. But now she was hungry.

She sat down at the tray and began to investigate the dishes they had brought her from the galley. The steaming food smelled wonderful. Trust Victor Kandinsky to have the best chef available to him.

She kept thinking about Chase as she ate.

Chapter 17

The coast guard had loaned Chase a small outboard speedboat from its store on the patrol vessel that had carried him early this morning from Moa to this position, then set him on a straight course for the *Sultana*. He would have covered half the distance when he could still make out the coast guard vessel behind him and the *Sultana* dead ahead.

After that midpoint, he would lose all sight of the coast guard ship. The positions were deliberately arranged this way, because the guard knew that if its vessel approached the *Sultana*, it could make Victor Kandinsky nervous. And Victor Kandinsky in a nervous state was known to be unpredictable, even though he was aware the coast guard could not legally board him in these neutral waters.

Chase was not to worry. The coast guard ship would remain at anchor right where they were and watch for his return. He was to stay in touch with them by the radio phone stowed in the speedboat. This way the patrol vessel could direct him safely back if it became necessary.

And Haley will be with me, he promised himself.

The *Sultana* loomed in front of him. Chase could see several expectant figures at the deck railing waiting for him. There was no sign of weapons, but he knew they would be ready for him if any trouble occurred. For Haley's safety, he would be careful to see it didn't.

He cut the engine, letting the speedboat coast into a hanging stairway pinned to the side of the yacht. Tying the speedboat off at the handrail, he picked up a basket, the contents covered with a cloth, and hooked it over his arm.

How quaint, Chase thought wryly, taking a deep breath as he began to climb the stairs. Just like taking goodies to Grandma's house.

The wolf was waiting for him at the top of the stairway, a tall, lean man with dark skin and a sedate voice. "The load looks heavy, Mr. McKinley. Or is it Lieutenant?"

"Either works."

"Would you like me to take it?"

Chase held the basket out of the way. "I'll deliver it personally to Grandma if you don't mind."

The guy plainly had no acquaintance with fairy tales. His brow furrowed in puzzlement. "I beg your pardon?"

"Never mind. Suppose you just take me to the man who ordered these jars and then give me what he's trading them for."

"Victor has also ordered that guests he doesn't know get searched before he sees them."

Figures that someone as rotten as he is would be nervous about concealed weapons. "Frisk away," Chase said.

The guy was obviously used to this routine. He made quick work of patting him down.

"I'm afraid I'll have to look inside the basket, too."

Chase was too eager to see Haley, too anxious to make sure she was all right, to argue about it. He lifted aside the cover, but he hung on to the basket. "Okay, take a look—uh—"

"Jamil. The name is Jamil."

Jamil looked.

"Satisfied?"

"For now. There will have to be a careful examination before Ms. Adams is released to you."

"And in the meantime?"

"I'll take you to Victor. He's waiting for you in the main lounge."

The only thing Chase was impressed by when he met Victor Kandinsky was his size. He wouldn't try to guess the man's weight, but it had to be considerable. Everything else about Kandinsky, especially his history, disgusted him, even his voice like the squeak of a mouse.

Chase removed the three jars from the basket and placed them on the table. Kandinsky's small eyes gleamed at the sight of them. Chase had to admit that the ancient containers alone were ceramic works of art. The two squat, wide-waisted Mayan ones, although not elaborately decorated, were graceful in form. The Egyptian jar was exceptional in both form and rich decoration, worthy of a pharaoh's royal burial.

Victor's stubby fingers removed the lids and peered into all three, nodding at their contents.

"You've got what you demanded," Chase said. "When do I get my girl back?"

"When the seeds themselves have been verified as still viable and of the right period."

Chase could understand the importance of the seed vault itself. In a time of widespread plant failure, its contents could renew crops to feed whole populations. But to go to the lengths Kandinsky had to acquire the contents of those jars was not just criminal. It was insane.

"And who takes care of that job?" Chase wanted to know.

"My valuable friend here, Jamil. Jamil is an agronomist with a special knowledge of seeds. With a few tests, he'll know whether these seeds are what they've been claimed to be."

"How long will that take?"

"An hour or so, maybe a bit more. While you're waiting, I'll have one of the crew take you to Ms. Adams's cabin." He picked up a phone and stabbed a button that apparently connected him to another part of the yacht. "Eno, I need you in the main lounge. No, not when you can get here. Now."

Chase made a silent wish as Victor replaced the phone. *Not too fast, Eno. Take your time.* This was the opportunity he'd been hoping for and was afraid he might not get. Kandinsky probably wouldn't like his asking, maybe would refuse to discuss it, but Chase was willing to risk that.

"Mind if I ask a question while we're waiting?"

Was he mistaken, or was that a suspicious gleam in those piggy eyes that looked back at him? Kandinsky was the sort who'd suspect just about everything and everyone, and be ready to strike if he didn't like it. "I'll hear it. That's all I'll guarantee."

"Thing is, I have this brother. A half brother really, which is why his name is Matthews. Josh Matthews."

"What about him?"

"Well, I seem to have misplaced him."

"Careless of you, I'd say."

"I've been looking for him here in Alaska, and I was just wondering…"

"Yeah?"

"If you had any idea where he could be."

Victor laughed, an ugly laugh. "Now why would I know where this brother of yours is when I've never heard of him?"

"I just guessed you might since I understood he was doing a story about you."

"Flattering, but I can't help you."

"Maybe not you personally, but you have a lot of people out there working for you, and maybe one of them…"

"Can help you? I wouldn't count on it. They know I don't like people talking or writing about me."

Was it his imagination, Chase wondered, or had he glimpsed Victor and Jamil exchange a fast, understanding glance? Something that had a nasty quality to it.

Victor knows about Josh all right. Whatever happened to his brother was ordered by this man. But Chase couldn't try pressuring him any further. It could endanger his getting Haley back, and that was all-important. He had no choice but to let the question of Josh go for now, frustrated though that made him.

A young crewman with a picture gallery of tattoos covering his arms entered the lounge, nodding at Chase by way of introduction.

"This is Eno," Victor said. "Eno, take the soldier here to Ms. Adams's cabin and lock him in. He shouldn't mind that. When you're finished later with cleaning and loading the guns, go back to the cabin and take our friends out on deck. No, Lieutenant, we're not planning to use you for target practice. We just believe in being prepared. Learned that way back on the streets of Detroit."

He cackled with laughter, as if he'd created a fine joke, then swung his attention back to Eno. "They can walk the decks. Ms. Adams ought to appreciate that after being locked away since yesterday. Just make sure they stay on the decks and that you stick with them."

The crewman saluted Victor as if he were addressing his captain. Well, maybe Victor *was* the acting captain on the *Sultana.*

Eno silently conducted Chase to the deck below and along a corridor. Stopping at the end, he fished a key out of his pocket and unlocked the door. There had never been a more beautiful sight than the one Chase saw when he entered the cabin behind that door.

Haley stood half-turned looking out the single porthole, her profile bathed in morning light, ivory skin seeming to glow from within, mouth parted.

She must have sensed him behind her. Her blue eyes widened when she wheeled around. For a moment they just stood there, gazing at each other. Then she was across the cabin and in his arms. He couldn't get enough of her, the soft, womanly feel of her body crushed against his, his mouth devouring hers.

Chase hadn't known it was possible to miss someone so much, to understand she was everything to you. Was this reunion as emotional for Haley? Was that why he felt a dampness on her cheeks?

He held her away just far enough to look down into her face. "Are those tears?"

"Don't tease me. I can't help it. It was hell being without you."

"Come here." He caught her by the hand and led her over to the bunk, where they seated themselves side by side.

They were alone in the cabin. Chase was just now aware that at some point, Eno had withdrawn and re-locked the door.

He had a furious longing to lay Haley down on this bunk, tear off her clothes and bury himself deep inside her. He would have done just that, too, if there wasn't the risk of Eno returning at any time. Instead, he had to settle for a few more wet kisses.

"Better than tears, huh?"

God, he couldn't wait to get them back to Anchorage and the uninterrupted privacy of their suite. Apparently Haley was thinking along those same lines.

"When are they going to release us?"

"It could take a while. It seems that Victor won't be satisfied until the seeds are authenticated by his expert in residence. That would be Jamil."

"I feel so guilty about this whole thing," Haley said.

"Why? It wasn't you who demanded that ransom."

"I wish I'd had the choice. I would have made it money, not something beyond price that belongs to the whole world, instead of one grasping SOB who thinks he's entitled to what should be in a museum."

"Maybe they will wind up in a museum one day."

"Oh, come on. Can you see Victor Kandinsky will-ing these treasures to a museum?"

"No, but I can see Dr. Hansen donating them. The seeds and the jars belonged to her, Haley. She had them in the vault for safekeeping until she could decide whether they should be kept there or publicly displayed in a secure facility. But when Dr. Schneider contacted her from Moa, she didn't hesitate to agree they should be used to free you."

"Now they're lost to both Dr. Hansen and the pub-lic. And all because of one miserable excuse for a man who's probably committed every crime there is and can't be touched."

"Not necessarily."

"What does that mean?"

"That I've been thinking ever since we heard about Kandinsky," Chase said slowly, "that if anyone deserves to be caught and punished, he does. And I think I know how to make that happen."

"All right. How?"

"This is a big yacht. It's bound to have two engines, and that means two propellers. It has to have that much force to drive it. If one of those props is disabled, just one, the *Sultana* will have no choice but to limp into the nearest port for repair, and that means Kandinsky is no longer in international waters."

"He's vulnerable. He can be seized by the authorities," Haley murmured.

"Right."

"But, Chase, how can you possibly get down into the engine room to cripple the boat?"

"I don't have to. All I need is a few minutes on deck. A simple little business I learned when I was in the rangers. It's not a guarantee, but when it works, it's an effective form of sabotage."

"A few minutes on deck? That's as bad as the possibility of sneaking into the engine room."

"Not so. As soon as Eno finishes the job he's working on, he's been instructed to take us strolling up on deck. The beauty of that is it was Victor's magnanimous idea." Chase chuckled over the irony of Kandinsky contributing to his own downfall.

"This piece of sabotage..."

"I don't have time to explain it, sweetheart, except to say there is a problem with it. I have the impression

Eno isn't the sharpest knife in the drawer, but he's not a fool, either. He's got to be distracted somehow for that minute or two I'll need. I don't suppose you have any ideas about that?"

Haley smiled. "As a matter of fact, I think I do. Something believable that Eno overheard when Jamil and I talked about it in here yesterday. Give me some sign when you need it, and I'll do my best to make it work."

They had discussed the essentials. There was no need for any further conversation. Until Eno arrived, they were content to sit there quietly on the edge of the bunk, holding hands like a pair of teenagers. The deckhand seemed pleased to find them being romantic like this.

"We can go out on deck now," he said shyly.

"That would be a treat," Haley said. "I've been hoping to see a whale from the porthole here, but so far, I haven't spotted any."

"Maybe you'll have better luck on deck," Chase encouraged her.

Smiling and nodding, Eno led them into the open, where there was a bracing wind. Looking eager, Haley went to the rail, where she scanned the open ocean, hair blowing in the wind. When she didn't find any sign of what she wanted, she moved on without delay, as if afraid she might miss the sight.

Chase deliberately trailed behind, searching more carefully for the elusive whale that neither he nor Haley cared about. Poor Eno didn't know which one of them to stick with.

"Eno," Haley called back to him, "I need a pair of extra eyes up here."

The deckhand hurried to catch up with her, leaving Chase standing at the bow. It was just where he wanted to be. Leaning on the rail, he looked down over the side of the yacht.

It took some straining before he located it, but there it was, nearly out of sight below the inward curve of the prow. The circular opening behind which one of the nylon lines used only in port to moor the yacht was coiled on its drum.

Fearing Eno might be suspiciously checking on him, he stood erect and looked casually in Eno and Haley's direction. The deckhand wasn't watching him. Nor was any other member of the crew around, but Chase was able to catch Haley's gaze. He grinned and waved casually. She understood it as her signal and went into action.

Racing around Eno, she flew along the deck, squealing in excitement. "It's a whale surfacing out there! Can you see it? Maybe we'll be lucky enough to see it blow a spout!"

Eno didn't hesitate to follow her. By the time they stopped, Chase knew he was out of sight. It cost him a full minute to find what he needed hiding under the lip at the top of the gunwale—the lever that released the brake on the winch. Although a bit stiff, he was able to slide it forward by exerting some muscle.

The automatic winch began to roll, dropping the line out of its dark cavity. It uncurled rapidly, descending into the sea, most of its length disappearing beneath the murky waters. Unless you had a reason to look for it—not likely when anchored out in the middle of the ocean like this—you wouldn't see this mooring line trailing beneath the thrust of the prow and under the surface.

It might all depend on chance after this, but Chase was satisfied he had accomplished what he could when he got to his feet. Dusting off his hands, he joined Haley and Eno. If the deckhand had missed him, he didn't indicate it.

"Any luck, you two?" he asked them cheerfully.

Haley shook her head in disappointment. "No, I thought I had a surfacing whale, but I was wrong."

"Me, too."

Jamil found the three of them standing there when he appeared behind them ten minutes or so later.

"You look glum, even our young Eno here. But I have news that should please you. I have verified the authenticity of the seeds. You are free to go."

Chase waited until the speedboat had sped them back to the coast guard ship to explain to both its captain and Haley what he had done to injure the *Sultana*.

"So," Chase continued, about to reveal the purpose of dropping the tie line overboard, "unless someone on the yacht spots that line in the water, and I pray they don't, then there's every reason—"

"I think I get it," the captain interrupted him.

Chase wasn't surprised. With his lengthy nautical experience, the captain would have heard of this kind of thing occurring before, either intentionally or by accident. But Haley remained puzzled.

"Well, I don't. Will one of you please explain it to me?"

"If that line isn't disturbed in the water," Chase said, "then this is what's bound to happen when the yacht fires up its twin engines and starts to head out. The line will get sucked back under the bottom of the hull by the draw of the propellers, and when it meets the blades of the first prop—"

It was Haley who cut in this time. "I do understand! The line will wind around that propeller and keep on winding until it runs out its entire length! It will be so tangled in the blades, it will choke off the power."

Chase nodded. "The engine will seize up and quit. Before it can run again, the line will have to be cut piece by piece off the blades. That would require the kind of diving equipment the *Sultana* isn't at all likely to be carrying. Either that, or she'll have to go into dry dock."

"And with only one engine still operating," the captain said, "a vessel that size is like a man with one of his legs not working."

"That's what you meant," Haley said, "by disabling the *Sultana* so that she'd have to limp into port somewhere for repair. She'd have no choice about leaving international waters."

"She'd certainly never make it all the way home on one engine," Chase said.

"Which means," the captain added, "that Victor Kandinsky and any of his gang on board are subject to arrest and prosecution. I'm going to radio every one of our coast guard ships and planes that patrol the Alaskan coast to be watching for that yacht. We'll get her as soon as she ducks into what she thinks is a safe port. Meanwhile, I've got a helicopter on the way to take you two back to Anchorage. We'll keep you posted at your hotel of any developments."

Haley and Chase barely got inside their Kodiak suite before their arms were wrapped around each other while they kissed fiercely and at the same time clawed at each other's clothes.

You'd think we'd never made love before, she thought.

Actually, that's what it did feel like. A man and a woman coming together for the first time. Not because she and Chase had been separated for any real length of time, but because they'd been so deeply worried about each other, and their passion and urgency reflected that.

Why, she asked herself afterward as she nestled against his naked warmth, *did it take me so long to admit to myself how much I love this man?*

She decided it had to be because she feared being hurt, feared he was incapable of loving her back. But it was time to pump up her courage and risk that.

"Chase, about us…"

"I know about us," he said without hesitation. "I've known about us since before Moa, but I wanted to wait until after that business was settled before I told you."

She propped herself up on one elbow and gazed down at him. "Tell me what?"

"Haley, I'm in love with you."

"I've been waiting to hear that. I've been waiting a long time to hear it." And lest he have any doubt about her own feelings, she bent down and kissed him tenderly.

"There's just one thing."

"Must there be?" she asked.

"I'm afraid so."

She knew what was coming. "It's about Josh, isn't it? Josh and me."

"I have to know how you feel about him. I have to be sure that—"

She placed her hand over his mouth. "Don't say it, because it doesn't exist. It never existed. I enjoyed his company when we dated, but it was never at any time a serious relationship."

"That was how you felt, but I can't not worry about how he felt. About how he might still feel. Haley, I don't want to hurt him because of us. And I still need to find him."

She couldn't stand this. He talked as though Josh

was still out there somewhere. She'd been so convinced that, after Moa had been fought and won and there was still no word or sign of Josh, he would accept at last his brother was gone.

She was so frustrated she wanted to scream at him, "He's dead! There is no other explanation that makes sense! Why can't you realize that? Why can't you stop tormenting both of us by hanging on to something that's no longer possible?"

But she couldn't bring herself to put any of it into words. Confessing her inability to believe that Josh still existed somewhere would only wound Chase deeply, and she couldn't do that to the man she loved with all her heart.

He must have sensed she was upset. That's why he drew her down and laid his cheek against hers. "We won't talk about it anymore, sweetheart. It can wait for another time. There's too much loving for us to do to spoil it."

That was all she both wanted and needed to hear.

They were about to go down for dinner that evening when the phone in their sitting room rang. Chase answered it, and when he heard who was calling, he motioned for Haley to get on the extension in her bedroom.

"I've got some great news," the caller said, "and you're going to love it."

Chase interrupted him. "Excuse me, sir. Haley is on the extension, but she would have picked up a few seconds too late to hear you identify yourself."

"Sorry about that. Ms. Adams, this is Colonel Micelli. You'll want to be in on this since it involves both of you. The captain of the coast guard ship that helped us out contacted me less than half an hour ago. He felt that since I was Second Lieutenant McKinley's commanding officer for the Moa operation, I should be the one to communicate the results to you."

Haley's immediate thought was that Chase's sabotage had worked. Victor Kandinsky was caught in his trap.

The colonel's explanation that followed proved she was right.

"What you did, Lieutenant, was an inspiration. It apparently took no time for that engine to freeze up and quit. The yacht thought they had a safe little harbor, with a small boat repair on a remote piece of the coast, that they could duck into without anyone in authority knowing they were there. They were wrong. The coast guard tracked them into that hole in no time at all."

"Kandinsky?" Chase wanted to know.

"Captured, along with everyone else on board who was in his gang. Now that they have King Kandinsky himself, I understand they'll soon be rounding up his operatives elsewhere."

Haley could imagine Victor's apoplectic fury when, in spite of his years of cunning evasion and all his money, he had been cornered. Once convicted and locked up, he would no longer enjoy the power and diet he relished.

"Here's a piece of news especially for you, Ms. Adams, that I think will please you. Your ransom was recovered from the *Sultana* and will be returned to Dr. Hansen at the first opportunity."

The colonel was right. It did please her, and it reminded her of a promise to herself. Tomorrow Haley would phone the seed vault headquarters and thank the director for her sacrifice on her behalf.

It's over, finished, Haley thought with a sweet relief

when the call ended. *We can't do any more here. We need to go home.*

But what were her chances of convincing Chase of that?

Chapter 18

"Chase, it's time to go back, don't you think?"

"Not yet, sweetheart."

They both knew why. He wasn't ready to give up his search for Josh, fruitless though it had been. She felt they must have exhausted every possible lead.

This time his voice turned reluctant when he said, "I guess you could go back to Portland ahead of me if you needed to, but I'd be sad as hell to lose you."

"Then don't," she wanted to say. "Go with me." Pointless. Instead, what she told him was, "Right now where I need to go is for a walk."

It was the truth. She and Chase were in conflict. She feared that if she stayed in the suite, they would end up arguing, and she was in no mood for that. She had to be alone for a while. Had some serious thinking to do.

"I thought you meant to work on one of your work projects."

"Maybe this afternoon. I could use this walk while you make your calls. There's no reason anymore for me not to be out there alone."

He hesitated briefly before agreeing. "No, I suppose there's no risk. But, hey, make sure your cell phone is on, huh?"

They parted after leaving the dining room, Chase heading back to their sitting room and the phone, and Haley exiting the rear of the hotel. She wanted this walk to be along the waterfront, but there was a question about that.

Which way? she asked herself when she reached the walkway below the terrace. She had already traveled on foot a couple of times to the left and was familiar with that direction, but neither she nor Chase had ever ventured to the right. That made her choice an easy one. New territory.

It occurred to her as she headed to the right along the harbor that she had another choice facing her here. One that was in no way easy.

If there was going to be any future for Chase and her, he would have to let this obsession with Josh go. Because that's just what it was. Nearly his whole life he'd been protecting and caring for his little brother. A brother who very likely no longer existed.

She would either have to confront Chase with all of this and demand he drop the load he'd been carrying for far too long, or stay with him without further opposition and be haunted always by the ghost of his half brother. That was the tough choice Haley had to make.

The walkway along the harbor was an elevated one, with steps at intervals descending to piers where boats of different kinds and dimensions were tethered. She didn't remember having seen any houseboats in the other direction, but there seemed to be a fair number of them moored here. They made for interesting viewing. No two were alike in size, color or design.

There was one in particular that Haley found appealing, probably because of the unique designs stenciled on its walls. She had never seen a motif like that before.

She was about to move on when her attention was captured by two figures who emerged from the interior of the houseboat. One of them was a slim young woman with an attractive face and the dark skin of a Native American. The other was an elderly man, a bit stooped, with a slow, shuffling gait.

He clearly had difficulty walking. The woman patiently helped him cross the open deck to a deck chair, which he sank into with apparent relief. It was when his caregiver bent over him with some murmured concern, and he lifted his face to her, that Haley realized this wasn't an old man at all.

His face was young, although battered, which possibly explained his shuffle. He had been injured somehow. Just her imagination, Haley wondered, or was that face familiar? Hard to tell with the healing wounds on it, but there was something...

Being one of life's totally unexpected revelations as it was, it came to her with a shock of sudden recognition. Dear God, it was him! Actually *him*! All the time he had been right here under their noses, and they had never known it!

The two people on the houseboat below Haley were too involved in each other to realize she was there. The presence of strangers passing on the walkway would be a common occurrence, probably. Nor did they pay any attention when she backed away, turned around and made her escape.

It was imperative that she get back to the hotel.

She alternately ran and speed-walked the distance, her mind churning out a dozen how and why and who questions. Not a one of them could be answered. That would have to wait for explanations.

There was only one certainty. Chase had been right, and she had been wrong.

He was just hanging up the phone when she burst into the sitting room.

"Arnie," he said. "My bail bond boss. He's in a stew because his other bounty hunters can't seem to locate missing jumpers. He wants to know when I'm coming back. He thinks I'm the only one who has a real talent for tracking them down. Can you beat the irony of that? I can find strangers, but I can't find my own brother."

Chase stopped there. He must have finally gotten a good look at her face. He came slowly to his feet.

"What is it, Haley? What's wrong? Are you all right?"

She waved her hand while he waited impatiently for her to recover her breath.

"Tell me!"

"You've got your miracle, Chase."

He stared at her for a long moment, somehow understanding her, first in disbelief and then in a joyous acceptance. "Josh! Are you actually saying—"

"Yes, it's Josh."

Chase followed her out of the hotel and down to the harbor walkway. By the time they were halfway to their destination, he was in the lead and she was struggling to keep up with him. When they reached the houseboat, Chase didn't hesitate to board it.

Josh and his friend were still on the deck. Startled by Chase's arrival, the woman came sharply to her feet from her own chair. Standing protectively in front of Josh's deck chair, she barred the way.

"Would you move out of the way so he can see me?" Chase asked her. "Please."

She didn't budge. "What are you doing here?" she challenged them. "This is a private houseboat. You have no right to be here."

"I'm sorry I didn't ask permission first to come on board. I was too excited to wait. I promise you it's all right, though. If you'll just let him see me, he'll tell you that himself."

"Who are you, anyway? Why should I trust you?"

"I'm Josh's half brother, Chase McKinley."

When she glanced at Haley, who had followed him on board, Haley murmured, "Haley Adams, a concerned friend."

The woman was hesitant, undecided, but in the end, she did move just enough out of the way to let Chase through. Haley saw the shock that registered on his face when, up close like this, he was able to get a look at Josh's face with its bruises and healing cuts.

Hunkering down beside the deck chair, he made his earnest appeal. "Josh, it's me. Don't you recognize me?"

Frowning, Josh searched his brother's face. *Did whatever happened to him injure his mind as well as his body?* Haley asked herself. *Is that why he hasn't spoken yet, hasn't even reacted to any of this?*

"Give him a minute," the woman defended him. "It's hard sometimes for him to remember."

Chase did wait, as patiently as a man of his character could wait, but Haley could see this whole thing was hurting him.

In the end, however, when Josh finally did utter a

slow but still puzzled, "Chase? Is it really you?" it was a relief to both Haley and Chase.

"Yes, buddy, it's me. We've been looking everywhere for you." He clasped his brother's hand, and even from here, Haley was ready to swear there were tears in the eyes of both men.

"Don't try to hug him," his protector warned Chase. "His ribs are still sore."

Josh has recognized Chase, Haley thought, but she could tell by the confusion in his look when he glanced in her direction that he didn't know who she was yet.

She and Josh had both changed. She'd known another man back in Portland. She just hoped Josh had weathered his changes okay.

Chase noticed the changes, too, and remarked on one of them. "Kid, you could use some color. You're too pale."

It was the woman who once again came to his defense. "This is the first time in days he's been outside. I thought we could risk it because he needed the sun, and then when you showed up like that out of nowhere—"

"I promise you he's safe now from what I think you must have been worried about. I'll explain why later, but shouldn't he be in the hospital?"

"He refused to go. But he's had a doctor's regular care. She stops by periodically to check on him."

Chase gazed at her in gratitude. "We owe you our thanks. It's obvious you've been caring for him, Ms.…"

"Beth Ann Raven. Raven is the English translation for the Aleut name of the bird."

Meaning she's an Aleut Indian, Haley thought.

Chase spoke to Beth Ann, but it was a silent Josh he looked at in concern. "But what happened? How did he get this way?"

"I knew that one day someone would come and find him, that I could no longer hide him and that I'd have to reveal how he came to be with me. But you can't go on squatting there like that listening to me. You'll get cramps in your legs. Both of you, help yourselves to a couple of chairs."

She indicated deck chairs stacked against the wall of the houseboat. Chase secured two of them and opened them. When all of them were seated, Beth Ann told her story.

"I've lived on this boat for years, and I work from here. What happened was late at night a few weeks ago. I was already in bed with the lights out when I heard this loud splash outside off the pier here. At first I didn't think it could be anything to worry about, probably because I was just too sleepy to go look. But then I thought, well, maybe I'd better check it out."

She looked over at Josh, making sure he was all right before she went on.

"So I turned on the lights, got into slippers and a robe, took a flashlight with me and went out on deck. I searched with the flashlight on the water, but it was a minute or so before I saw him out there. Like someone had dumped a large sack of trash off the walkway. It took me a few seconds to realize it was a floating body."

Haley shuddered over the image of Josh being flung into the harbor.

"It was a miracle he hadn't sunk," Chase said, the anger hard in his voice.

"The real miracle was that I was able to rescue him, because to begin with, I figured this was a dead body. But I couldn't be sure of that, which is why I got the pole. I'm pretty strong, but Josh is no lightweight, and with his clothes soaked through…"

Haley had nothing but admiration for this woman for the strength and courage she had to save Josh and take him into her home. Maybe it came from her heritage as an Aleut. Most women would have been too afraid to do anything but phone the police. Beth Ann continued while Josh sat there quietly, contributing nothing.

"The second miracle came when I checked him and found he was still breathing. He couldn't have inhaled much water, if any, or he would have drowned. The way I figured it, he must have been robbed and severely beaten when he tried to fight back, and whoever did it thought he was dead when they tossed him in the harbor. What actually had to have happened was that he'd lost consciousness, and the cold water revived him enough for him to hold his head above the water instinctively."

"But he doesn't remember any of this?" Chase asked her.

"Not clearly, no. Anyway, I learned he couldn't have been robbed. That was when I got blankets to cover him, which meant getting him out of his wet things and finding his wallet still with him. Everything soaked clean through but all there—money, credit cards, driver's license, even the watch on his wrist. It was all a mystery."

Not a mystery, Haley determined. It had to have been the work of Victor Kandinsky, who'd learned Josh was getting too close to his secrets and ordered the attack on him.

Beth Ann gazed at Josh again to be certain he was still okay before she went on. "I couldn't have gotten him inside and on one of the bunks if he hadn't stirred. With me supporting him, he was able to limp that far before he collapsed. I could see he'd been so badly worked over that he needed to be in a hospital. But he got very agitated when I told him I was going to phone for an ambulance. He begged me not to call anyone, said that no one could know he was here. I know I shouldn't have listened to him, but I was afraid I'd make him worse if I didn't promise him."

"I don't blame you," Haley said. "I would have done the same."

Chase wanted to be sure of something. "But you did say Josh has regular medical treatment, didn't you?"

"I did. I have a friend who's interning at one of the hospitals. I asked her to come over without telling her why. Dirty trick, but I was afraid she'd refuse if I explained the situation on the phone. When she saw Josh, the first thing she said was I should call an ambulance, that he needed a hospital. She argued she'd get in trouble if she treated him here in the houseboat, and if anyone found out she didn't report the attack, she could be denied her right to practice."

"And in the end?" Chase asked.

"I promised after pleading with her that I'd somehow make it up to her. She wound up cleaning and bandaging his wounds while grumbling he ought to be x-rayed. She gave me painkillers for him and refused to make an opinion on his recovery. But she's stopped by regularly since to check on his progress. I know he must look to you like he can't have made any, but you didn't see him that night and the first days afterward."

Josh finally spoke. "Guess I've been a pain in the ass. Just like I was when I was a kid. Remember those times, Chase?"

"I remember, but that's all in the past. And so is what happened to you out there that awful night. You're safe now, Josh. Kandinsky and his gang can't come after you anymore."

Beth Ann must have sensed that Chase was about to relate his own story of what had been happening, Haley thought. Just as her sharp eye, ever mindful of her patient, noticed he was starting to droop in his deck chair. She came abruptly to her feet.

"I know you must have a lot to tell him, but would you mind if I ask you to save it for…say, tomorrow? He's beginning to look tired. I need to get him back in his bunk."

Chase didn't hesitate to agree. He helped her to get Josh back into bed, and after promising they wouldn't return too soon in the morning, he and Haley left.

It was on their way back to the hotel that Chase asked her, "What do you think? Should we try to get Josh into a hospital now that he no longer needs to hide out?"

Haley's answer was immediate. "No. Leave him just where he is. He couldn't get any better or more attentive care than he's getting on that houseboat."

They were bearing Josh's notebook and his luggage when they returned to the houseboat the next morning. Josh and Beth Ann were once again settled on the deck in their chairs, Beth Ann working on a piece of embroidery in her lap and Josh peacefully idle.

Chase immediately wanted to know, "How is he this morning?"

"He had a good night, and he's alert. What's that you've brought with you?"

Chase held up one of the two suitcases. "Josh left this stuff behind in the rooming house where he was staying. It's packed with all of his clothes. We figured they'd be wanted."

"For sure. All he had was the outfit he was wearing when he was heaved into the harbor. I had to use some of the funds in his wallet to buy new essentials, so these additions are very welcome."

Chase indicated the blue journal. "You remember this, Josh?"

He looked a bit unsure at first and then nodded.

Chase placed the journal in his lap. "I thought maybe when you were up to it you'd like to work on it again."

"Yes, maybe."

Haley didn't think he sounded at all enthusiastic about the idea. Since Chase clearly wanted to remain at his brother's side, Haley volunteered to move the luggage out of the way.

"If you'll tell me where you'd like the cases, Beth Ann, I'll be happy to place them there for you."

"Here, I'll show you." Rising from her chair, she seized the bigger of the two suitcases and led the way into the houseboat. "We'll just shove them into this cabin here. I'll unpack them later and store the cases under the bunk. As you can see, the space on a houseboat has to be rationed."

Cramped or not, Haley thought it was charmingly decorated and told Beth Ann so.

"I made coffee. Would you and Chase like some?"

"I doubt Chase would. He's much too involved with Josh, but I'd love a mug."

Haley could see she was right about Chase when she and Beth Ann returned to the deck with their steaming mugs and settled into the same chairs they had occupied yesterday. Chase had already launched into the full account of how he and Haley had turned up in Alaska in search of Josh, starting with the early events in Portland.

When he gets to it finally, she thought, *and that's not*

going to be anytime soon, he's going to give his brother the last chapter on Victor Kandinsky and why he's no longer a threat. And Josh? Well, it wasn't evident to Chase, but Haley was aware Josh wasn't focused on any of this, that Kandinsky had ceased to matter to him. The man had left his mark.

She hadn't the heart, though, to suggest this to Chase. He was too happy telling his story, and she suspected Josh didn't mind listening to it.

Forgetting about the two men, Haley became fascinated with the needlework Beth Ann was industriously laboring over. "Those are beautiful designs. What's the piece going to be?"

Beth Ann held it up. "It's a wall hanging. The designs I'm embroidering on it are traditional Aleutian ones my people used to decorate their clothing. The needles were made from seagull bones."

"Is it going on one of your walls when it's finished?"

Beth Ann laughed. "There are already enough of them up there. This is going into one of the Anchorage shops. They're popular with the tourists. The shops will take as many as I can give them, along with my wood carvings and jewelry from the jade that's Alaska's state gem. All of it is how I make my living."

"With that kind of talent I can't see you starving."

"I do all right."

It was back at the hotel that Haley noticed how quiet Chase was. "Is something bothering you?"

"I'm not sure."

"Do I get to hear?"

"If he's up to it, I need to speak privately to Josh tomorrow."

"About?"

"A couple of things, but specifically you. I have to learn just how much he still cares for you. It *matters*."

She stared at him. "I don't know whether to laugh or weep over your ignorance."

"What's that supposed to mean?"

"It means, dear heart, that you are both ignorant and blind. Josh scarcely looked at me or spoke to me either yesterday or today. All of his glances were for Beth Ann, and hers were for him."

"Are you saying—?"

"That they're in love with each other, yes."

"How can that be when they've known each other only a matter of days?"

"Weeks, days, hours. It happens."

Chase seemed dazed over the possibility. *Maybe he'll wake up to the reality of it*, she thought, *and the realization that it happened to us.* In the meantime…

"We owe Sergeant Blackfeather a call. He deserves to hear Josh has been found alive and safe. It's all right to let him know. I had a moment to ask Beth Ann, and since Josh is no longer in danger, she gave her permission."

"I won't go with you today," Haley told Chase the next morning.

He looked at her in concern. "Is something wrong?"

"Nothing is wrong. I just think you prefer to have Josh to yourself, and that's perfectly understandable. Also, if I go along on a third visit, Beth Ann is going to feel that she has to entertain me again. But I imagine this way, with you watching over Josh, she can be free to work on the crafts she makes, the work she does."

What Haley told him was all true, but she omitted her most important reason for staying behind. She had a serious decision to make, and she wasn't ready to share it.

"What'll you do on your own?"

"It's another great weather day. I'll probably take a long walk, and if there's any time afterward, I may get in some licks on the laptop."

When Chase left, she exited the hotel by the front entrance and wandered down one street after another with no destination in mind.

I probably should have told him what I've been thinking, Haley told herself. *That would have been the fair thing to do. But I need to prepare myself. I need to know what to say to him if he wants to stay on here in Anchorage for a bit longer, and most likely expects me to stay with him. Beth Ann or not, he'll want to be here for the brother he was asked by his parents to watch over all those years ago.* Maybe, when Josh was well enough, he'd try to take him back to Seattle, even ask Beth Ann to come along.

By the time Haley started back to the hotel, she knew conclusively what she was going to do. Within the next day or two, she was going home, and she wanted Chase to go with her. But if he couldn't, or wouldn't, she could see no future for them. She needed to come first in his life, as he would in hers, instead of his brother.

Leaving the man she loved so deeply here in Alaska would be devastating, but it would be necessary.

Chase was halfway to the houseboat when his cell phone rang. It turned out to be Arnie, his bail bond boss, calling him from Seattle. Arnie begged him to spare a few minutes of his time to talk. Chase stood there on the walkway and listened. Arnie had a couple of highly interesting things to tell him. He promised the man he would think about them and let him know.

Josh was in his familiar deck chair when Chase arrived at the houseboat.

"What?" Beth Ann asked. "No Haley this morning?"

"She had some work to do," Chase explained.

"Me, too. I have a jewelry order overdue. If you don't mind keeping Josh company, I'll head in to my work-table."

She left the deck, and he settled down beside his brother. He was pleased to see that Josh was more of his old self today. Ready to listen and understand.

When Chase finished telling him what he wanted to happen whenever he was well enough for it, Josh looked at him for a long moment before responding, "This is where I belong now, not Seattle. I don't know if I want to be a reporter any longer, but I'll find my way here somehow."

"You telling me you want to make your home in Alaska?"

"Wherever Beth Ann is *is* my home."

Sonofagun. Haley knew what she was talking about. Josh and Beth Ann *were* in love.

Did Josh see disappointment on his face?

"There's something I need to tell you, Chase, that I should have said long ago. I appreciate how you've looked out for me all these years. Don't think I didn't value it growing up. I did, but the point is I'm no longer a kid. I'm a man now, have been for some time."

Chase stared at him in wonder, thinking, *That mind of his is a lot stronger than I imagined.* "What are you telling me? That it's time to let go?"

Josh smiled. "Something like that. I can care for myself now, or will again as soon as I get out of this chair."

"Then you won't mind if, in the next day or so, Haley and I fly back to Seattle?"

"I won't mind, no. Wherever we are, Chase, we'll always be family, ready to be there for each other. By the way, if it matters, Haley and I had a lot of fun dating, but we were never serious."

Haley soared when Chase told her back at the hotel what he and Josh had settled. "He's a lot smarter than I thought, that little brother of mine."

"Then you and I are going home?"

"As soon as we can book a flight. Seattle or Portland. That's another thing we have to decide. Arnie called me on the way to the houseboat. He wants me to come into the bail bond business with him. He doesn't mind whether it's Seattle or whether we open a branch in Portland that I'd be in charge of. That way you wouldn't have to leave your clients in Portland."

"What are you saying?"

"Heck, it should be plain. I'm asking you to marry me. I may not have a little brother to protect anymore, but I've always got the woman I love to protect. And maybe we'll have our own kids to nurture and protect."

Chase demonstrated that by taking her into his arms and kissing her deeply and possessively.

When he finally released her, Haley couldn't help asking him, "So, what if it had turned out that, as you once mistakenly insisted, Josh loved me and still did? What would you have done?"

"Brother or no brother, I would have told him he couldn't have you. That you belong to me."

"I guess I can live with that. So, when do we start the kids?"

* * * * *

Available April 7, 2015

#1843 CAVANAUGH FORTUNE
Cavanaugh Justice • by Marie Ferrarella

Tech-savvy officer Valri Cavanaugh must track down a ring of hackers causing major destruction to businesses in Aurora. She's partnered with detective Alex Brody, an incorrigible flirt who keeps his distance because of her name. Will they find love even as the danger escalates?

#1844 SECRET AGENT BOYFRIEND
The Adair Affairs • by Addison Fox

When long-buried secrets surface for an American royal family, society princess Landry Adair and too-handsome FBI expert Derek Winchester must pretend to care for each other to trap a killer. But fake romance turns very real while they work to solve a decades-old kidnapping.

#1845 JOINT ENGAGEMENT
To Protect and Serve • by Karen Anders

Special agent Kinley Cooper and NCIS special agent Beau Jerrott don't work well together, but when a boat is found adrift with all personnel aboard dead, they must learn to trust each other, putting their careers—and their hearts—on the line.

#1846 McKINNON'S ROYAL MISSION
by Amelia Autin

Not a chance. Government ultrasecret agent Trace McKinnon won't babysit. He nearly refuses the assignment to guard Zakhar's princess Mara Theodora, but his fluency in the Zakharan language is what the State Department needs...to spy on the targeted—and far too appealing—princess!

REQUEST YOUR FREE BOOKS!
2 FREE NOVELS PLUS 2 FREE GIFTS!

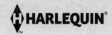

ROMANTIC suspense

Sparked by danger, fueled by passion

YES! Please send me 2 FREE Harlequin® Romantic Suspense novels and my 2 FREE gifts (gifts are worth about $10). After receiving them, if I don't wish to receive any more books, I can return the shipping statement marked "cancel." If I don't cancel, I will receive 4 brand-new novels every month and be billed just $4.74 per book in the U.S. or $5.24 per book in Canada. That's a savings of at least 14% off the cover price! It's quite a bargain! Shipping and handling is just 50¢ per book in the U.S. and 75¢ per book in Canada.* I understand that accepting the 2 free books and gifts places me under no obligation to buy anything. I can always return a shipment and cancel at any time. Even if I never buy another book, the two free books and gifts are mine to keep forever.

240/340 HDN F45N

Name	(PLEASE PRINT)	

Address		Apt. #

City	State/Prov.	Zip/Postal Code

Signature (if under 18, a parent or guardian must sign)

Mail to the **Harlequin®** Reader Service:
IN U.S.A.: P.O. Box 1867, Buffalo, NY 14240-1867
IN CANADA: P.O. Box 609, Fort Erie, Ontario L2A 5X3

Want to try two free books from another line?
Call 1-800-873-8635 or visit www.ReaderService.com.

* Terms and prices subject to change without notice. Prices do not include applicable taxes. Sales tax applicable in N.Y. Canadian residents will be charged applicable taxes. Offer not valid in Quebec. This offer is limited to one order per household. Not valid for current subscribers to Harlequin Romantic Suspense books. All orders subject to credit approval. Credit or debit balances in a customer's account(s) may be offset by any other outstanding balance owed by or to the customer. Please allow 4 to 6 weeks for delivery. Offer available while quantities last.

Your Privacy—The Harlequin® Reader Service is committed to protecting your privacy. Our Privacy Policy is available online at www.ReaderService.com or upon request from the Harlequin Reader Service.

We make a portion of our mailing list available to reputable third parties that offer products we believe may interest you. If you prefer that we not exchange your name with third parties, or if you wish to clarify or modify your communication preferences, please visit us at www.ReaderService.com/consumerschoice or write to us at Harlequin Reader Service Preference Service, P.O. Box 9062, Buffalo, NY 14269. Include your complete name and address.

HRS13R

Valri Cavanaugh is determined to make it up the ranks on her own merit, not because of her name. A new crime spree could make or break her career, but dealing with her new partner might prove just as difficult—and dangerous—as solving the case…

"Won't Detective Brody feel resentful, being paired up with a beat cop?" Valri Cavanaugh asked.

"Possibly," the chief acknowledged, his tone stern. "Which is why I'm issuing you a temporary promotion to detective for the duration of this investigation."

"Promotion? To detective?" she repeated in an awed whisper, never taking her eyes off the chief.

"Tell me—and think carefully—are you up for this?" he asked her.

There was no hesitation in Valri's voice this time as she gave him her answer. "Yes, sir."

"Good." He nodded, appearing pleased for a split second then once again stern. He hit the button on his intercom, connecting him to his administrative assistant out front. "You can send him in now, Raleigh."

"Right away, sir," the feminine voice on the intercom

promised.

The next moment the door to Brian Cavanaugh's inner office opened. A tall, broad-shouldered detective with dirty-blond hair that was slightly longer than regulation dictated walked in as if he owned every square inch of space he passed.

Sparing an appreciative glance at the officer sitting in front of the chief of detectives—Brody was not one who didn't note beauty wherever he came in contact with it—he then focused his attention entirely on the chief.

Alex had spent his morning with a dead man in a dingy apartment that desperately needed a thorough cleaning and a massive dose of fresh air. The chief's immaculate, spacious office was a very welcome contrast. He stood behind the only empty chair in the room, waiting to find out if this was going to be something he needed to sit down for, or just a quick, "touch base" sort of a meeting.

"You sent for me, sir?" he asked the chief.

Brian smiled then gestured for the young detective to sit down. "I did indeed, Detective Brody."

What came next, Alex knew, would test him to the limit. He hadn't spent years in the trenches for this. But then, you didn't say no to a Cavanaugh…

Don't miss
CAVANAUGH FORTUNE
by USA TODAY *bestselling author*
Marie Ferrarella.
Available April 2015 wherever
Harlequin® Romantic Suspense
books and ebooks are sold.

www.Harlequin.com

HRSEXP0315

Love the Harlequin book you just read?

Your opinion matters.

Review this book on your favorite book site, review site, blog or your own social media properties and share your opinion with other readers!

Be sure to connect with us at:
Harlequin.com/Newsletters
Facebook.com/HarlequinBooks
Twitter.com/HarlequinBooks

JUST CAN'T GET ENOUGH?

Join our social communities
and talk to us online.

You will have access to the latest
news on upcoming titles and special
promotions, but most importantly,
you can talk to other fans about your
favorite Harlequin reads.

Harlequin.com/Community

Facebook.com/HarlequinBooks

Twitter.com/HarlequinBooks

Pinterest.com/HarlequinBooks

HARLEQUIN®

A *Romance* FOR EVERY MOOD™

**Stay up-to-date on all your
romance-reading news with the
Harlequin Shopping Guide,
featuring bestselling authors, exciting new
miniseries, books to watch and more!**

The newest issue will be delivered right to you
with our compliments! There are 4 each year.

Signing up is easy.

EMAIL

ShoppingGuide@Harlequin.ca

WRITE TO US

HARLEQUIN BOOKS
Attention: Customer Service Department
P.O. Box 9057, Buffalo, NY 14269-9057

OR PHONE

1-800-873-8635 in the United States
1-888-343-9777 in Canada

Please allow 4-6 weeks for delivery of the first issue by mail.

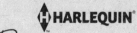